ALSO BY KARISSA KNIGHT

THE CLIENT
Mina's Choice Book One

THE CONTRACT
Mina's Choice Book Two

The
CLIENT
MINA'S CHOICE BOOK ONE

KARISSA KNIGHT

A NOVEL OF ROMANTIC SUSPENSE

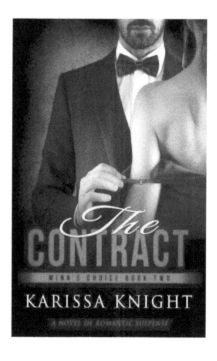

The
CONTRACT
MINA'S CHOICE BOOK TWO

KARISSA KNIGHT

A NOVEL OF ROMANTIC SUSPENSE

PRAISE FOR THE CLIENT

"**Sexy Suspense!** Love the main character-an in-control-professional law-yer, mixed with a thrill-seeking cliff diver who has other steamy secrets. The author puts this intriguing character in the middle of a perfectly twist-y psychological thriller, creating a delicious beginning to a series that will have readers anxious for the next book. (I know I can't wait.)" Valerie B. Johnson, Author of the Circle of Nine Series

"**Intriguing mystery with hot sex.** When high profile attorney Wilhelmina Green takes on a handsome billionaire client, she gets more than she bargained for—or exactly what she wants. You'll need a fan and a cold glass of water close by when you read this one." Sheila Lowe, author of the Claudia Rose Mysteries

"**LOVED this.** The settings, the atmosphere, the clever use of physical danger in more than the obvious... I'm inspired and want more novels with this kind of plotting. When will #2 be available???" Gisele Vezelay, author of Pride and Prejudice fan fiction books.

PRAISE FOR THE CONTRACT

"**Tantalizing the reader-** The Contract is nearly perfect—in pacing, in characterization, in keeping me on the edge of my seat for two days, while I gobbled chapter after chapter. Karissa Knight knows how to tantalize the reader. She is unrelenting with suspense and nail-biting drama. If you want a book that you can submit to, that will take over your life until you read the last page—this is it!" -Saralyn Richard, author of the Detective Parrott mysteries.

"**Enjoyed-** This book was fast-paced and intriguing. It was very, very, steamy, angsty, fun read. The characters were relatable and believable. I flew through this book and I am looking forward to reading the last book whenever it comes out. Would I go back and find the first book in the trilogy? Probably. If only to connect the dots better. Do I want to read more by Karissa Knight? Definitely." -Net Galley Reader.

"**A thrilling ride of suspense and romance-** Take a deep breath before you dive into The Contract, the second book in the Mina's Choice romantic suspense series. As Mina tries to redeem herself from the shame she feels in defending slimy sexual predators, she takes control over her professional and personal choices. But all choices have consequences, and in this gripping novel, it seems the past is catching up with both Mina and her new lover. Get ready for an adrenaline rush in every chapter." -Joy Ann Ribar, Wisconsin mystery author.

"**Hot, hot, hot!** – The second in the Mina's Choice Series dives deeper into tombstoning, Mina's punishing habit, but also explores Jonathan's darker side. Knight masterfully balances the narrative between the characters' erotic desires with a compelling, twisting mystery that involves a long-forgotten meeting and the Russian mob in Chicago. Every aspect

is tightly controlled, leaving the reader breathless and wanting more."
-Sharon Lynn, author of The Bath mysteries.

"**The Contract has it ALL!** – Love, lust, and angst, THE CONTRACT has it all. The antagonists are evil personified, the kind I love to hate, and the protagonists are fallible, the kind I love to root for. The nail-biting action and emotional tension held me captive as I tore through the sizzling pages." -Laurie Buchanan, author of the Sean McPherson thrillers.

THE CLIFF DIVER

THE CLIFF DIVER

Book Three

Mina's Choice

~ Karissa Knight ~

GENRE: Romantic Suspense

This is a work of fiction. All of the names, characters, organizations, places, and events portrayed in this novel are either products of the author's imagination or are used fictitiously. While some locations and locales are real, the author has added fictional touches to further the story. Any resemblance to real or actual events, locales, or persons living or dead, is purely coincidental.

Copyright © 2024 by Karissa Knight
All rights reserved.
Published in the United States by 3 Elements Publishing

ISBN (ebook)

ISBN (paperback) 979-8-3241151-3-5

Edited by Stacey Donovan at Book Editing Associates and Karen at Barren Acres Editing

Cover Design by Tatiana Villa of Vila Designs

Cover image and internal images licensed with Adobe Stock Images

First Edition: August 2024

For Michael. Our story will always have a happy ending.

"I admired the water's ability to rage against the wind and then become tranquil after the storm."

— Wilhelmina Green

"The evil act once committed, one of two things must follow: either the act is punished, or it is not."

— Marquis De Sade

~1~

MINA

"I will possess your heart."

Ben Gibbard, Death Cab for Cutie's singer, calmed me with his lyric voice as the buzz of the tattooist's electric needle grated like a dentist's drill. I tried to focus on the words and the rhythmic bass guitar humming in the background.

Lo Rain, a purple-haired artist, bent over my hip and thigh. Nag Champa incense filled the air. She drew wild lavender and a waterfall that reminded me of several cliffs I'd tombstoned. The waterfall would circle past the scar on my leg. Once, in Croatia, I'd made a bad judgment. When I plunged into the water, I hit coral, and it tore my leg wide open. The tattoo would always remind me that the choices I made were mine to own.

With my cell phone pressed to my ear, I lay back on the narrow padded table, my gaze locked on the painted ceiling above me. Gray clouds swirled around Greek gods, demons, and cartoon characters all peering down as if laughing at my pain.

"How's it feel?" Jonathon asked. He would have sat in on the session if he could.

"Can't you guess?" My teeth ground together. I tried not to think about the burning sensation from the needle pressed into my skin.

"Tell me." His deep voice resonated with me. I missed him.

"She's drawing a lavender flower with the fine needle tool."

"And?"

"It stings. But I'm tough."

"You're the toughest woman I know, Mina."

"I miss you. When are you coming home?" Jonathon was in an undisclosed location in Greece. He could have been on one of the thousands of islands or on the mainland. I had no idea.

"I don't know," he said. "I haven't been able to find her."

Three weeks earlier, he had stepped down as CEO of Prevail Pharmaceutical Software to follow a lead. The woman he'd dated years ago had orchestrated an elaborate plan to kidnap me and extort millions from Jonathon. He had traveled to Greece to find her—Rory Bradford, his ex-girlfriend. She was the mastermind behind the extortion plan orchestrated by Janko Vorobiev less than a month ago.

Her heart must have been shattered when Jonathon left her. When their love turned sour. Her revenge was cruel and unforgiving. Her thugs killed Jonathon's personal bodyguard and ruined my best friend Traci Lambert's life.

Jonathon wasn't out for revenge. He planned to stop her reign of terror.

Though I longed for him to hold my hand during this self-imposed ordeal, the pain of the tattoo artist's needle was nothing compared to the thought of losing him. "Are you being careful?" I asked.

"Of course." It was a throwaway answer and one I didn't believe. He refused to tell me what plans he had to ruin Rory.

"Tell me about Greece," I said.

"I haven't had much time to enjoy it."

"You must be joking. The cerulean blue sky and Mediterranean Sea? I've been there and smelled the salty air. You *must* have found something to enjoy."

"It would be so much better if you were here."

"I miss you too." I missed his stormy gaze and the smooth tone of voice. I missed the sting of his studded paddle on my ass. "Where are you now?"

"I'm drinking iced coffee at a small table on a busy street—"

"Paved or brick?"

"The street is paved with stones. Nearby, there's a statue of Poseidon holding his staff. There's a Mythos beer umbrella above me with the name in bold green cursive. It's so hot, I'm trying to stay in the shade, even though the sun's setting."

"Are you in Athens?"

"No."

"Mykonos?"

"No."

"Chalcis?"

"Stop. You know I can't tell you where I am. She could be listening."

"But you're using a burner phone."

"You know her reach is far and wide." He'd told me about how insanely controlling Rory was. Though she claimed to be a submissive, she worked hard to fill that role and to deserve Jonathon's punishment. She taught him how to be a dominant in the bedroom.

"I want to see you," I said. "I could be there this weekend—"

"No. It's too dangerous, Mina. Erik Edwards gave his life. Janko almost killed Greg. If I hadn't come home in time, he would have killed you."

When Rory paid Janko Vorobiev to extort a seven-figure sum from Jonathon, the plan failed, so Janko came after Jonathon. He killed Jonathon's personal bodyguard, Erik, and shot Greg Hauser, a good friend and confidant, in the knee. Luckily, Jonathon came home in time. He fought Janko, who got what he deserved, and now that man was serving time in federal prison.

"I won't put you in danger ever again," Jonathon said.

"I'd like to get my hands on Rory. I can hold my own. You know I'm a black belt."

"Martial arts won't protect you against semi-automatic weapons," he said.

The needle dug into the flesh above my hip bone. I sucked air through my teeth. "What have you learned about Rory?"

"I've hired mercenaries to fight her. I've got to be strategic and calculating. And ...I'm worried she knows I'm here."

Rory's far-reaching influence was deadly. I'd be devastated if I lost him.

Our relationship began early last summer when he hired me to represent him. Jonathon had become a person of interest in the murder of his personal assistant. When I learned that he was into a certain lifestyle, I became a person interested in him.

Lo Rain turned the tattoo pen off. "I need you to roll onto your side."

"Hold on." I situated myself on the narrow padded table with my left arm raised up under my head, I pressed the phone to my right ear.

"Are you getting close to finding Rory?"

"There's so much I can't tell you over the phone."

I noted the fear in his voice. "How much longer?"

Lo Rain answered, "About an hour. I'm filling in the waterfall with color now." She started up the pen again. The needle dug into my flesh, and I grimaced.

"There's no telling," Jonathon said. "It could be weeks or months before I locate her. I wish it were over and I could come home. I love you, Mina."

"I love you too."

-2-

JONATHON

The hardest part of being in Greece was being a half a world away from Mina. I missed her more than anything. I missed her sass, and her soft lips. I missed her brilliant conversation and her long, graceful arms. Last month we became closer than I ever dreamed possible. In all the ways no one ever understood me before, Mina got *me*. She saw *me*.

I looked out across the street at pedestrians hurrying to evening meetups, couples hand in hand, peering into shop windows, a young mother pushing a stroller. It had been a week since I called Mina. I thought of her and smoothed the beard I'd grown since I arrived in Greece.

Mina cried when she heard I was leaving. But when I explained I needed to find Rory—to stop her—Mina understood. All her work defending sociopaths, felons, and psychotic scumbags had taught her something about the criminal mind. Mina understood Rory would never let up. In fact, it was her idea to dismantle Rory's scaffolding. To infect Rory's tower of power and bring her to the ground.

The rest came easily. Rory and I went to college together. We'd had a very dysfunctional relationship and when we parted ways, she returned to Europe. To her crime-boss father. She told me once that she was born in Europe when I questioned her ability to speak Italian. But I didn't know she also spoke Russian. Or that Russian was her first language.

Rory Bradford, the woman I dated for four years, was actually Rory Protsenko, the daughter of Artur Protsenko, king of a well-known Russian crime syndicate. More recently she tried to extort money from me. And worse, she sicced her thug Janko Vorobiev on the woman I loved. To get her revenge, Rory tried to ruin the best thing I had going. Now it was my turn. I could never let Rory get away with what she'd done. I needed to put an end to this before she became even more desperate.

In the last month, I'd learned Rory oversaw production of fentanyl from her factory near Izmir, Turkey. Though her father was the leader of a criminal empire, Rory had branched out on her own. She was power hungry and hated being under anyone's thumb—including her father's. She sold the deadly drugs to criminals and mercenaries from all over the world. For various reasons, most of them would rather do business with her than the Chinese.

Stan Moorlehem and I staked out the fentanyl plant one night while they loaded crates into the backs of four Sprinter vans. Mayhem—Stan's nickname—and I followed the vans to the port in Izmir. I alerted Nico Fortunato—a Navy SEAL I met through Bujinkan training—and his team tracked the shipment. Nico commanded a team of highly trained men and women who intercepted a small freighter headed toward Bari, Italy. PHMSA, the Pipeline and Hazardous Materials Safety Administration, confiscated three tons of the deadly drug made by Rory's company.

While sipping iced coffee, I made notes about what happened on a Chromebook, then sent them to Mayhem. "Rory seems undaunted by our attempts to destroy her. When PHMSA officials traced the shipment back to one of her factories, they found it had been burned to the ground. No trace of that operation was left. She had many, though, so we move to phase two. Find Rory's headquarters. Find her other manufacturing locations. And find Sotoris."

I hit send, then transferred the communication and all my notes to a thumb drive.

Across the road, a fifteen-foot metal statue of Poseidon towered above the stone circle. His fish tail swept waves made of aging blue iron. Brightly colored compact cars drove around the circle past the café—a blue and white Twizy, a red Mini Cooper, a yellow Mercedes-Benz MB Smart Coupe—so close, I could almost touch them. The road was too narrow for more than one at a time.

I looked at each driver, trying to see if they made the briefest eye contact. If so, I would leave. I would hide and cover my tracks. Rory's people were everywhere.

Javier Garrido, my new personal bodyguard, stood against the patio entrance in the shade of the setting sun. Javier had only been working for me for about a month. I'd selected him from a handful of well-trained bodyguards after Janko Vorobiev killed my right-hand man, Erik Edwards. I signaled for him to join me.

"Sir?"

"Sit down, Javier." I dragged the metal chair away from the table for him. Javier previously worked for a former governor of Illinois. He managed difficult scenarios and bomb threats. Originally trained in the Army, his transition to protective services earned him high scores. More than that, he was fiercely loyal. He stayed with the past governor until he died of old age.

"Sir?"

"We need to talk, Javier." I was still getting to know him.

He unbuttoned his black suit jacket and sat beside me. It might have been the heat, but he looked uncomfortable. This was never going to work between us if he couldn't relax with me.

"Have I done something wrong, sir?"

"No. Of course not." I finished the iced espresso and signaled the waitress to bring two more. *"Ena akomi, parakalo."*

She nodded and went back inside.

"Javier, what did you expect to get out of this job?"

"What do you mean, sir?"

"And stop calling me sir. It gives me a superiority complex. Besides, I think we're about the same age."

"Yes, si—" Javier nodded.

"Just Jonathon."

Javier lowered his head.

He was trained to be respectful. I had to respect that. "Mr. Heun, then."

"Mr. Heun." He nodded.

The waitress set two iced espressos on paper napkins. I handed her the cash payment and a tip in euros.

"Tell me something about yourself. Where did you grow up?" My track record this year with personal bodyguards was not good. My last personal bodyguard was a close friend. The one before that betrayed me and tried to kill Mina. Though I debated the wisdom of befriending Javier, it was important to learn about the people working for me. I never wanted to take them for granted. Especially when their lives were on the line.

Javier cleared his throat. His eyes were hidden behind slim, dark sunglasses. "I immigrated from Mexico to the U.S. with my family about twenty years ago. My father and mother gained citizenship after living and working in Chicago for ten years."

"Where did you go to school?"

"Phoenix Military Academy in Chicago. After that, I enrolled in the Army."

"Where were you stationed?"

"I was never deployed to the front lines." Javier downed a big swallow of the iced coffee.

"How do you feel about that?"

Javier looked at the table. "I'm not sure."

"Look, I have some hand-to-hand combat skills. I'm a twelfth-degree black-belt in Kendo martial arts." Sword fighting was more than a hobby of mine. It was an obsession. I collected rare katanas and when I was home, I trained daily. "I'm telling you this so you know I can hold my own in the right circumstances."

"Forgive me for saying so, but you're a legend among my colleagues. How you stopped that international criminal—I mean—you cut off his hand!" His eyes lit up, but he quickly stifled the emotion and composed himself.

Legend? "I'm not proud of it." It had taken every ounce of restraint to keep from killing Janko.

He squinted at the setting sun. "If I may, si—ah, Mr. Heun—I'm happy to be working for you. I believe in what you're doing here. It's the work of a saint. If you know what I mean."

"Javier, you think too highly of me. I'm not a saint . . . or a superhero.

I'm a man risking my life to hopefully save others' lives. That includes my fiancée." Technically, I hadn't asked Mina to marry me yet. I didn't want her to make plans that may or may not become reality. I knew the deadly risks I faced here.

Javier fidgeted with a white-gold ring on his left hand. I'd noticed it before.

"Are you married?" I asked.

His eyes lit briefly. "Her name is Rachel."

I could see it in the way he caressed the ring. Javier would never tell me he was afraid he wouldn't make it back to Chicago.

"The men working for me are professionals. They have experience with the Russian mob and have helped police track and kill terrorist cells of ISIS and other groups. I don't want you to worry that we won't make it home."

Javier looked down at his shoes and gave a slight nod.

"I will make sure you get home." I reached across the table and gripped his arm. I understood his fear.

Beginning to doubt Javier had the balls for this job, I finished the last of my coffee. "Let's get back to the villa where it's more private."

Javier nodded. "No disrespect, Mr. Heun, I'd like to spar with you someday."

As I pushed the metal chair away from the table, I saw an orange Ford Fiesta rounding the curve and coming for us. Javier leapt at me and shoved the table out of the way.

Javier thrust me into the building as the Fiesta crashed into our table, just missing us. The car hit the building. With a blinding flash, an explosion deafened me. The force of the bomb threw me into the wall. I fell to the ground.

Hot flames licked my hands as I rolled on top of Javier. He seemed to be unconscious and as I tried to get up, a second explosion knocked me to the sidewalk. My cheek lay against hard pavement. Before my eyes fluttered closed, I saw burning bodies lying on the ground, tables overturned, and linen on fire. Smoke poured out of the blackened shell of the orange car.

I woke with the taste of blood on my teeth and my ears ringing a high-pitched *shree*. The space was pitch-black around me, not even the night sky glowed through a window. Yet somehow I knew it was past midnight. The last thing I remembered was Javier lunging for me as a car careened toward us.

I was sitting upright in a wooden chair. When I hitched my shoulder, pain shot through my arm. It was dislocated. I tried to adjust myself in the seat and quickly learned my ankles were bound to the chair legs. My arms were tied behind my back and ropes held me to the chair. My shirt and shoes had been removed. I assessed other body parts. My teeth were intact, but my lip had split. My cheekbone, knuckles, and elbows felt bruised. The back of one hand burned with extreme pain. I tried to feel the injury and touched an open wound.

There could only be one person who would want to do this to me.

Beyond the intense ringing in my ears, I heard someone breathing. I wasn't alone. "Javier?" I croaked.

A blinding spotlight came on and I squinted. "What do you want from me?"

"In time, my friend. In time."

I heard the strike of a match and through the glare of the spotlight, the coal of a cigarette glowed orange.

~3~

MINA

Like an idiot, I let Greg Hauser take me on this day trip. It was his bright idea to get me out of the climbing gym onto a real cliff face, where my taped fingers curled around white quartzite and my toes balanced on the narrow outcroppings. I pressed my belly into the outward jut of the rock face. Though a cool autumn breeze rustled tree leaves, my red Northface T-shirt was moist with sweat. I took a deep breath, searching for the next handhold.

"A little farther to your right . . . a little farther . . . there it is." Greg knew I needed a distraction. Rock climbing was completely new to me, but for some stupid reason, I thought it might be a handy skill for one of my next tombstoning dives.

Greg secured the ropes and carabiners that we used to climb to the top of the crag. He chose the route and belayed me when I lost contact. "How am I—"

"It's a crimp, a small hold, but it's enough. Grab it." He encouraged me through the crux, the most technically difficult part of the climb. With his butt safely on solid *flat* ground, he looked down from above with a smug look of satisfaction on his face. Sure, he'd made it to the top.

I'd never climb this high without assurances, like a secured rope. I reached to my right.

"There you go." He tightened the belaying rope and it pulled snugly against my hips. "Now step up with your right foot."

Come on, you need to take your training outside, he'd said. Devil's Lake, Wisconsin, was only two and a half hours from Chicago. Though he'd climbed these cliffs before, I hadn't. And though I loved to dive from heights that made most people woozy, I'd never scaled more than a half-dozen meters.

Ugh. I had no fear of heights, but I'd much rather be falling one hundred meters—diving into an ocean or sea or deep lake—than clinging like a bug to a freaking wall.

I slid my foot up to the next rock and it crumbled. Rocks and debris tumbled down the wall and landed sixty feet below. "That's no good. Now what?" My foot dangled. I held on by my fingertips. If only there was water below, then it wouldn't freak me out as much. But hitting the ground from this height? That wasn't on my bucket list.

"You'll have to smear it."

"What's that mean?"

"Press the ball of your foot against the face and propel yourself upward. You can grab the next pocket. Do you see it? It's about one foot above your left hand."

With sweaty palms and my heart racing, I felt the granite for a viable hold. I looked up. There was a shadowed indentation that looked like nothing from here. "That?"

"Yes. Trust me."

"I don't have much of a choice, do I?" The thought of my skull crushed on a rock made my stomach flip. At least I wouldn't fall far. The harness would catch me.

I tucked my knee to my chest and pressed the ball of my right foot into the granite face.

"Keep your eye on the pocket." He was so freaking perky.

"I am." *One, two, three*—I shoved off with my right foot and lunged for the pocket. My left fingers just missed the handhold and I scrambled to find a grab. I fell.

My shoulder bounced against the wall and the harness ripped against my recent, still healing tattoo. Though it had been a few weeks since my ink, the area now felt like a fresh sunburn. I dangled a few feet from where I previously balanced. "Dammit!"

"It's fine. You're fine." Greg laughed. "You're almost there. Come on, I'm right here for you."

"How did I let you talk me into this?" I reached for the nearest handhold and slipped my toes onto an outcrop. I looked up, found the next grips, and pulled myself to the crux again. *Again.*

"I won't let you fail, Mina. I see another way if you skid left. I'll just need to secure the top roping to this tree behind me." Greg disappeared.

I searched the wall to my upper left and spotted a crack that I could easily slip my fingers into. I pulled my body and shoved my toes into a jug. Before Greg returned, I was five feet past the point where I fell from moments ago. I reached the top edge. "Greg?"

"I'm here." He cranked the ropes tighter as I elbowed my way onto the top of the bluff. "Take my hand."

I gripped his wrist as he gripped mine and pulled me safely to the bluff. I sat on the ground and took a long deep breath, looking out at the view. Far below, the blue surface of Devil's Lake glistened in the sun. Fall colors, yellows, oranges, and bright reds, dotted the landscape for miles.

"See? You didn't need my help at all. You're a natural climber, your instincts are good." Greg grabbed his discarded backpack and sat down beside me. He peeled off a bright yellow jacket and threw his feet over the side of the cliff. His red shoes and lime green socks shone like a beacon in the sun, but I was drawn to the spectacle farther away. His gaze followed mine. "Worth it, eh?"

I looked sideways at him. "I could have hiked up this boulder from the south and it would have been just as beautiful."

His laughter warmed my heart. I punched his arm playfully.

"What was that for?"

"For making me work so hard for it. How did you become such a good climber?"

"I grew up in Colorado. As kids, my brothers and I were always scaling boulders. We grew up, and so did the sizes of the rocks."

Greg had grown a short beard since his knee surgery. It suited him and gave him a scholarly look. He'd climbed this rock face using mostly hand and arm strength. While he scaled the rock face above me, I noticed he favored the uninjured left leg. He was fit from the waist up, but still wore a knee brace on the leg Janko Vorobiev shot. He'd been lucky.

He told me the knee replacement surgery had gone well, and he was doing most activities at about fifty-five percent.

Though Jonathon hired Greg to be my bodyguard this summer, I knew very little about Greg's past. "How many brothers do you have?"

"Two. I'm in the middle." He dug into his backpack and pulled out two energy bars.

I took one and unclipped the water bottle from my belt. As we sat and munched our bars, Greg talked about his brothers and their climbing adventures, but I didn't really listen. I couldn't help thinking about Jonathon. What kind of view was he looking at right now? Could he see the teal-blue Mediterranean? Could he feel the white sand? The warm water?

I'd been to the Mediterranean and loved it. But Jonathon wasn't there for pleasure. He was seeking one of the most powerful women in the criminal world. Rory Bradford was a dangerous adversary. According to Jonathon, she had mercenaries and criminals at her beck and call. When he knew her in college, she was just a young woman with a penchant for punishment. She hid her past well. After they separated, she went back to Europe. I supposed he hoped to never see her again.

In the last month, he learned Rory manufactured and sold fentanyl to anyone who would buy it, including the Russians, the Chinese, and North Koreans. What they did with it, she didn't care. They shipped it to places like New York and Chicago, with no regard for the lives they took. It was poison. And she controlled much of the market.

"Are you ready to rappel back down?"

"Sorry?" I hadn't been listening to Greg.

"You've got your mind on other things. I get it. I'm worried about him too." He stood on one leg, awkwardly avoiding his healing knee and zipped his backpack.

"Are you sore? Does your physical therapist know you went climbing today?"

"Of course not. How is Jonathon, anyway?"

"I haven't heard from him in two weeks." I stood up and brushed the dirt off my butt and hands.

"That long?"

"I tried to reach him." After the first few days, his phone went straight to voicemail. I'd be devastated if I lost him. "I'm worried, Greg."

~4~

MINA

$\mathcal{J}$ onathon curled his leg over mine and pulled me closer. "I don't want to leave you," he said.

It was past midnight. We lay awake in my queen-sized bed. My spacious, Lincoln Park condo faced Lake Michigan. Lights out on the water—what we could see from my bed—moved slowly. I snuggled into his warmth. His fresh clean smell. "I don't want you to go. Let me come with you."

"Rory will try to hurt you."

As soon as he spoke her name, every cell in my body stood at attention. I refused to give up Jonathon's embrace for her. "How will she know I'm with you?"

"She has a terrorist army. They're everywhere, Mina."

"I know. They're in Chicago too."

"But she's in Greece. I'm the lure. If she's hunting me, and I told her I'm coming for her, she'll be waiting for me. She is relentless and as compulsive as a child. If I don't finish what she started, she'll never stop looking for you."

This was no game of cat and mouse. This game was deadly warfare. "We'll run away. We'll go to some remote island in Southeast Asia and live quietly for the rest of our lives. Where she'll never find us—"

His lips raised in a smile, and he scratched the dark stubble on his chin. "Run away? That doesn't sound like you. Diving into the fire—now that's what I'd expect."

I embraced what scared me most: representing killers and psychopaths to follow the dream, to earn money and prestige. At the expense of inner peace.

I adjusted my pillow and sat up against the headboard, pulling the sheet up to my armpits. "Let me help you catch your ex. I've spent years helping criminals get away with murder. I need this chance to redeem myself."

His forehead furrowed with concern.

"I was twenty-four when I passed the bar with such high marks that three top firms in Chicago had a bidding war," I said. "I went with Milton, Wallace, and Edwards because they offered the highest paycheck. I was too naïve to ask what kinds of cases they would give me or what types of criminals I'd have to represent. I was a defense lawyer fresh out of law school, and I was hungry to get inside the courtroom. I wanted to defend people. I was ambitious and focused on making six figures a year.

"From all I've seen, from all I've learned . . ." I shook my head and closed my eyes. I hated myself for helping acquit evil people. I knew now I wanted—no, needed—the opportunity to *fight* criminals. To put them where they belong. "I want to do something good for society as a whole. This is my chance. This is what I've dreamed of. Rory is just like every heinous murderer I've represented in the courtroom. You must let me help you."

"She's not just a sociopath, Mina. She's a psychopath and a terrorist with an army of trained guerillas. She's out of your league."

"I know the difference. A psychopath is someone who lacks empathy and is extremely antisocial. A sociopath has those traits combined with a tendency toward abnormally violent behavior. They are brilliant and manipulative. I've worked with many people just like her. I know how to deal with them."

"You haven't met Rory."

"Introduce me."

Jonathon looked away. He shook his head and toyed with the sheets.

Discussing sociopaths brought the first man I represented to mind. I'd never told anyone this story before. Wealthy sociopathic criminals with no hearts and no remorse were chosen for me by my firm because I was very good at talking the jury into an acquittal. Those wealthy bastards paid a fortune for me.

As I recalled that time in my life, my shoulders tightened. I drew my arms to my side and crossed them tightly over my chest. "The first case Jim Milton assigned to me was a man accused of murdering his wife and two children."

Jonathon looked at me with interest. "That must have been difficult."

"I remember wondering how bad could it be? Milton had confidence in me, and he wanted a woman to defend the man. My presence as his defense attorney would suggest to the jurors that the accused had empathy. The fact he had a woman backing him up would show them that a woman—someone who may someday have a family of her own—believed he was innocent. My presence would surely sway the jury that this man could never hurt a woman. Let alone children."

"Did you believe he was innocent?"

"At first, I thought the arresting officer was full of crap. The accused—I won't tell you his name because you might actually know him—appeared to be depressed and so shaken by the aftermath. By his arrest. By the deaths—the *murders*—of his beloved wife and children. They were six and nine years old." I recalled their faces from photographs I used in the courtroom and paused to clear my throat.

"He wanted help arranging their funerals and didn't seem to grasp why he'd been arrested," I said. "As time went on and I got to know him, I never suspected it was all an act. In the courtroom he cried. He seemed distraught and anguished. During our private meetings he would burst into tears. He wanted me to believe he was innocent."

"What happened?"

"At the time, I believed him. I believed in my work. Most importantly, I believed I was doing good for a man and for society."

Jonathon placed a hand over mine. I made a fist.

"The jury proclaimed him innocent of all charges. He thanked me for helping acquit him. Then he smiled. My client saved the reveal for after the trial. He saved it for me alone."

Jonathon looked away.

I continued, "He bared his teeth, but it wasn't a smile. His wolflike grin was full of cold heartless cruelty. It was as if he was so pleased with himself. And in that moment, I knew I was damned. I knew I had just stepped into a hell of my own making."

"Maybe his act protected you from the truth."

"Protected me? Those aren't the words I would choose." I clutched the sheet and drew it to my chin. "I will never forgive myself for helping acquit him." For the hundredth time, I delayed the onset of grief for what I'd done, although deep inside I longed to be punished for it.

"Mina . . ."

"He told me he couldn't live with the person his wife had become. He planned the entire murder from the time the youngest was born. Before he thanked me for convincing the jury, he asked if I believed him. *'Did you like it? My performance?'* he asked. My skin crawled like a thousand beetles had been dumped down my shirt. The evil he emitted poured over me. I couldn't forgive myself, and I had no way to escape my life."

"Let me hold you." Jonathon pulled me close and embraced me. His warm hug comforted me. "I'm so sorry, Mina."

I leaned into his hug and let him rock me back and forth. He rubbed my back and softly cooed soothing words. "It isn't your fault. You were doing your job."

I sniffed tears away and laid my head on Jonathon's warm chest. *It was my fault.*

"Is that when you began tombstoning?" he asked.

"Diving was my whole life. Shortly after that case, I took a personal vacation to Lake Havasu, Arizona. That was the first time I used tombstoning as a way to punish myself. I dove during the early hours of the morning during a violent thunderstorm." I would never tell Jonathon that sometimes, standing at the top of those cliffs, I had wished for death. But when I dove, the muscle memory kicked in. My body did the things it remembered—as if saving me from myself—and I always landed with grace.

"You told me about that dive. You were lucky you weren't struck by lightning."

"Lucky? Lucky that for the next six years, Jim Milton assigned to me

Chicago's worst sociopaths? Lucky I helped acquit murderers and rap-ists? No. I don't see it that way."

"Well, at least one good thing came out of your years in the court-room. I found you. I'm so happy, Mina, that I found you." Jonathon's white teeth gleamed in the dim light.

I kissed his stubbly chin and cupped his face in my hand. "You are the best thing that happened to me too," I said. "If it weren't for meeting you, I might not have changed a thing. But for the rest . . ." Grief choked me. I wiped my eyes.

Jonathon said, "I love you, Mina. Your past doesn't matter to me, I don't care about that. I wish you could understand—as I do—what a fierce woman you are. You are smart and talented. You have drive and ambition. You are everything I want in a partner."

My breath caught in my throat. *Partner?* Warmth filled every cell in my body. That moment, love that I never thought I was capable of bloomed in my heart. Jonathon confirmed that all I'd been through may have been worth it. If finding him was the reason I'd traveled through hell, I would travel back again to keep him close.

Only one thing, one woman, stood between me and that goal. Rory Bradford. I refused to become her prey and the only way to solve that was . . . "Jonathon, take me to her."

He sat up on his elbow. His cerulean-blue gaze met mine.

"I need to do this with you, Jonathon. I need to help you entrap Rory and put her away. So, don't tell me I can't. I won't take no for an answer."

The next morning, he was gone.

-5-

JONATHON

"Who are you working with?" The strike to my face came immediately this time.

I spit blood on the floor. Five cigarette burns on my chest oozed. I could ignore the wounds—my throbbing head, a split lip, and dislocated shoulder—when I thought of returning to Mina. The man asking the questions would get nothing out of me.

"Who is working with you?"

Thick, black, combed-back hair fell to his shoulders. His dark, hollow eyes glared at me with contempt. My captor, currently the man irritating me the most, didn't know that I knew him. Marco Vorobiev was the younger brother of Janko. He'd been trafficking drugs for Rory Bradford, aka, Rory Protsenko, for more than a decade. Like his brother, he was a wicked man, working for one of the most powerful organized crime groups in the world.

"You know very well that I work alone," I said. "If you don't, you're more stupid than she realizes." The wiry man paced back to the dark corner of the room where a table on wheels contained many instruments intended for torturing me. He pushed it toward me, to show me what was in store if I didn't answer his questions. He didn't know I'd never reveal a thing.

Marco and another man took turns torturing me. It seemed like it had been about three days since the car bombing, but I couldn't be sure. I blacked out after the explosion. It may have taken hours or a few days for the smoke to clear from my head. Except for the spotlight shining in my eyes, the windowless room was dark. They didn't give me water or food—not that I remember. Now that I was fully conscious, I pretended to be out of it. I let my head hang. I groaned.

"How did you intercept the shipment? The fentanyl was worth billions on the street. More than you've made in a lifetime. She wants you to pay for what you've stolen. With blood. Now—" He picked up a pair of cable snips from the table. "I will ask you one last time, then I'll start to remove your toes, one by one. Who are you working with?"

He looked so much like his brother Janko I wanted to kill him. I let my head hang from my shoulders and allowed my hatred to bloom. I let it build up a fire and feed me energy. My chin hung to my chest but behind my back, I worked on the ropes binding my wrists. I picked at them until the knot came loose. I moaned and under my breath mumbled a question of my own.

He put a hand to his ear. "Did you say something?"

I whispered my question again.

"I can't hear you. Who are you working with?" He dropped the snips and picked up a hammer, then kicked the table out of the way. He gazed down at my bare feet, my ankles bound to the legs of the chair. "Perhaps some incentive."

"Wait, I'll tell you," I said, this time so he could hear me.

Just as I hoped, he approached.

I released my wrists as he drew nearer. "Well?" he asked.

I whispered, "No one." Swiftly, I grabbed his neck and pulled him toward me, ignoring the shooting pain in my dislocated shoulder. It threw him off-balance, and as I'd planned, the weight of his body tipped over the chair I was bound to. He fought to recover, but I held his throat in a viselike grip. Cutting off his breath and vital blood flow to his brain. He struggled to get away, and I swiveled the chair, pinning one arm beneath it with my weight on top of him. My knee and the corner of the chair pressed into his lower back.

He tried to cry out, but I wouldn't let him take a breath. I could hold him in this lock as long as it took. I had all the time in the world.

As he let out his final breath and the fight released from his body, the door to the cell swung open.

"I want him alive." It was *her* voice.

The butt of a rifle poised above my head. Then blackness.

~6~

MINA

Janko Vorobiev was held in MCC Chicago with a twenty-four-hour military guard. When I entered the federal prison, I told the security guards I was Janko's lawyer. I was, in fact, a criminal lawyer who represented the worst of society's dregs. My name, Wilhelmina Green, had become a household word in the Chicago area, especially among law enforcement.

When the guards checked over the lists of approved visitors—there were none—I saw a lawyer had already been to see Janko. I lied and said his lawyer, the man who represented local Russian mob boss, Konstantin Tsezar, no longer wanted the case. I said I was his *new* attorney and threw a fit, telling them their paperwork wasn't up to date. They let me in.

Two guards brought Janko into the secure meeting room. They stood on either side holding his arms. He shrugged them off as he entered. "Surprise, surprise. Look who's here."

One of Janko's arms was handcuffed to a belt at his waist. The other hung from a sling. The guards backed up and stood on either side of the door. I didn't ask for privacy during the meeting. I wanted witnesses in case Janko did something regrettable.

Knowing what he was capable of, I locked my gaze on him. He wore ankle shackles, and in the sling, his right hand was covered with a pillow-sized bandage where they'd reattached the hand Jonathon took with his sword. I heard the surgery had gone well, but what did I care? Janko had nearly killed my best friend, Traci, blackmailed Jonathon, blown a bullet hole through Greg's knee, threatened my life, and killed Erik Edwards. I had zero sympathy for this man.

"Have a seat, Janko." I stood on the opposite side of the table.

"Why should I? I have no regrets. They said you are taking my case. Why?"

"I'm not."

His face drew tight with cynicism or pain. I hoped it was the latter. "You lied?"

I looked across at him. "You kidnapped my best friend and murdered Erik. I want you to rot in a Russian prison for the rest of your pathetic little life."

His cold laughter bounced off the concrete walls. "You see? You are no better than me."

"Perhaps not. But I'm not in federal prison."

He sat in the plastic chair. "You are not winning my friendship, Mina. Did you come to badger me? Because when I get out . . ." Janko yanked against the handcuff with his good hand, "You and your lover will be the first victims of my rage."

"Idle threats. Since you're going nowhere, I need something from you."

"Good luck to you." He turned his head and faced the wall.

"You'll do this for me, Janko, or I'll have a chat with Konstantin Tsezar. I hear he's favored by the leaders of the Russian mafia now. I'll bet he has connections right here in this prison." I had no way of knowing if this was true.

Konstantin Tsezar and Janko were working with the same Transnational Organized Crime syndicate. Tsezar ruled the Chicago area. His connections to law enforcement put him above the law in more ways than I could fathom. One thing was certain. In court, Janko could betray them all. Now that Janko was in prison, Kostya Tsezar would find a way to silence Janko. It was the reason Janko was in the highest security level and under twenty-four-hour guard.

"I'm not afraid of Kostya." Janko tipped his head as if he could care less.

"Fine. I'll go. Guards—"

One prison guard took a step forward.

"Wait." Janko lifted a lazy gaze to meet mine. "I'm willing to play your game. But you do something for me first."

It was simply luck he wanted to bargain. I had no intention of doing anything for him, yet I was curious. "What?"

He bared his teeth. His lip curled into a semi-smile as his good hand went to his crotch.

"When hell freezes over." I spun toward the door.

"When I get out, I will come looking for you." Janko's reptile gaze followed me.

"You'll never get out. And if I have my way, you'll die long before any trial."

His smile faded. "Contact the Croatian Embassy."

"There's nothing they can do for you. The Croatian Embassy has no jurisdiction. You committed murder in the United States of America."

He frowned. "Then I need you to contact Marco Vorobiev, my brother. If you can't reach him, there is another, Rahman Bishura. He is my business associate in Dubrovnik."

I had no intention of contacting them, but I committed the names to memory. "What will I tell them?"

"They will know what to do."

"My turn. How do I contact Rory Bradford?"

"Who?"

"Don't bullshit me." But for some reason, the look on his face was momentarily sheer confusion.

Janko's brow furrowed as he looked me in the eye. "What do you want with her?"

"That's none of your business."

"You don't know how powerful she is."

"Tell me."

Janko tried to stand then winced in pain. For the first time since I'd known this man, he faltered. "She will kill me."

"You're not afraid of Tsezar, but you're afraid of Rory?"

"She—" He glanced back at the guards. "She has people everywhere."

"You're a dead man any way you look at it. Do I care? Jonathon has gone after her, and I need to find him." I wouldn't tell Janko I hadn't heard from Jonathon in two weeks. No one had.

Until this year, I wasn't able to quit my job. The expense of the condo and lure of standing before a courtroom audience kept me chained to the firm. Until this year, I didn't think about pursuing a different tangent of my legal career—like representing victims of abuse or becoming a prosecuting attorney. Until this year, I didn't know how to tell my senior partners at Milton, Wallace, & Edwards whom I was willing—and unwilling—to represent. None of it was possible until I met Jonathon. He had given me more confidence and the courage to tell my employers exactly what I wanted.

And now he was missing. I would do everything in my power to find him.

Janko looked me in the eye, his pupils darting back and forth. "Jonathon is a worthy adversary, but Rory will know he is coming. She predicted it months ago. She hoped for it."

I grew impatient. "A deal is a deal, Janko. Tell me how to reach her."

"She knows who you are. She knows what you are to *him*."

"That's what I'm counting on."

Janko finally gave me an address in Bucharest and two cell phone numbers for his contacts. He told me Rory and her family owned an island in Greece. Its name: Sotoris. His information matched Jonathon's last communications.

I'd lied when I agreed to call Janko's people. I had no guilt about that. The information I needed was in my hand.

~ 7 ~

MINA

"*The number you have reached is no longer in service.*"

Why didn't he answer? Why was his phone disconnected? I dreaded to think he was hurt, or worse . . . dead.

Where are you, Jonathon?

Someone would have notified me. Someone would have called.

All I knew was, Jonathon was in Greece. Other than that, I had no idea. A friend's villa on an exclusive island? A chartered yacht? He told me he had boats and other resources and he'd hired a British mercenary to help with the dirty work. It didn't help. I wished I'd known their names.

I feared Jonathon's attempt to stop Rory Bradford had sealed his doom, and I had to go to Europe to find him.

Before booking my flight to Greece, I looked up the addresses Janko gave me. I found one location to be a collapsed stone edifice crumbled by recent attacks. Photos of the building verified news articles of a terrorist bombing. The house was empty. A dead end.

The other place Janko mentioned, Sotoris, was a privately owned island. Jonathon had once spoken of it. Yet there was no record of Sotoris Island in the Mediterranean. Google Maps didn't locate it. Historical archives had no record of it.

I changed my angle and looked for any information about Rory Bradford. Years ago, she was enrolled at UW Madison, but her job histories at U.S. companies had been erased. I found no trace of her birth, as if she never existed. I had nothing but Jonathon's stories of her to go on.

I couldn't allow my research to flatline. My most recent client, Bodhi Michaels, had been framed for laundering money for Kostya Tsezar. Bohdi was peripherally involved with the same organization Janko and

Tsezar worked for. Lucky for Bohdi, or lucky for me, I represented him in court. Per my counsel, he gave a list of names—people known to the Transnational Organized Crime group—in exchange for a lesser sentence. I perused the list of TOC members, this time looking for clues to Janko's connections in Russia, Croatia, and Greece.

One at a time, I eliminated them. They were wealthy businessmen and women. They were politicians and leaders. They were Russian expats and Saudi oil moguls. Some suffered moral ambiguation. Others got away with extortion, sexploitation, and other horrendous crimes. One of Bohdi's clients, R. O. Protsenko, had recently closed his accounts.

Protsenko seemed to have no past, no job history, and no address. I googled the name, and the search took me to the most notorious, Artur Myronovych Protsenko, the known leader of the Russian mafia. Artur was on every law enforcement watch list. Suspected of murdering hundreds of expatriates from Russia and Ukraine and dealing arms to terrorists, he was thought to be controlling numerous terrorist cells in Saudi Arabia, Uzbekistan, and Russia.

Was R. O. Protsenko his son? I dug deeper, reading as much as I could. An article dated almost twenty years ago spoke of an Interpol investigation into a series of terrorist attacks on the border between Austria and Hungary. During the investigation, Artur Protsenko was suspected of selling weapons to al Qaeda. At the time of the investigation, his ex-wife and child both fled Russia, eventually seeking asylum in Greece. The article gave their names: Olena Protsenko, his wife, and Rory Protsenko, his daughter.

I sat back in my leather desk chair as chilling waves washed over me.

Rory Bradford *was* Rory Protsenko. The daughter of TOC leader, Artur Protsenko.

Jonathon knew. That's why he didn't want me to go with him.

Rory had introduced Jonathon to Janko. She was clearly involved with the TOC group in more ways than one. He'd even seen her at an underground human auction where she was the auctioneer. Her name came up when Janko said, *She despises you!*

Jonathon had kept vital information from me.

In the days that followed, I called three police stations in Athens to ask if he'd been arrested. I studied the website for the International Commission on Missing Persons. The ICMP was *the* international authority for finding missing persons. They were overwhelmed with the searches for refugees from Ukraine and another massive earthquake in Turkey. They had no time or resources to help me find one missing man in Greece.

I was getting nowhere.

I needed to get out of my apartment. Pulling on yoga pants and a jacket, I took to the street in my jogging shoes. My cell phone was tucked into my pants pocket, and I pressed my Bluetooth earbuds into my ears.

A cold pre-winter blast hit me as I jogged toward Lake Michigan. The wind took my breath as I instructed Google to call Traci. She picked up on the first ring.

"I was just thinking about you, Wil." Traci still called me by an old nickname, short for Wilhelmina. Jonathon and his friends were the only ones who addressed me as Mina.

"How are you?" I stopped at a crosswalk and, jogging in place, waited for the signal to cross.

"Good. David and I were wondering if you want to go out to dinner this weekend. We wanted to try that new Korean place in Edgewater." She and David had been seeing each other since this summer. He'd kindly came to Traci's aid after Janko's men kidnapped her. David stood by her side throughout her recovery.

The walk signal flashed, and I crossed North Lakeview Avenue and headed toward the pedestrian path. "I'd love to, but I'm going out of town."

"That's sudden, isn't it?"

"Jonathon is missing, and I need to find him."

"You told me he hasn't called. But what can you do about it? He's in Greece, right?"

I'd told Traci everything about Jonathon's trip, except that he was on a mission to locate and stop his nemesis, Rory Bradford. At the time, I didn't know she was the only daughter of one of the world's most powerful Russian criminals.

"Are you and David still looking for a place to live together?"

Their romance began quickly and heated up fast. Lately, they'd spent so much time together, they decided to move in together as soon as Traci's lease was up for renewal.

"Yes. My lease ends this month and I have to put everything in storage. David's apartment near Northwestern is so tiny. We can't find a place we agree on. There's not much on the market right now."

"How would you like to stay at my place?" I jogged past the Laughter Gazebo and turned toward Sunshine Playground.

"What? How long will you be gone?"

"As long as it takes. Traci, I gave notice at Milton, Wallace, and Edwards. I'm taking an extended leave of absence. I might not be back by Christmas."

"You have the strangest ideas about vacations, Wil."

I had no preconceived notions that this would be a relaxing trip. "I'm worried about him. Besides, the Mediterranean sun will do me some good."

"We can stay at your place?"

"As long as you need."

"That would give us time to find a place we both agree on."

"It's a deal then. You can move in over the weekend."

"What has Jonathon gotten into this time, Wil?"

I couldn't tell Traci the level of Jonathon's involvement. I just didn't know.

– 8 –

JONATHON

TWO MONTHS AGO

"**I** like this one." Mina held the red leather handle of a flogger in one hand. She dragged the velvety twenty-four-inch straps across her arm, pausing to touch the soft leather.

I loved watching her peruse my collection of BDSM gear. After Rory, the last thing I wanted was another relationship. But for some reason, I obsessed about the gear. I collected whips and shackles, reeds, and ropes. I used them on a few willing women along the way. Women who I'd never share my feelings with. Or breakfast, for that matter.

"Is that what you want me to spank you with?" I asked.

"I'm not sure." She hung it on a hook between a stiff black crop and a bullwhip. "What's this?" She lifted a bondage strap away from the wall.

I took it off the hook and held it up for her. "These are ankle cuffs. The padded center of the strap goes behind your neck like so." I draped it over her neck with the ankle cuffs dangling from the strong elastic strap in front.

Mina fondled it as if trying on a new scarf. She toyed with the manacle. "My ankles go in here?"

"That's right."

"It would make the wearer very, um, accessible. My curiosity is piqued." She looked along the wall at my collection. "So this is a spreader?" She pointed nearby to a unique style of ankle cuffs with a metal bar between the straps.

I cleared my throat. I'd used that one on Rory—not at her request—many years ago. She'd made me very angry that day by showing up at an important meeting with the Mayo Clinic partners. We were discussing the best uses of PPS software for their hospitals and Rory walked in wearing a garter and lacy underwear with black stockings underneath a hip-length leather jacket. She pushed aside our laptops and paperwork and crawled up on the table.

That night I locked this very ankle spreader around Rory's legs and didn't let her go for forty-eight hours. I did unimaginable things to her during that time because I was so angry we'd almost lost the contract with the Mayo partners. In the aftermath, I sent hundreds of emails and apologies, and I lied to them—something I hate to do—telling them an employee had gone off the deep end. That she fantasized a relationship with me. And finally, I told them she was fired.

Rory never worked for PPS. She was cruel in her heartless attempts to get my attention. It always worked—she got what she wanted and laughed like a psycho bitch afterward. "See, Jonathon, you can be a dominant in the bedroom."

Shortly after that episode and dozens like it, I left her.

Mina took the spreader off the wall and examined it.

"Put it back," I said.

She locked her gaze on me for what seemed like an eternity. I took the spreader from her and hung it up.

"Why not that one?"

"You won't like it." I couldn't tell her the truth. I was afraid she wouldn't like *me* once I put it on her.

Her gaze was drawn to it, then me. "Are you afraid you'll hurt me?"

I couldn't answer. Mina was insightful. She was somehow attuned to me. I moved down the wall to a long length of rope. "Let me show you something else." I gathered the coil of smooth nylon rope in my hands and led Mina to the bed in the center of the room. On the way, she plucked the flogger off the wall and handed it to me.

"You know you can't hurt me," she said.

She didn't know me. "Kneel on the bed."

Mina was so willing. She was curious and excited. Like a kid in a candy shop. She was so unlike my last relationship with Rory, and I loved her more for that.

She held out her arms as I tied the ropes Japanese style around and around her chest—a bustier. Mina watched me lace the ends around her breasts, leaving her nipples free. Her breath was shallow as she looked me in the eye. "I want to feel the flogger. I want you to whip me."

I dragged my fingers between her moist folds. "You will. I'm going to own you tonight."

"I'd like that. I need to be punished."

I picked up the leather flogger and slapped it against the bed.

She flinched, but she also smiled seductively at me. "Don't hold back. I've been a very bad girl."

A puff of air exploded from my lungs. Mina was not a bad girl. Not to me. I longed to show her what I saw in her. She was strong and fierce, like a mother cougar. Protective and intense. Cautious and also timid. I longed to tell her how much I admired her.

I also longed—in my own strange way—to control her. Power play was like a dance. B&D play put the dominant–in this case, me—in a position of both caretaker, and punisher. To the sub, the ropes and bonds were really just a metaphor. When the submissive willingly let go, when she leaned into the restraints and finally submitted on the inside, it was like watching a flower bloom. It was like watching the unfolding of all the potency and vitality, the power of nature. A sunrise. A seed bursting with life. And having that power made me realize how small I really was. It made me feel...human.

Mina bent over the side of the bed and spread her legs. Tonight, if punishment was what she wanted, I would give it to her. I raised the flogger and let it fly at her ass.

− 9 −

MINA

As a submissive, you have all the control.

Jonathon told me not to come to Greece. I was never good at following his commands in the bedroom because ultimately, I wanted his punishment. My decision to go to Greece had nothing to do with our B&D relationship. I loved him. Despite our lifestyle, or because of it—because I could open up to him and share my darkest desires—I had to find him. If he was in danger, I needed to help. If he was hurt or suffering, I wanted to be there for him.

Traci and David moved into my apartment. I packed my suitcase with essentials and clothes for every possibility from formal to beachwear, including my cliff-diving gear. As I checked my closet one last time, I glanced at the new climbing shoes I wore to Devil's Lake. Greg's backpack and ropes accidentally ended up in my car.

I called an Uber, and on the way to Jonathon's condo, I called Greg.

"Hey. Your climbing gear is in my apartment. I let Traci know you'll come by to pick it up this week. She and David are moving in over the weekend."

"What?"

I told him the abridged version of my plan to go to Greece.

"That's the stupidest idea I've ever heard. You can't go, Mina!"

"Too late, Greg." I made the decision so fast, I hadn't even had time to make airline reservations.

"Why didn't you tell me? I'll book a flight and meet you there."

"Don't. There's no need for both of us to go." The last time he tried to help, he got shot. He was still recovering.

He breathed hard into the receiver.

"Geez. You don't need to get so worked up," I said.

"I'm on the treadmill. I'm putting in my 8000 steps for the day."

The Uber driver stopped at an intersection. Pedestrians crossed in front of the car. My gaze followed each man with dark hair in my subconscious search for Jonathon. "I need you to stay here, Greg. I need someone with stable internet access. There's no telling what kind of service there will be once I get there." Who knew what was available on the Mediterranean islands? "If one of Jonathon's associates calls, I need you to let me know."

Greg stayed silent for a few beats as the Uber moved through traffic toward Jonathan's Chicago apartment in the penthouse of the Waldorf Astoria. "Can I count on you?"

"I don't like it."

"I don't expect you to."

When I arrived at Jonathon's penthouse, the worst thoughts buzzed like a swarm of wasps in my head. Had Rory or Artur Protsenko's terrorists taken Jonathon? Was he hurt? Had he been tortured?

Dare I assume he was dead?

As I arrived at the penthouse with my suitcase in tow, the door opened. Assad Ridhwaan, Jonathon's driver and personal butler welcomed me. "We've been waiting for you."

"We?" Assad took my bag and led me to the spacious living room overlooking Lake Michigan. It had been six weeks since I'd been here. Everything was exactly as he'd left it except for one detail.

A man I didn't recognize stood near one of the Swedish chrome chairs. "Wilhelmina Green? It's a pleasure to meet you." His high-pitched voice coming from such a large man seemed almost cartoonish.

"And who are you?"

He approached me with his hand extended. The diamond and gold cufflinks on his crisp white shirt glistened from beneath the cuffs of his finely tailored dark-gray suit. A bright, lime green and yellow paisley tie hugged his plump, pale neck. His complexion was as white as any vampire portrayed in the movies. "Kent Whitaker. I'm Jonathon's personal banker."

I shook his hand and set my purse on a chair. "I don't understand."

"In the event Jonathon broke off contact, I was to meet with you."

"Who set this up?"

"Jonathon did," Asaad said. "Before he left. I called Mr. Whitaker right after you told me you were flying to Greece."

The possibility that my worst-case scenarios rang true swelled to enormous size.

A thick black-leather file pouch sat on the coffee table. I sank into the couch, my knees suddenly weak. "Have you heard from him?"

"No." Kent pinched his slacks above the knee and sat stiffly in the stylized Swedish chair. "But that's the point, isn't it? In the event that something happened to Jonathon, he wanted to give you power of attorney over all his finances."

"All?" I balked.

"Yes. He wants you to take control."

Assad came to my side. "Please have a seat. You have a lot to go over with Mr. Whitaker. Can I get you anything, sir? Water? Coffee? A drink?"

"I'll take coffee with skim milk and stevia sweetener if you have it," Whitaker said. "Otherwise, I'll take it with milk, not cream, and any sugar-free sweetener you have."

"We have stevia and two percent."

"Go light on the milk then."

"Mina?" Assad waited expectantly.

I couldn't believe this was happening. "Coffee would be nice. Thank you, Assad," I said.

Assad nodded and backed out of the room.

Whitaker opened the leather pouch and pulled out a stack of pre-prepared legal documents and two pens. We got to work.

An hour and a half later after we'd finished the coffee, my hand was tired from signing all the paperwork. The banker stood to leave. "What will you do now, Ms. Green?"

"I'm going to find him. Mr. Whitaker—"

"Please call me Kent."

I nodded. "Kent. The TOC groups we're dealing with won't respond to puny, half-assed attempts. It's going to require big guns. And by big guns, I mean large sums of money. Perhaps that's why Jonathon gave me POA."

"I'm in complete agreement, Ms. Green." He tucked the pouch with all the signed documents under his arm.

"Mr. Whitaker, Kent, I'd like you to free up 100 million dollars and move it to a cash account. Just in case."

"Just in case," he repeated. "Anything you need."

"I'm glad you're in agreement." I walked him to the door. "I'll need that to be available by the morning."

He took a sharp breath and stuck a finger beneath the knot of his tie. "I'll do what I can."

"Thank you."

When I closed the door, I looked at my phone. Still no phone calls from Jonathon. I tried calling his number again. The automated recording answered.

Where are you? I couldn't believe this was happening.

During our last conversation, he'd said two or three men he couldn't identify were following him. His bodyguards were on high alert. The last thing he'd spoken of was a statue of Poseidon in the center of a square. How many statues like that could there be?

I needed to make airline reservations, so I went to the kitchen and sat on a stool next to Assad.

"Are you hungry? I can cook something for you," he said.

"Not right now. I need to buy an airline ticket."

"No, you don't." Assad smiled. "Mr. Huen has a private jet."

I lowered my phone and gazed at him. I'd forgotten that Jonathon flew me from Wollongong back to the States. "How do I get hold of his pilot?"

In the morning, Assad would drive me to the airport, and I'd board Jonathon's private jet. My heart pounded with the familiar adrenaline rush of escaping my life as if I were going on an exotic, extreme-sport vacation. In the past few years, I'd traveled to Mexico, Lake Champlain,

Croatia, and Wollongong, Australia. I'd taken these clandestine trips with one purpose in mind.

Tombstoning.

To dive from the highest cliff I could find into deep, pristine waters. To attain the thrill that comes with falling sixty or more feet through the air at high velocity. When I hit the water it was the nearest thing to death that I would ever experience. And as the water swallowed me, it silenced my thoughts. My guilt. I felt forgiven. It was the only thing that purged me of the negative rhetoric buzzing in my brain. I knew it was an unhealthy addiction. My therapist agreed. But nothing else freed me from the bonds of guilt . . .

Until Jonathon came along with his bondage gear and whips, diving was the only thing that gave me the feeling of atonement. His punishment absolved me. In his torture chamber, I paid for my sins. I paid for helping to acquit evil men. For helping them get away with murder.

Though I craved Jonathon's dominance, his control, and I missed the sting of his crop on my ass, most of all, I missed his forgiveness. His tenderness. His kind understanding of what I'd been through.

Once again, I recalled the stories Jonathon told me about Rory. Was I jealous? Perhaps. She had been Jonathon's submissive in sex, but that's where our similarities ended. She was obsessed about being a submissive and constantly asked him to treat her as such. She acted out and misbehaved in order to get Jonathon's attention. They argued constantly, according to him.

She was the reason Jonathon asked me to sign a dominant and submissive contract. Before he left, he tore it up. He professed his love. A feeling that I strongly reciprocated.

This trip was to rescue my missing lover.

-10-

MINA

Leo Thibodeaux, Jonathon's pilot, flew a Gulfstream G650. "One of the fastest mid-sized jets," he said. "I'll get you there in no time."

We flew to New York for refueling then across the Atlantic to Attiki Odos, the bustling Athens International Airport. There was a flight attendant on board, and though I was the only passenger, I felt utterly spoiled by the luxury treatment.

We arrived around four thirty in the afternoon and deboarded the plane. A warm, salty breeze smelling of diesel fuel and bus exhaust whipped hair from my face.

Leo handed me my suitcase. He towered over me, but leaned in slightly to ask, "When will you return to the States?"

"I'm not sure. Can I reach out if I need to go . . . somewhere?" I wasn't sure if I'd need to fly around Europe. I certainly had no idea when I'd return to Chicago.

"I'll be available whenever you need me. Just call."

"Thank you, Leo."

He shook my hand. "Good luck, Ms. Green. I hope you're able to find Mr. Heun."

As did I.

I collected my luggage and hailed a cab. I didn't know if Jonathon had people here in Greece. In case Rory was watching, waiting for me, I decided to stay offline and remain inconspicuous.

"Where are you headed, *despoinída?*" the cab driver asked.

For a month I'd been listening to Greek language tapes and knew the cab driver had called me *miss*. "The Acropolis View Hotel," I said. The same hotel Jonathon stayed in when he arrived in Greece almost six weeks ago.

Almost an hour later, I stood my rose-colored, Samsonite suitcase upright beside the front desk and waited. The painted arched ceiling soared above me. Potted palms and long, pale diaphanous curtains added warmth to the large windows and marble floors. A middle-aged gentleman with short gray hair finished typing on his keyboard and glanced my way.

"May I help you?" he asked.

"I'm checking in, and I'd like to speak to someone about guest records. Is it possible to find out when my friend checked out of your hotel?"

"Let me check you in, then I'll get a manager to help you."

He took my information then handed me an agreement to sign and a key card. "Your room has already been paid for."

"What? How?"

"A gentleman named J. T. Heun was expecting you."

My heart missed a beat. "Is he here? Is he still here?"

"Let me get the manager to help you," he said.

A uniformed woman wearing her hair in a tight bun came from behind a closed door. As she approached, she straightened her navy blue jacket. "Let's see." She gazed at a computer screen turned away from me. "It looks like Mr. Heun checked out on October eleventh."

The date struck me. "That was one week ago."

"That's correct. Mr. Heun was with us for . . . let's see . . . five weeks. That's a very long stay." This information made no sense to me. Jonathon didn't stay in one location. He moved around. He was looking for Rory.

It had been two weeks since I'd spoken with my lover. At the time, I didn't know I'd be traveling to Greece. So how . . .? "How did he arrange to pay for my room? How did he anticipate my trip?"

"He left explicit instructions and a credit card number when he checked out." She asked if I was his wife.

I wished I were. Then all this would surely be over. "No, I'm his fiancée." The word slid out as easily as water from a fountain cherub's mouth. "I don't know where to find him. *Leipei. Mou leipei.*" He's missing. I miss him.

"I'm so sorry."

"Did he say where he was going? Someone must have spoken with him."

"It looks like he checked out digitally. I'm sorry, that's all the information I can give you," the manager said.

It didn't make sense. I rubbed my dry, tired eyes and slung my purse over my shoulder. I took my key card and suitcase to the elevator.

As the hotel name Acropolis View suggested, my room had a small balcony with a view of the Parthenon. Weary from the long flight, I sank into the mattress and plugged my phone into the European travel adaptor.

There was plenty of time to recover that night, and my body began to adjust to the eight-hour time difference. After showering, I changed from my travel clothes into yoga pants and a T-shirt. Unlike my tombstoning trips—which were my secret pleasure—I let my family and all of my colleagues know I was going to Greece. Greg insisted. And unlike my secret trips, the dangers I faced here were out of my control. Rory was unpredictable. She was a terrorist.

I responded to texts from my dad. *"I made it to Greece. It's beautiful here."*

My brother, James, wrote, *"Living the life, I hear. I want photos."*

I answered, *"I'm testing the water. Someday we'll take this trip with your family."* James's wife, Sienna, and their two young boys would love a vacation without the dangers I sailed into.

Finally, I called Jonathon. Like the hundreds of times I'd called before, the call was picked up by his provider. *This number is no longer available.*

Before I left Chicago, I'd called three Athens police stations and received very little help. The problem was, there were a half-dozen police stations in this area. Now, I made my first call to the Athens Foreigners Division Police Station.

After I chose English language in the menu, the automated answering service prompted, "How may I direct your call? Please select from the following services."

I skipped the second menu and hit o for the operator.

"*Pósous se voithâo?* How may I help you?" The man's languid way of talking made me think I made a mistake calling. *Would he take me seriously? Would he even care?*

I let out the breath I'd been holding. "I'd like to know if a friend of mine has been arrested." It was a long shot for sure. Jonathon wouldn't have done anything criminal. Not on purpose.

"Is he American?"

"Yes. His name's Jonathon Heun. I'd like you to check records from the past two weeks." I opened the sliding door to my small private balcony. The fresh-but-tepid air did nothing to revive my tired senses.

"Are you working with the U.S. Embassy?" he asked.

I had already asked the embassy if an arrest had been reported. The embassy wasn't in the business of finding missing persons. They were there to help with legal matters and foreign affairs related to crime. They didn't waiver in their response that no one had reported or contacted them about Jonathon Heun.

The man on the phone droned on while, I assumed, he looked through some file on his computer. The conversation was going nowhere. ". . . I see no record of arrest for the man you speak of. Contact your embassy to report a missing American. If your friend is missing, the embassy will contact us. Or contact the International Commission on Missing Persons. The IMCP should be able to help you."

Seriously? Bureaucracy.

He hung up. At least it was more than I'd gotten so far.

Before I left Chicago, I'd visited the IMCP website. They worked with government agencies and the United Nations Human Rights Council to ensure individual rights and to protect individuals from trafficking or other crimes related to forced disappearance. Their vast mission—to find the collective missing after tragedies such as 9/11 in New York City and the mass exodus in Ukraine—was a colossal undertaking. The organization also ensured the agencies involved in investigative work maintained transparency and protocol.

And yet, without a crime to investigate, I had nowhere to turn.

Standing on my balcony, my gaze fell on the Acropolis and the Parthenon atop it. Scaffolding for repair work laced around the pillars. In the distance, small gray clouds dotted the sky over the mountain range. My cab driver had proudly pointed to the Paneion Oros Mountain peak in the near distance. The largest mountain in Greece, Hymettus, was hidden today by the hazy horizon.

Jonathon had seen these sights. When he first arrived, he told me all about them. Now, I wondered if he could see these mountains from wherever he was.

Determined to find him, I could not let bureaucracy get in the way. I needed sleep.

The next morning, a half-eaten croissant lay in ruins on my plate, surrounded by a smattering of black fig seeds and an apricot pit. My laptop open, I continued my search for Sotoris Island through more than two thousand Greek islands. These islands dotted the Aegean Sea all the way to Turkey's shore. Almost two hundred were inhabited.

Was Jonathon mistaken about the name of the island? No such island with that name existed in the Aegean Sea, the Sea of Crete, or the Ionian Sea. If the Protsenko family owned an island, it would surely be unregistered. I was looking for a four-leaf clover on a mountainside.

Feeling defeated, I sat back and looked up at the ancient temple. The gods were laughing at me. Hecate, the goddess of death, was probably collecting wagers about my ability to find Jonathon.

–11–

JONATHON

For days—maybe a week?—I slept on a four-poster bed draped in sheer white fabric and white sheets. I was aware of someone caring for wounds. A burn on my hand. A lump on the back of my head. A split lip.

The young girl caring for me never spoke. Once, I opened my eyes and a huge Black man stood behind her with an Uzi pointed at me. I closed my eyes again. When I recovered enough to get out of bed, I paced in the small, elegant room. Behind me, a comfortable, thickly upholstered chair with too many pillows was angled in the corner. A heavy wooden desk situated under the window had no stool to sit on. A simple bathroom had a toilet, pedestal sink, and electronic touch controlled shower.

There were no paintings on the white walls, no decorations. And no instruments. No razor to shave my scruffy facial hair. Not even a pencil and paper to write with at the desk.

I gazed out the window of my prison cell—because that's what it was—and the view was breathtaking and clear because the villa was—I gasped—on a cliff.

Small islands dotted the horizon and an endless blue sea. I thought only of Mina.

From this height . . . I inched to the window and dared myself to look down. I hated heights. I hated that feeling of my stomach rising up to meet my heart. In Chicago, I'd forced myself to stand near the windows. I forced myself to look down and face my fear. My phobia was a weakness I hoped to someday conquer.

Mina, on the other hand, would love this. I envied her bravery. I felt only awe for the stories she'd told. And as I gazed out at the edge of the cliff, I tried to imagine coming from a place of strength. Like hers.

Nausea rushed up, filling my mouth with saliva and that weak feeling of fear—acrophobia. I rushed to the bathroom and crouched over the toilet. My stomach emptied, and I rinsed my mouth in the sink.

Before I left the U.S., I'd sent Mina a fiery red flare. If something were to happen to me, I needed someone to have access to my accounts. They would need resources to find me. And only Mina knew the kind of danger I faced here in Greece. By giving her POA over my accounts, she would suspect I was in grave danger. *Was there any other kind?* Of course not. And by sending up that flare, I expected Mina to do whatever it took. She would come for me.

But now . . .

Somehow I needed to warn her not to. I didn't want her to become Rory's next victim. Did Stan Moorlehem know I was alive? And what about Javier? I had no memory of the blast, or the hours afterward. I only know that I woke in the clutches of terrorists.

Stay in Chicago, Mina. Don't come looking for me.

I wanted desperately to call her. Tell her to stay home. To tell her I deeply missed her.

Rory and two of her men had entered the basement where Marco Vorobiev held me captive. After I killed Marco, Rory brought me here, the island I believe to be called Sotoris. The flight by helicopter took hours, and I determined the island must be on the eastern side of the Aegean Sea near Turkey. I assumed this because we knew one of her fentanyl manufacturing plants was in Izmir. Whether I was right made no difference. Here, she locked me in a tower bedroom in her villa. The locked and guarded room had no doorknob, only two deadbolts that could only be opened with keys.

I had a gnawing suspicion that I'd see Mina sooner than I wished. She was tenacious. Rory was a psycho bitch. I dreaded what Rory would do to her.

Days passed and I longed for a razor to shave my beard. The young Muslim girl brought me clean, soft clothes every day and took the dirty ones away. She never brought shoes or a belt—though I asked for them.

She didn't seem to speak English. I was unfamiliar with her dialect—a form of Arabic—and I wondered why she was here.

Other than the girl's twice-daily visits, I was left alone. Alone with the expansive, terrifying view. Alone with the rise and set of the sun. Alone with my thoughts. And this gave my wounds time to heal. My beard grew in and, day by day, I watched the scabs from cigarette burns on my chest peel and turn pink. It gave me time to scheme.

After ten days, I heard her voice in the hall outside my door. *She* had finally come to talk.

A key unlocked the deadbolts. When Rory opened the door, her bodyguards stood between us.

"You look like hell, Jonathon."

"What do you want, Rory?"

She crossed her arms and locked her gaze on mine, as if daring me to look away. Though she looked elegant in her white linen pants and silky off-white camisole, her features had hardened. She dressed her black hair in an elegant chignon at the base of her neck. Her sinewy arms and her narrow waist were no longer sexy. Time had not been her friend. The ropey tendons in her neck gave her a gaunt, cadaverous look. Yet there was power and ownership in her hard gaze. It was clear that she feared nothing, and no one dared get in her way.

In that I saw her weakness. Me.

"Your lover is right on schedule," she said. "She flew to Greece and she's walking right into my trap. I reserved a room at the Acropolis Hotel, assuming she would go where you did. She's so predictable. What could you possibly see in her?"

I lunged at Rory. The two large Black men caught me by the arms and held me back. One swiftly put me in a lock from behind and held me. I kicked at his shins with my bare feet, and it certainly hurt me more than it did him. A head taller than me, he swiftly locked my neck in his elbow as his strong hands gripped my wrists. I was weak—healing—and lost the fight. The other guard, more my size, aimed his automatic weapon at my face.

Rory threw her head back as wicked laughter erupted from her. "Still *practicing* martial arts, Jon? My men are prepared for you. You won't escape. Answer my questions, and maybe I'll let you go to her."

"What questions?"

"Thanks to you, Interpol is investigating now. Making my life a living hell. I'm keeping you here like a rat in a cage where you'll be much less of a pest to me."

I spit at her feet.

"Maybe when Mina is pleading for her life, you'll give in to me. Maybe then you'll kneel at *my* feet."

"Leave Mina out of this." I fought to get away from the guard holding my arms. "I have nothing to say to you."

Rory walked to the window. "Janko told me you found true love. He told me all about your little arrangement with Wilhelmina Green, the hottest criminal defense attorney in Chicago."

"You don't know anything about her."

"She lives in Lincoln Park in a secured high-rise facing the lake. Her good friend Traci Lambert and boyfriend David Maccoby moved into her flat. They'll stay there while she's away. So nice to see that Traci recovered from that tragic abduction this summer."

Her sarcastic tone sickened me. "You did that *to her!*"

Rory didn't miss a beat. "Wilhelmina—what a ridiculous name, by the way— most recently represented Bohdi Michaels. Made a fool of Federal Prosecutor Harvey Slater, don't you think? Oh, and you hired her when your dear little right-hand assistant, Kymani Zhao, was brutally murdered. So ugly what they did to her. But you're not capable of murder, are you?"

"Let's test that theory, shall we?" I struggled to get free, and her terrorist soldier held me tighter.

She faced me. "It's funny, isn't it? You told me you'd never play with whips and chains ever again."

The guard choked me with his thick arm. "You're pure evil," I coughed.

"I wished you'd told me the truth about BDSM back then, Jonathon."

"What truth?" I had no idea where the one-sided conversation was leading.

"Dominance is like an addiction. Once you feel the power of control, you never want to submit ever again. Do you?" She stood less than a foot from me.

"I'm not power hungry like you are."

"Oh? I have no doubt she's the submissive in your relationship." She squinted at me and smiled evilly. "Wait. That's not true, is it? Is she the dominant one?"

"What difference does it make?" I'd had enough of her teasing. I fought to get away, but the man held me fast. The other cocked and raised his automatic weapon at my head.

"Oh, it makes all the difference, Jon. Don't you see? Now that I have you back, I want you to suffer, the way I suffered when we were together. I won't kill her, no. Do you know why not? I want you to beg me to keep her alive. I want you to beg me, to offer your very soul, for her freedom. And you will. Can you guess why?"

"I have no idea." I ground my teeth together.

"Because there are men in this world who would love to have a successful, American woman kneel at their feet. There are men who want *that* kind of control. They want to break women like her, and they'll pay a very nice sum. In fact, the money I earn from selling her to the highest bidder will almost replace the money you took from me when you stole my shipment of fentanyl."

"You wouldn't."

"Yes, I would, Jon." Her lashes fluttered as she narrowed her mean gaze. "You're the lucky one. You get to watch her submit to these men."

"You'll never catch her. I'll make sure of it." I pitied her. "You have no idea what you're up against."

She walked to the door. "You're wrong. In case you haven't noticed, you're a prisoner. I'm going to keep you like a bird in a cage. So you'll never fly again. You'll wither and die up here. The world will pass you by, and no one will miss you."

-12-

MINA

While I was holed up in my Athens hotel room, I had a lot of time to think about the past. Four months ago, a few weeks after Jonathon and I met—after we signed the legal documents, and I officially became his criminal defense attorney—he took me out to dinner. He loved to show off his knowledge of five-star restaurants and had a taste for expensive food. The attraction between us was still fresh, the heat almost unbearable, making me worry about having sex with a client.

We returned to his apartment together. I knew it was a bad idea, but my sexual curiosity had been teased. Jonathon had professed to being dominant in the bedroom. It was something I had always wanted to explore with the right person.

He had barely closed the door before pulling me close, pressing his body against mine in a heated embrace. I wrapped my arms around his narrow waist. His hands made their way down to my hips. Standing on my toes, I stretched upward to meet his lips. His kiss was soft, and his breath smelled of cinnamon. I opened my mouth, letting him in. Letting him take me. Jonathon tugged at my lips with his teeth then bit harder. When I moaned, he kissed my chin and neck, making his way down to my shoulders.

I let my hands drop onto his firm ass and lost myself in the moment. He smelled of expensive cologne: a heady aroma conjuring memories of exotic beaches and fresh greenery. "I want you," I whispered. "I want to submit to you. I want to explore BDSM."

"Do you?" Jonathon pushed me against the wall, placed his hands on my shoulders and pressed one leg between both of mine. I straddled him, pressing into his thigh, and coaxed my arousal. He pushed the strap of my sundress down and reached behind me for my zipper.

"Yes." My dress fell to the floor. When I stepped out if it, he scooped me into his arms. While we kissed, firmly locking our lips together, he carried me through the doorway of the nearest room. His muscles were solid and strong. Jonathon's strength was my aphrodisiac.

I grappled with the buttons on his shirt as he bit at my neck and earlobe, toying with my skin, teasing with his teeth. He pushed the strap of my bra aside and kissed my shoulder and arm. Then he casually put my small wrists into one of his strong hands and backed me into a wall. Holding me there, he unfastened his belt with his other hand.

"What are you doing?"

Jonathon maintained eye contact. Once his belt was free, he looped it around my wrists, shifting his hold to the belt.

I gasped at the swiftness with which he overpowered me. A surge of adrenaline went through me when I realized he now had control of me.

"Feeling helpless, Mina?" His voice was calm and cool, seductive.

My lips parted.

"I'm going to outline some rules," he said.

I liked rules. My heart raced with excitement, like riding a new roller coaster for the first time. I didn't reply.

"I want you to call me Master."

Master. The meaning carried dark notes of control which implied consequences. I nodded. I knew what was in store and heated with desire.

"It's not a request. You will say, 'yes, Master' or, 'no, Master.' Is that clear?"

Broken rules meant punishment. I was curious where it would lead. I needed to know the consequences if I screwed up. My vulva pulsed when I nodded again.

Still holding my wrists in the belt loop, he swiftly bent me over his knees so I lay across his lap. It happened so fast I didn't have time to fight back. His domination and complete control, immediate.

He spanked me hard. "Answer the question, Mina. Do you understand the rule?"

It stung when he hit me two more times. I likened it to the sting of the water's surface when I dove from several dozen meters. It was punishing, yes, but the pain removed all my worry and fear. Somehow, it brought peace of mind.

"Yes, Master." I inwardly smiled.

"Louder," he commanded, spanking me again.

"Yes, Master."

I locked my gaze on him, curious what other plans he had for this encounter.

"Now we're getting somewhere." While still holding my hands in the belt loop, Jonathon walked with me toward a heavy curtain.

He drew back the curtain and revealed a tall X-shaped board in the shadows.

"Wait, Master . . . Jonathon . . ."

The look in his eyes frightened me.

"Master." I met his gaze.

"Are you nervous? Are you afraid, Mina?" He cuffed one wrist to a ring on the top of the X.

I nodded.

"You said you were curious about BDSM. Here's how it works. Use your safe word, *red*. When you say it, I will stop immediately."

I was wary now. "I don't want you to hurt me so badly that I have to use my safe word."

"I am not going to hurt you unless you don't follow the rules. But if you don't like it, you'll have a way of stopping me from going too far. You have control." He unlocked a trunk on the floor and pulled out a pair of handcuffs.

I wanted to explore bondage and discipline, and I thought I'd be giving all the power to the man I chose. What I hadn't realized was, he gave me the power to stop it all. I tugged at the cool handcuffs and delighted in the feeling of helplessness coursing through my veins.

"Yes, Master," I said.

He ran his fingers across my lips. I kissed them. Sucked on them. His breathing became slow and deep. I matched it with deep breaths of my own. He dragged his moist fingers down the center of my throat to the dip above my collarbone, to my breasts. I arched into him, and he cupped my breasts in both hands, squeezing my nipples between his thumb and fingers.

I closed my eyes and let the sensation trickle to my moist pussy. One of his hands flattened against my belly and moved to my thigh. The other, he dragged to my panties. He tugged on them. Pressed his fingers against my mound, teasing my little nub to an erection beneath the cloth. I moaned.

"Do you want me to touch you?"

"Yes, Master."

He slid his fingers beneath the panties and fingered my moist folds. I throbbed with desire. I groaned and pressed my hips into his hands.

He pulled my panties off and fingered me gently. I began to climax.

He stopped, stood, and moved deliberately to my neck. My chest.

"Take me, Jonathon. Please, make me come."

The bright, awakening sting of his hand against my inner thigh forced air into my lungs. He locked his gaze on me. Even in the dim light, the whites of his eyes frightened me. He slapped me again, this time on the other thigh. I gritted my teeth and sucked in air.

It went on this way, the sting of his hand warming the flesh on my thighs, until heat poured off my skin. I was about to say the safe word when Jonathon stopped and dropped to his knees in front of me.

He began licking my clitoris, teasing me then stopping. Slapping my hot, burning thighs then stroking my clit with his firm tongue. I craved the release. I longed for it with obsessive fixation. I pulled on the chains. I wanted to touch myself, to relieve the fervor building down there. The torture was unbearable.

The orgasm took me gradually at first, beginning as a spasm, then growing in heat and intensity. I slipped into the black hole of uncontrolled release. It enveloped me like a warm blanket on a wintry night, and I disappeared into its darkness.

"Oh, Jonathon." I moaned.

He stood. Looking me in the eyes, he removed his pants. "Do you want me, Mina?"

"Yes, Master." No hesitation.

He tossed his pants aside and approached me. His hot throbbing cock brushed against my legs. He kissed my breasts. I pulled hard at my bonds, longing to touch him and run my fingers through his hair. "Oh, please," I begged.

He slapped my tender thighs and this time I knew. "Please, *Master.*" I begged. "Please fuck me, Master. Please!"

He spread my legs wide, causing the handcuffs holding my wrists to tighten against the board. He slid his hot, hard cock into my dripping wet sex. With my arms stretched above my head, I was unable to return his thrusts. It was so raw. He slid up and down, pressing me against the board. His carnal need and engorged cock filled me, bringing me to the edge of release again. I gloried in it, allowing him to control me.

He built up a fervor as fierce and violent as a criminal attack—then thrust into me—slamming me against the rigid wood. Faster. Harder. When he reached his threshold he cried out in ecstasy. I too, reached a peak and moaned with him.

Jonathon rested his forehead on my shoulder for a moment. Our sweat mingled where he pressed his body against mine. Moments later, he unlocked the handcuffs and lowered my arms. Then he picked me up, carried me to the bed, and collapsed next to me. We lay naked together, quiet in the afterglow.

"You never used your safe word."

Heat still radiated off my tender thighs. It was the first time Jonathon delivered so much pain and my first experience with the X-rack. But I didn't need to use the safe word. Somehow, I always felt safe with Jonathon, even when he was at his steeliest.

I didn't need to wonder about Rory's first time with Jonathon. He told me all about her. Most women wouldn't want to hear how their lover fucked another woman, but at the time I'd been starved for him. Janko Vorobiev was threatening Jonathon, using me against him. It was then Jonathon first admitted his love for me. He stayed true to me. No matter how I resisted him, he always came through. He'd shot a love arrow through my heart, and now I couldn't imagine life without him.

–13–

MINA

I finished my coffee with cream and gazed out at the ancient ruins in the distance. From my hotel balcony, I could see distant statues of Orpheus and Eurydice, and Eros and Psyche. They had stood the test of time. A pleasant breeze brushed my skin, and I thought of Jonathon. I didn't know if our love would last, but I was oh so willing to try. I missed his untamable black hair and steely blue eyes. I missed his sultry voice and the way he took control of me. The way he could punish then forgive me with a tender kiss. I missed his clean, fresh smell.

You said you were hopelessly in love. Why haven't you called?

Tendrils of jealousy curled along my skin. He'd gone looking for Rory. Was he with her now? Was that why he didn't call?

When Jonathon first met Rory, he didn't know she was the daughter of a crime syndicate leader. She was studying Japanese culture as part of a foreign studies major. She spoke Japanese, Russian, French, and German, according to Jonathon. Later, she introduced him to Janko Vorobiev. Most recently, she'd been a translator for government officials in Austria and Hungary. Jonathon last saw her at a private auction of trafficked men and women. She was the auctioneer.

As Janko had put it, she *despised* Jonathon. She was part of Janko's blackmail operation, we just didn't know to what degree. How could I be jealous? He assured me that he hated her.

I gazed out at the pillars and ruins and people going about their daily lives. Could we ever have a normal life like that? Listening to the traffic on the street below, I heard something else rise above Athens' low hum. The buzz of a remote-control airplane or—there it was, flying just above the trees—a drone.

The black, bug-like craft had four sets of copter-like blades and hovered in the air three stories below my room. The X-shaped device—about a foot in diameter—rose slowly. As it came nearer, I saw the round lens of a camera mounted on the top beneath the whirling blades. As if scanning each balcony, the camera turned side to side.

Could the controller of the device see inside the hotel rooms? *What is it looking for?*

Before it reached the level of my balcony, I went inside and tightly closed the curtains. In case I was its target, I was afraid to look outside again,. Still, sitting here in this hotel room was not helping me find Jonathon.

Ready to hit the pavement, I dressed and slipped on my comfortable Sorels and glanced down at my suitcase. My dad's police issue Browning lay inside. After debating whether to carry it with me—the drone spooked me—I opened the safe in the closet and locked the gun inside. Bringing it on this trip made me feel safer. Jonathon had made the dangers clear.

Within an hour, a cab driver left me at Alimos Marina, the one Jonathon had spoken of during one of our calls. Masts of hundreds of sailing yachts and catamarans lined the shore and docks. Yachts bobbed in the clear blue-green water, moored and awaiting their owners' next adventure. The vertical masts of sailboats pointed to the sky like a forest of leafless trees.

I pulled the photo of Jonathon out of my purse and got to work, walking down each dock, and stopping every pedestrian, boat owner, and fisherman. *"Echete dei aftón ton ánthropo?"* Have you seen this man?

I asked a group of chattering women loading their sailboat for a day trip. I asked an elderly couple untying their boat and shoving off from the dock. I asked the cashier at the marina gas station and everyone whose path I crossed.

"No. I'm sorry I can't help you," they replied.

The day wore on. The hot sun heated my cheeks, and my shoulders had begun to pink with the coming of a sunburn. I hadn't thought to put on sunscreen. My stomach growled and I looked at my cell phone for the time. It was well after noon.

An approaching man wore belted cargo shorts and a white, short sleeve, button-front shirt. His dark, weathered skin had seen years of Mediterranean sun.

I stood up from a wooden bench and held out Jonathon's picture. "Excuse me. Have you seen this man?" I asked in Greek.

To my surprise, he nodded and set down a tackle box and the armful of towels he'd been carrying. "Speak English?"

"Yes." My heart thumped in double-time.

"He is a striking man, unforgettable." His English was good. "He was here at the marina, was it last month?" The man's kind eyes searched mine as he took the photo in a well-manicured but callused hand.

"Yes. Last month," I said. "He rented a boat—a yacht—from someone here. He's missing now."

"Oh. I'm not sure I can help you." He handed back the photo and leaned to pick up his tackle box.

"Please. I need to find him. The police are no help. He's been missing for almost three weeks. Can you at least tell me who he rented the yacht from?"

The man shook his head. "He wanted to charter from me, but I was booked that week."

"When was that exactly?"

"It was around the beginning of September. I remember because I wished your man had chartered my boat. Instead, I booked a family of seven. Two brothers from Texas with their wives and three children. They were an unruly group from the moment we set sail. Let the kids run wild while the brothers and their wives drank all day. I speak good English, no? But I'm no babysitter. Those kids . . ."

"You do speak English very well." I tried to be conversational.

"I learn so I can do business with everyone, no?"

I steered the conversation back on track. "Do you know whose yacht Jonathon chartered?"

The man looked down the pier. "I recommended another charter. I don't know if they worked something out or not."

"What's your friend's name?" I wished he would just tell me. "Which sailboat is his?"

"Alex Buccino. I haven't seen Alex in weeks. He's probably anchored in Kriti where he spends the winter."

The island of Crete, as we say in English, was another airplane ride away. "Do you have his phone number?"

"That I do, my lady." He dictated from his cell phone contact as I typed the number in.

"My name is Karolos Samaroulis."

"Wilhelmina Green. Nice to meet you, Karolos. Thank you for your help."

"Call me Karl. I'm happy to help a beautiful woman out. Good luck with your quest, *despoinída*." He walked away.

I made the call. After I introduced myself and told him Jonathon was missing, I asked, "Mr. Buccino, did Jonathon Heun charter your yacht?"

"Slow down, slow down, *despoinída*. What's your name?"

This time, I didn't hesitate. "Mina. I'm Jonathon's fiancée."

"Ah. Jonathon anticipated your call. He said you are tenacious."

"Believe it." I sat on the bench near the docks as my heart raced. Alex brought me one step closer to finding Jonathon. "I've come all the way from Chicago to find him. Now I'm tracing his last known locations. Please tell me the last time you saw him."

Alex paused for a moment. I thought he hung up. "Alex?"

"I took him to Mikonos where he stayed in a villa owned by a friend."

"I need to know everything." Now that I had Alex's attention, I was interviewing a witness. "What day was that? Where else did you go? Did he meet someone? Was he taken by force?"

"Where are you now?"

"I'm at the Alimos Marina in Athens. Can we meet?" I stared out at the vast blue Mediterranean. "You need to tell me what's going on. He's in danger."

"No more than you are, Ms. Green. He is afraid for you."

His use of present tense didn't get past me. "Where is he?"

"Ms. Green, I can send someone for you. Tell me exactly where you are."

"I'm on the docks. Is he alive? Will you take me to him?"

"No, *despoinída.*"

I sat back. "Why the hell not?"

"Because I made a promise."

"How good is his promise if he's dead?"

"He is not dead," Alex said.

"You're sure?" I felt so close to finding Jonathon, yet a thousand miles separated us.

"Positive. He is with *her* now."

"What are you saying?"

"She is convinced he will come back to her."

"Impossible. Jonathon loves me." Pangs of jealousy drove needles into my heart.

"There is nothing like the rage of a jilted lover. Especially when she has a means to an end."

"How long ago did you leave him with her?"

"About two weeks."

My breathing grew shallow. *Who was the jilted lover now? Rory or me?* I gazed at the puffy gray clouds on the horizon where a storm gave back to the sea beneath it. From somewhere above, I heard the sound of a drone flying above the trees. I ducked under the eaves of a nearby building. "Can you meet me in Athens? I'm afraid to talk on the phone."

"I'll find you. Just stay where you are."

The drone hovered high above the docks, slowly turning toward me. I asked again, "Will you take me to him?"

My gut tightened. For some reason, Alex didn't make me feel safer. "Okay. When can I expect you?"

"Soon, *despoinída.*"

I thanked him and hung up the phone. Something wasn't right. I had no time to lose. As the buzz of the drone drew nearer, I decided not to wait. I pulled a scarf over my head and jogged after Karolos.

Since I hadn't seen which boat he boarded, I called, "Karolos? Hello?

Mr. Samaroulis?" Near the end of the dock, I spotted him on a handsome catamaran where he looped a length of rope around his elbow.

"You said that you'll charter a yacht?"

He sucked in his lower lip. "The *Dragonfly* happens to be free this week. But only until Friday."

Five days. It gave me five days. "Are you available?"

"Yes."

He set the rope aside and disembarked the catamaran. Facing me with a friendly smile, he stuck out his hand to shake mine. My search was on course again and—for now—no longer stuck in the doldrums.

Near the shore, a drone hovered over the sailing yachts.

-14-

JONATHON

When Rory had entered my room with her guerillas, she didn't know I'd find a way to get something—anything—to help me get out of here. As one guerilla was holding my arms behind my back, I struggled to get free, and he momentarily released my wrists. Calling upon my years of martial arts training, I was vigilant. Observant. Swift. In that moment, I slipped a hand into his pants' pocket and palmed the first thing I could find. I couldn't have hoped for better luck. The prize I retrieved was his utility knife.

Rory and her mercenaries had long since left. I now sat on the padded chair and with my overgrown thumbnail, I pried the knife open. A small blade, a bottle opener, a can opener, tweezers, and a reamer. It was an aged, ordinary Swiss Army knife crusted between the metal grooves with dirt and possibly dried blood. The larger blade was broken off. I pried the toothpick from the slot on the end and went to work on the deadbolts.

The day the car bomb exploded near the café, I'd been watching out for an attack. Earlier that day, my old friend Stan Moorlehem—aka, Mayhem—called with a tip. He'd received intel from his spies in Turkey that Rory Protsenko had finally learned who intercepted her fentanyl shipment.

And she was pissed.

Mayhem was born in Eastbourne, England, and he served in the British Army. He became SAS about ten years ago and was discharged after sustaining an injury in Ukraine. He walked with a limp now, but still carried all the hatred of a new recruit for terrorists. When I told him my plans to destroy Rory, Artur Protsenko's daughter, he leaped in with both feet.

The wide plastic toothpick wasn't exactly the right tool for picking a lock. I needed a straight pin and so examined the Swiss Army knife again. Using the tweezers, I pried apart the tiny, quarter-inch lanyard ring and twisted it off. The patience I practiced during years of Bujinkan training became useful. I flipped the small knife out and worked on that half-inch ring for two hours until it was as straight as a needle. By then, the sound of a key in the lock signaled my lunchtime.

I tucked my tools under the pillow on my bed.

"Stand back!" The guard opened the door.

The big guy who I'd stolen the Swiss Army knife from stood behind the Muslim serving girl with his Uzi pointed at me. She set a paper plate with fruit, hummus, and pita on the desk. I guessed she was eleven or twelve, and I began to really wonder who she was. She wore a silk dress with flowers—too elegant for someone her age—and a white chador. She was too young for a hijab. Also, she never smiled. Was she forced to work here? Was she someone's child? She ducked out quickly and passed the guard like a scared little marmoset.

This had become my routine. He brought the girl, she left clothes, food, necessities, then he locked me in again. The guard stood in her wake and flicked the barrel of his gun at me before he closed the door. I stared him down, but this time I took stock of what was on the other side of him. A narrow hallway and a staircase.

Soon, I'd escape from this prison cell. Soon, I'd be face-to-face with Rory.

-15-

MINA

A month ago, Jonathon had chartered a boat from Alex Buccino to find Rory's island hideaway. Now I followed in his footsteps. I was no closer to finding Sotoris, but I was determined to find something.

I hastily returned to the hotel and checked out. Greg called a few times, but I let it go to voicemail. When I had time, I would call him back. After thanking the cab driver and tipping him, I rolled my bag to the head of the long dock and down a pier with dozens of tethered sailing yachts and catamarans on either side. Karolos jogged toward me. He'd changed into khaki slacks and a short-sleeved captain's shirt. When he reached me, he removed his white captain's cap and bowed.

"Let me take your bag."

"I've got it," I said.

He took it from me anyway. "For the next five days, you are in my care. I'll make sure you're well-fed, and the bar is stocked. I'll translate when you need me to, and I'll tell you everything you need to know about the islands. I'm here to pamper you, Ms. Green. I am at your service, as they say."

I wasn't here to be pampered, but jet lag still made me tired. I worried that five days wasn't long enough. Karolos thought he'd heard of Sotoris Island but didn't know where it was. He did, however, know someone who he thought could help. Michael Bettencourt was anchored on Milos, an overnight sail from Athens. I made a mental note to search his name on Google later.

Karl headed down the dock and I followed. He asked, "Are you expecting any guests to join you? Family? Friends?"

"No. Not unless we find my . . .dear friend." *Fiancé? Lover?* I had described Jonathon as my fiancé to the hotel manager. It was the closest to my true feelings for Jonathon. Now that he was with Rory . . .

Karl looked at me sideways with his mouth pinched. "This man is more than a friend. He's your lover, no?"

"Yes."

"You have called him?"

"His phone is dead. I'm afraid something happened to him."

"It's a mystery, then. We are on a manhunt." Karl smiled.

"Something like that." I didn't warn Karl that Jonathon's life was in danger and by association, so was mine.

He tilted his head, examining my face. "But there is something else," he said. "Are you sure you want to find your lover? Every man is complex and has many passions. Could he have run off with another woman?"

Alex implied Rory thought she could get Jonathon back. He would never run off with her. He hated her. *Didn't he?*

Some complicated feelings had arisen since Jonathon disappeared. I hated to think of him with her again, but he'd planted all those stories in my head. He told me all about their deviant sexual practices and her seductive ways. Had she been able to lure him into her bed again? Is that why he hadn't called?

I dropped my gaze. How could I explain this to Karl? "I'm not willing to let him go. I fear for his life."

Karl nodded. "He is a lucky man to have you. Come, I'll introduce you to the crew." He took me to the end of the dock. Awaiting me was the handsome, sixty-foot sailing catamaran with three staterooms and crew. Two people stood on the dock beside the boarding gate.

"Welcome, my lady," a young man said.

"This is Nathan Matthiessen, my first mate." Karl introduced us. "Nathan is a Greek, like me. But his English is good."

Nathan wore belted jeans and a sleek, white athletic T-shirt. He said something in Greek then explained. "That means, *What's up.*"

I shook his hand and said hello.

"And this is Luna Hennings, our cook and entertainment specialist," Karl said.

Middle-aged Luna wore a knee-length white dress with elastic short sleeves pinching her plump arms. Her sun-bleached hair was tied in a knot with a yellow scarf. "So nice to meet you," she said in her pleasant, slightly posh British accent.

I shook her hand.

Karl handed my bag to Nathan and led me onto the boat. He showed me around the lounge area in the aft section. A comfortable-looking U-shaped couch with tan cushions was ensconced in a covered seating area in the cockpit. A folding table in the center of the space converted it into a dining room. On one side, a few steep stairs led to the captain's cockpit and navigational area, where an array of electronic screens blinked with red and green lights.

We held on to the side rail and mast stays to climb toward the bow where a trampoline stretched tightly between the two pontoons. "This is a nice area to suntan," Karl said.

I nodded. Lounging in the sun wasn't on my list of things to do during my stay. "Where is my cabin?"

"Your berth is below. Come this way." We walked back through the cockpit to a central sliding door. "This is the saloon." He pronounced it like salon. "In inclement weather, you stay inside."

The living room had more seating, the comfortable couches and tables secured to the floor. The shelving had rails to keep things from falling out. A fully stocked bar, the bottles also behind rails, with affixed stools filled one corner. "Beyond the bar is the galley where Luna prepares delicious meals for you. Your berth is this way." Karl led me through the saloon to a master suite fit for a queen.

My berth had a queen-sized bed and tiny bathroom—called the *head* in boating lingo —with just enough room to stand in the shower. Lightly stained wood walls curved to the shape of the hull. Drawers and cabinets in secured furniture, under the bed, and in the walls would keep things from rolling around when we hit a squall or high seas. It made me wonder what tempest might lie ahead.

Nathan brought my bags down and said, "Make yourself at home."

They showed me how to lock the closets and secure drawers so my things would stay put. I wondered how rough the Mediterranean Sea would get on this journey.

An hour later, we shoved off from the Alimos Marina pier. Nathan started up the engines, the twin motors churning the saltwater behind us, and we slowly cruised past the row of docked vessels. A cool evening breeze blew strands of my light brown hair away from my face.

I was usually drawn to the ocean for the rush of escape. For the thrill of diving from great heights into the roiling waves of the planet's most powerful bodies of water. My tombstone diving trips gave me a sense of closure. This trip didn't thrill me. On the contrary, I feared for Jonathon's life. I was terrified I'd never find him. The only closure I would feel would be when I finally held Jonathon in my arms.

I stood on the bow and watched as the shore, safety, and my sense of security moved farther away.

-16-

MINA

I hadn't been on a ship since I was about twelve, and my grandparents took the family on a Caribbean cruise. My older brothers, James and Eddie, and I had such fun leaning over the railings and peering down six stories at the sea moving beneath the ship. I remember the lure of that height—even then—and I wanted to dive. I'd climb up onto the railing and scare James. He'd pull me down before one of the ship's crew yelled at me. James told me to save it for the pool.

He didn't know that later, during my diving competitions, I often imagined what it was like to jump from the promenade deck. He still doesn't know that since that cruise I've jumped from much higher cliffs. No one—except Jonathon and my best friend Traci—knew.

A cruise ship that size was much more stable on the ocean than a sixty-foot boat like Karl's. The hum of the catamaran's motor and the soft easy movements of the boat cutting through the water would lull me to sleep if I let them. I freshened up and unpacked a few outfits from my bag. I tucked my shoes and cosmetics into drawers so they wouldn't roll around. I then hung up a few garments before sitting on the bed and looking out the narrow, shoulder-level window at the azure sky. The same sky I imagined Jonathon looking at.

Where are you?

Greg called once more and left a message. "Have you arrived in Greece? Where are you?"

Greg still thought he was my bodyguard. My stomach growled because I skipped lunch today, so I decided to call him later tonight. The sun was sinking below the horizon when I exited my berth. Nathan had the helm. He'd shut off the engine and now the main sail filled with wind and carried us on a course from the western shore of the Athenian peninsula to the Saronic Gulf.

I joined Karl on deck, where he sat at a long table with a map of the Mediterranean spread out in front of him. He leaned forward, studying a chain of islands surrounding the Aegean Sea.

"A paper map. Don't you use the internet for navigation?" I sat in a wooden folding chair and looked closer.

"No, *despoinída*. A captain should always have his paper navigational tools. There are many times at sea when there is no internet. Sometimes, no electricity. A captain should always be prepared."

I imagined the havoc a storm created, and I didn't want to be on board when that occurred. "How far is Milos?"

"About one hundred forty-five kilometers, or ninety miles."

His finger rested beside a medium-sized island between the mainland, Greece, and Kriti.

"How long will it take to get there?"

"Eight hours. We will be there by the time you wake in the morning."

"That soon?" I was really thinking, *That long?* Every minute counted in this search. I wondered if I'd made the right choice sailing with Karolos. Could I have flown?

"There are some beautiful bays on Milos for snorkeling. Are you a scuba diver?"

"I've done a little snorkeling, but I'm not a scuba diver." I didn't want to talk about my brand of diving. "You say you don't know where Sotoris is."

"Correct." Karl sat back and wiped his brow with a handkerchief. "I don't know of it, but there are two thousand islands in Greece. Many are uninhabited. Many are private."

"Sotoris must exist. Jonathon told me he was headed there."

"Small islands are not always named on the big maps. Especially so if they are owned privately."

Luna came outside with a platter of olives and cheese slices alongside stuffed grape leaves. "Here you are, love. Goat cheese, kalamata olives, and dolmas stuffed with rice, mint, and pinyon nuts." She set the dish on the table in front of me and asked if I'd like something to drink.

"Do you have Perrier?" Jonathon's go-to drink had become my preferred choice and jet lag still made me too drowsy for wine.

"We have sparkling water," she said. "Perhaps something stronger?"

"No thanks. I'll take it with lime." Coming out of a long day of traveling had made me hungry. My hand hovered over her snack plate as I made my choice then popped an olive into my mouth.

She retreated to the galley to prepare drinks and our meal.

"My friend, Michael Bettencourt, may know how to find the island. We are headed to Milos, where he is staying for a few weeks. Michael is, at least, predictable."

"I hope he knows where Sotoris is."

"If not, Michael will know someone who does. I'm sure he can help."

Luna brought my sparkling water. "Oh no. We're not meeting that louse, are we?"

Karl laughed. "Luna lost a friendly cooking competition to Michael, and now she's bitter."

"Not bitter, love. He gave me the recipe. But where did he get asafetida and hibiscus flowers that time of year? I'm sure he cheated." The sparkle in her blue eyes made me smile.

"He cooks?" I asked before biting into a minty dolma.

"He can do many things *very well*," Karl said.

"At least he claims he can." Luna waved in disgust and walked away.

"Michael lives on his fifty-foot Oyster sailboat. He bought the yacht five years ago after divorcing a duchess. I won't say who she was, but Michael got the better end of that deal. Let me show you." Karl pulled up a link with photos on his cell phone. Though I knew nothing about sailing yachts, this one was low to the water and sleek as an arrow. It had black sails and looked as fast as a race car.

"That's some boat," I said.

Karl's half grin seemed full of admiration. "They are the very best. He cruises from island to island, working from his computer when he has internet."

"What sort of work does he do?" I bit into a soft, fragrant dolma.

"I don't know. Rumor has it he's invested in stocks, so he watches the market. He's been sailing these waters for ten years, since before he married the duchess. He knows all the cruisers—the ones who live on their boats—and those of us who work for a living. He is generous with his time, and if you need a hand, he will always help a friend."

We chatted through Luna's tasty feast of zucchini stuffed with cream cheese and nuts. She preferred vegetarian fare and took most of her recipes from New York's *Moosewood Cookbook*. She laughed when I shared a story about the worst meal I ever cooked, macaroni and cheese from scratch. The pasta was hard, and the cheese formed into globs. It tasted like scratch because I knew so little about cooking.

"In the meantime, enjoy Greece," Karl said. "You may not find your true love this week but look at the sky. Enjoy the islands and the sea. The water is warm this time of year."

I wanted to take his suggestion to heart—to relax—but couldn't allow myself the luxury until I found Jonathon.

After our meal, Karolos let me sit in the captain's chair and *drive*. He'd lowered the sails, and the yacht was set on autopilot for the long straightaway to Milos. Electronic navigational tools made boating seem easy. For an hour or so, we cruised with the main deck lights turned off. This far from shore the stars seemed so much brighter. Bioluminescent algae glowed in our wake. It turned the sea into a green, glimmering, and in some way, spiritual body.

Around midnight, after Karl and Luna had gone to bed, Nathan took the helm. I went to my quarters and checked my cell phone. The conversation with Alex left me unsettled. And I needed to return Greg's call. I lay back on the queen-sized bed and let the gentle rocking waves lull me into a state of relaxation. My finger poised over Greg's number when he called.

"Where the hell are you?"

"I told you—"

"Why didn't you call when you arrived?"

"I've been busy looking for Jonathon. I'm on a catamaran headed to Milos."

That shut him up.

"Jonathon set me the task of keeping you out of trouble. I need you to stay in touch, Mina." He sounded anxious, more so than usual.

"That worked so well in the past. How's your knee?"

"Okay, smart aleck. It's dangerous there."

"Don't be angry at me, okay? I spoke to Alex Buccino, Jonathon's friend. Though Alex refused to take me to Jonathon, he said he could help. But I don't know. I got a funny feeling about him. The captain of my charter has a friend named Michael Bettencourt, who knows the islands better than anyone. He may know how to find Sotoris, the island where Rory lives."

"Jonathon's—"

The line was staticky for a moment, I thought he said Jonathon was dead. "What?"

"Stan Moorlehem called me. Javier Garrido is in the hospital with multiple injuries and burns. There was a car bombing in Mikonos. Jonathon is assumed to be dead."

My mouth hung open. It couldn't be true.

"Several bodies of victims were not able to be identified. They suspect that one is Jonathon."

"It can't be." I swallowed hard and carried my cell phone above deck. My heart felt wounded, and exhaustion led to tears. I sniffed it all back and sat on the trampoline. Alex Buccino said Jonathon was with Rory. *Who was I to believe?* "He can't be dead."

"Mina, I'm so sorry."

The pontoons beneath the trampoline sliced through the waves like a knife through room-temperature butter. "Jonathon once told me that if he was in danger, he'd give me POA of his finances. He told me that if this ever happened, I was to come looking for him." I filled Greg in on the meeting with Kent Whitaker before I left.

"Then what?"

"I don't know. I came here and I'm looking for clues."

"So you don't have a plan."

Sheepish, I looked down at the water rushing beneath the boat. "I'm making it up as I go."

"Come home, Mina. You shouldn't be there alone, it's too dangerous." Greg's anxiety filtered through the phone line like poisonous gas.

"I'm not coming home. I'm going to find Jonathon. Dead or alive."

"Mina—"

"If he has failed, then someone needs to continue his work. Someone has to stop her."

The fentanyl she produced killed people all around the world. If Jonathon were dead—which I didn't want to believe—I would stick to his plan to stop Rory.

"I'll take the next flight."

I cleared my throat. "You can't. Your knee—"

"Is fine. I took you rock climbing, didn't I? The leg's at eighty-five percent. And I don't need it to shoot a gun."

"Greg, I'm on a catamaran in the middle of the Mediterranean Sea. Stay where you are and do some research for me. Who is Michael Bettencourt? Where is Sotoris?"

"You can't be serious."

"I'm going after her."

"Oh my God, Mina. You have no idea what you're getting into."

"Will you help me?"

"I'll do whatever you need," he said. "Whatever it takes."

Greg, like me, cared deeply for his friend. He would risk his life for him. And so would I.

Stars above seemed bright enough to light the way. Tiny green and red lights from other boats dotted the horizon. The orange harvest moon rising in the east was the only familiar thing in the sky. It gave me no comfort.

Jonathon couldn't be dead. But if he was, Rory Protsenko would pay dearly. I'd make certain of it.

-17-

JONATHON

I gazed out my tower window at dark gray clouds on the horizon. Tall cumulonimbus storm clouds moved closer by the minute. By now Mina would think I was dead. Stan Mayhem would have called her, and if he couldn't reach her, he would have called Greg. He would have told Mina the news.

Don't give up on me, Mina.

We never expected Rory to take out civilians. And what about Javier? Though I was not a religious man, I prayed for Javier's life. The car bomb screwed up everything. If I couldn't escape, I hoped Stan would move forward and continue the work I started. Rory must be stopped from manufacturing fentanyl. I must stop her from preying on people. And especially, from stalking Mina.

I took stock of the scabby burns on my chest. Yellowed bruises darkened my arms and chest. I went through my plan once more. My first barrier to escape were the two deadbolts on the door. I plunged the straightened bale loop and toothpick from the Swiss Army knife into the first keyhole. The pin depressed the spring, and I jiggled the tooth-pick to raise the tumblers. *Click.*

The second lock was an older model cast iron lock, but the keyhole size was about the same. I slipped the homemade lockpick into the hole. This was a more complicated device and required some search-ing, some trial and error, before I was able to release the cylinder. *Chink.*

Success. I tucked the Swiss Army knife into the pocket of the pale-blue cotton pajama pants they'd given me. Since there was no doorknob, I stuck my fingers beneath the gap at the floor and tugged the door open. No guards were stationed outside my room. The white cotton

V-neck T-shirt blended nicely with the white walls in the hall. Like camouflage. Deprived of shoes, my bare feet were as silent as a declawed cat.

I tiptoed down the hallway to the top of an enclosed spiral stairwell. Two men's voices reverberated off the plaster walls. I listened for a few minutes as they said a man's name, Vadym, and chuckled, then I dropped to the floor at the top step to see around the corner.

One soldier was sitting in a chair near the base of the stairs. The other ended the conversation and walked off. I hopped to my feet again and looked around. Quietly, I tried one of the doors in the hallway. The first was locked with deadbolts. I listened with my ear pressed against the door and heard someone inside. At first it sounded like humming, but I soon realized it was the sorrowful sound of a child weeping. Was the Muslim girl in here?

I knocked softly and the whimpering stopped. "Is that you, little marmoset?" I whispered. Could the girl caring for me also be a prisoner?

I heard rustling, and four fingers appeared under the door. I recognized the hand, the slim fingers belonging to the girl who looked after me. I squatted down and touched her. I whispered, "I'll get us out of here, I promise."

"My name is Sitaara. Sitaara el Attar."

El Attar? "Sitaara, is your father Allawi? Alawi el Attar?" Alawi was an old friend who I hadn't seen in years. We met at a hospital grand opening in Dubai several years ago. We hit it off like we'd known each other since high school. He invited me to his older daughter's wedding. Sitaara was there and she was only five.

"Yes." She sounded so sad.

"Have patience, Sitaara. I will help you." It angered me that Rory kept a child locked in a room. I opened the other door looking for something, a tool or weapon. The closet was filled with toiletries and towels. I took a hand towel, gripped both ends and twisted it into a rope.

Now armed with a garrote, I crept down the steps with the towel wrapped between my palms.

The soldier still sat at the base of the steps, facing away from me. Ahead, an arched passageway was open to the outside elements. A strong wind blew off the sea, bringing the storm I'd seen earlier. At the end of the passageway, a closed door led—I supposed—to the main building. No one else was around.

The smaller of the two guards Rory had brought to my room leaned forward with his elbows on his knees, gazing down at his cell phone. He swiped through images on some social media app. I snuck up behind him while he read a post and laughed. As he thumbed his response, I swiftly swung the garrote over his head and tightened my grip, cutting off his scream and precious air. He struggled and kicked the chair out from under him. The clatter made too much noise, but I held him tight with his back pressed into me until he passed out.

I let him fall to the floor, then took the Uzi off his shoulder, and slung it over mine. I frisked him and found ammo for the Uzi and a pistol, then looked for anything else I could use. He had a small knife holstered to his leg, so I clipped it to my calf and hid it under my pajama leg.

When I was through with him, I wrapped the towel around the pistol and shot his thigh at close range so that when he woke, he couldn't follow me. Then I moved swiftly to the door at the end of the hall.

Storm clouds darkened the sky. The storm was nearly upon us.

I pushed the unlocked door open a crack. Just enough to see what was on the other side: a vacant room with a grand stairway leading up to a balcony. Voices carried, bouncing off the white plaster and black marble floors. I let the door go wide and sprung to the stairs, taking them two at a time. When I reached the top, I darted toward a set of double doors, toward the voices.

"She's not in Athens? How did she get away from you?" Rory sounded pissed.

Was she talking about Mina? Rory wanted to capture Mina. This was an unacceptable possibility, one that we had strategized for. Stan Mayhem would know what to do.

If . . . if he knew Mina was here in Greece.

An indistinct man's voice mumbled a reply to Rory's question. I strained to hear over the clap of thunder.

A bang, as if someone slapped a hand on a desk or table, startled me. "What the hell am I paying you for?" Rory said. "Find her, Alex. Do it now."

Mina is in danger!

Barely holding my rage at bay, I pushed the door open another inch. Armed guards stood in the corners of the room. Rory sat at the end of a dining table with a plate of fruit and cheese in front of her and a glass of sparkling wine in one hand. In a red golf shirt, Alex sat next to her. He sipped from a tumbler.

I'd trusted *Alex Buccino*. He was clearly more motivated by money than anything else.

Rage seethed inside me. At Alex for betraying me. At Rory for threatening my lover.

Without opening the door, I aimed the Uzi at Rory. I had her in my sights. My finger hooked the trigger.

As I depressed the trigger something hard knocked against my skull. I fired and missed. The bullets ricocheted off the wall.

At the sound of gunfire, Rory and Alex leapt up from the table in a frenzied attempt to escape the gunfire.

"Drop the weapon." A guard behind me pressed the barrel of a gun to my head. He kicked the door open.

Without me, Mina and now Sitaara had no chance at all. I took my finger off the trigger and lowered the weapon.

Rory's gaze turned on me as if she were bored. "Have a seat, Jon. We expected you."

"Hello, Jon." Alex tipped back his drink. "Nice to see you again."

I turned slowly, made eye contact with the guard, and raised my hands in defeat. He yanked the Uzi off my shoulder and shoved me into the room.

Thunder boomed overhead.

~18~

MINA

Jonathon's dead.

Denial? Rage? These feelings swarmed through my body like angry wasps. The fact that Jonathon's POA had gone into effect after he stopped communicating with his banker worried me. Greg's words kept me up half the night, and now I struggled to keep my emotions from pouring over.

With a warm cup of morning coffee in my hand, I stood on deck watching the sunrise behind the rocky coast of Milos. To the south, black rain clouds hovered near Kriti. Though I wore sunglasses, I shaded my eyes against the sun sparkling on the water.

I needed to stay focused. I needed to believe Jonathon was alive.

As we motored closer to a big island, Karolos shouted out the names of landmarks from the captain's chair above deck. "The big island is Milos. There's Antimilos, the smaller island on the right. Want to go for a swim? That's Plathiena Beach on your left. It's where the locals swim. We can stop if you like."

Karl still seemed to think I was on vacation, not in a life and death race to locate Jonathon. "No thanks. Let's keep going."

Nathan held the rail and pointed to the rocky cove. "We can drop anchor whenever you like. There's calmer water sheltered by cliffs on the other side of the island."

"Cliffs?" He had my attention.

"Sarakiniko Beach is famous for white cliffs made of rare volcanic formations. Some people like to jump from them. The water is deep enough," Nathan said. "Extreme sports like cliff diving are popular in Greece. And thrilling. I've done it. It's exhilarating."

Though curious about the cliffs, I had one agenda. "Maybe once we find Jonathon—"

"Look there!" Karl called out. "You can see Placa Castle."

Nathan pointed to a white dot high above green-and-orange shrubs on the top of the stony island.

An hour later, we docked at Adamantas, the port city on Milos. While Nathan handed our paperwork to the port authority officials, Karl looked out over the bay. "There. See the black yacht with the satellite dishes on top? That belongs to Michael Bettencourt."

Michael's sleek yacht stood out among the fishing boats and catamarans. "That's impressive," I said.

Shaped like a dart and nearly twice the length of the cat, it had black canvas wrapped around the sails. The tall mast was equipped with satellite dishes and an array of other electronic devices. A shiny canopy strapped to cleats on the deck protected the navigational area from the harsh sun and weather. "Where is Michael?"

"I know where to find him," Karl said. "The one thing I love about Michael, he is predictable. He loves women."

At the port authority, Karl followed protocols and handed our passports to officials. He gave a list of goods on board and our reason for traveling. He seemed to know one of the officials, so the process went smoothly. Once we passed inspection, the official handed us back our passports. Karl and I got off the yacht and hailed a cab.

"Don't you want to do some shopping? See the sights?" Karl asked.

"We don't have time for shopping."

I had my comfortable Sorel walking shoes on, prepared to hike the hills if necessary. We took to the streets and began to climb away from the sea. The hot sun had bleached everything on Milos Island. Box-shaped buildings were painted a glossy eggshell to match the seawall along the shore. Pearl and ivory walls looked as if they could sustain hurricane-force winds. Cerulean-blue doors and window casings threw a blast of color onto the pale canvas, inviting tourists and visitors to come inside. Green flowering bushes hung over stone walls and punctuated the hillside.

Karl proudly chattered about the landmark features, the church and the castle on the hill, the history of the island. We arrived at a home where flower boxes lined a cornflower-blue doorway, and the windows were open. From inside, we heard a woman's agitated voice arguing with someone. Indeed, a man's casual response punctuated her rants with occasional *yays* or *nays*.

Karl knocked on the door, interrupting the woman's passionate speech.

"Yah." A tanned woman in a yellow sundress came to the screen door. She was about my age but shorter and plump, with striking sea-green eyes that stood out against her jet-black hair. She spoke Greek to Karolos.

Karl removed his ball cap and spoke with her.

She turned her head and shouted at someone inside the room. Equally indignant, a man responded and came to the door.

"Michael, I am so sorry to bother you, but I need a favor." Karl twisted the cap in his hands.

"Karolos! My old friend." Michael stepped outside to embrace him.

Michael Bettencourt was tall and muscular, like Jonathon. His sun-bleached auburn hair was combed into a sleek ponytail. His long, sunburnt nose looked as if it had been broken, maybe more than once.

The men's heartfelt greeting made me smile. Behind them, the woman clenched her jaw and gave Michael a furious glare.

"Is this a good time?" Karl asked.

"As good as any. How can I help you?"

Karl put his hand on Michael's shoulder. "My passenger is on a mission, and she needs help."

"Anything, friend."

"This is Wilhelmina Green. She is looking for her lover, Jonathon Heun."

A look of recognition lit Michael's eyes, then he gave me a hearty embrace that almost took the wind out of me. "Mina, I am honored. My good friend Jonathon told me you would come."

"He did?"

"He told me you are the best criminal defense lawyer in Chicago. He adores you," Michael said with a glimmer in his eye.

I stepped back. The woman in the door locked her gaze on Michael. "I don't have the same advantage. How do you know Jonathon?"

"We met in Japan," he said.

The woman glowered at him then burst out of the house with her finger pointed. She launched into another tirade as if she understood more than I did. Michael shouted back in defense. She had the last word.

"I'm sorry if this is a bad time," Karl repeated.

"Not at all." He gave her a signal to stop, then said in a pleasant voice, "How can I help you?"

The two men walked away. I was left standing beside the woman with arms crossed in frustration.

"Men," I said.

"Infuriating." Her Greek accent peppered her speech as her gaze followed Michael's backside. He walked around the side of the house out of our view. She dropped her arms and relaxed, "But, oh, how I love him."

I knew the feeling well. I longed to see Jonathon's face. To touch his shoulders. It would even be a pleasure to argue with him again.

Her features smoothed and she smiled, holding out her hand. "My name's Emilya Tsoukopolis. You are looking for your husband?"

"We're not married. But yes. I'm looking for my boyfriend." I didn't realize how tight my grip had been on my purse strap as I let go, shook her hand, and introduced myself.

"I hope Michael can help you." The sincerity in Emilya's voice almost made me cry. She looked me up and down with dark-rimmed, sea-green irises that seemed to glow like the bioluminescents in the sea.

"Come inside," she said. "I have espresso."

The rich, hot espresso and cream made my heart race with hope that I was closer to finding Jonathon. The four of us sat in mismatched painted chairs at Emilya's well-worn, square wooden table. Karl shook his head. "The reason you can't find Sotoris Island is that it doesn't exist."

I disagreed. "But Jonathon said . . ."

"There's no such island." Karolos picked at a small scratch on one finger. "I have lived in Greece my whole life. I know the Aegean like my own mother. And if it's not on Google Maps, it doesn't exist."

"How will I ever find Jonathon?" I asked.

Michael adjusted the ponytail at the base of his skull. "I hate to disagree, but . . . there are many, many unnamed islands in the Aegean. And private owners don't always want Google's search engine to find them. Take a different approach to finding him. If I were you, I'd look for the most dangerous yacht in the sea. It's owned by an organized crime boss, and no one approaches it . . . and it's probably anchored near this Sotoris."

Karl sat back and rested an elbow in the palm of one hand. With the other, he squeezed the sides of his mouth with his thumb and forefinger.

"I keep track of that particular yacht because I don't want to cross paths with it," Michael said. "Lately, it's anchored here." He picked up a pen and pointed to an island in the eastern region of the Aegean Sea.

Karolos leaned over the map and shook his head. "There's a resort on the nearby island, Karpathos. There are beaches and the snorkeling is lovely. However, I cannot make it that far and return to Athens for my next charter. Why don't you take her? Your boat is faster."

I looked from Karl to Michael. "But Michael said it's dangerous."

"It is." Emilya placed her hand on Michael's thigh. "The yacht is owned by the Russian mafia. Tell them what you heard."

Michael's dark amber gaze rested on Emilya, then Karl, then me. "They have armed guerillas guarding the decks. I've heard they'll fire missile launchers at boats when they come too close. That's not the worst of it. Those same guerillas dump buckets of chum off the sides of the boat. It draws every shark and killer whale for miles."

Back in Chicago, the Russian mafia left their mark all over the city. They beheaded and tortured people. They carried out execution-style killings, exactly what they'd done to my private investigator friend, Gary Underwood. While investigating Janko for me, Gary had been strapped to a chair while someone gouged his eyes out. I was quite aware what this TOC group was capable of. The question was, did Karl or Michael have the stomach for it?

"That's crazy talk," Karl said.

"It's true," Michael said. "I heard of two vacationers snorkeling too close to the yacht. The guerillas dumped five gallon buckets of blood into the ocean near their boat. Sharks attacked the vacationers. A friend of a friend said the woman's leg was torn off." He finished his espresso.

Karl burped out a stilted laugh. "Guerillas? Sharks? You're joking, right? This is hearsay."

"Maybe, but that's not all. They use drones to scout out the surrounding area. The yacht is equipped with the finest pirate-proof technology. They use photonic disruptors to temporarily blind anyone who comes near the ship. They have a fleet of weaponized drones and if that doesn't deter you, they also have long-range acoustic devices to disrupt any other ships' navigational equipment. I'm pretty sure they deal with terrorists."

"They deal in weapons and ship fentanyl by the ton." My statement bounced off the small kitchen walls.

The others stared at me.

"I assume Artur Protsenko owns the yacht. He's the leader of the TOC syndicate we believe is the Russian mafia. Their sickness has contaminated Chicago, New York, and many other American cities. They have cells all over the world," I said.

"Artur's daughter, Rory, was in a relationship with Jonathon a number of years ago. He thought he was in love with her until she became bitter over their arrangement. Her rage infected their relationship and destroyed it. I'm happy about that. If it hadn't been for her, I might not have met Jonathon." I stopped to wet my dry throat with what was left of my espresso. I could feel the others' gazes on me like a cold silk shroud.

"A few months ago, Jonathon and I were threatened by an old colleague of his. He tried to extort millions from Jonathon. I've since learned Rory Protsenko now runs the largest fentanyl manufacturing plant in this region. They distribute their deadly, addictive drugs to Eastern Europe, South Africa, and some regions of the Middle East.

Jonathon discovered this after we helped the FBI capture members of the TOC group in Chicago. He came here to destroy her."

"By himself?" Karl asked, his question laced with suspicion. He sucked on his lower lip.

"Once he arrived here in Greece, he assembled a team of mercenaries. He had help, and Jonathon has always been a fighter. And he can defend himself. He is a twelfth degree blackbelt in martial arts and a certified Kendo master."

"No kidding? I've only reached the eighth don." Michael's eyebrows floated upward with admiration.

Emilya elbowed him.

"I met Hideo for the first time the year I went to Japan to train for my sixth don. That's where I met Jonathon," Michael said.

"You know him?" I asked.

"Yes. He's a formidable fighter. It was the only chance I've had to watch those masters at work. They are phenomenal. Their speed and precision—"

"Tell us more about the TOC group." Emilya nodded at me.

"Yesterday I spoke to a friend of ours," I said. "A car bomb explosion in Mikonos killed several people. Jonathon's bodyguard was hospitalized. There were a handful of unidentified bodies and—" I choked on the next words. "They never found Jonathon's body."

"I heard about the explosion," Emilya said. "Four were killed in Poseidon Square. They suspected the terrorist group known as Ivan's Militsya. Was Jonathon . . . do you think he lived?"

I shook my head. "I don't know. I have this feeling he's alive. And if Rory used the bomb as a diversion to kidnap him, then he's in her clutches."

Karl looked out the window. "I'm so sorry, *despoinída*."

Michael scratched his shoulder and looked at the floor. "What are you hoping for here?"

"It was an arrogant and ambitious risk for him to come here." I laughed, but not because it was funny, and looked at the deep brown ring at the bottom of my empty espresso cup. "He's *not* dead. I just know it. Jonathon gathered a mercenary army to fight against Rory and Artur. They're waiting in Naxos for his next command. They're willing to fight for what's right and what's good in this world. I know it sounds clichéd. Idealistic and, in a way, ridiculous. But Interpol was doing nothing. Protsenko's group is so widespread—they infiltrate all levels of society and use the most wicked psychological tactics to employ people. Jonathon thought, since he knew Rory, he could get close to her and somehow subvert the organization. At the very least, he was hoping to alert authorities of her whereabouts. Three weeks ago, they finally got Interpol to cooperate. He and his team intercepted one shipment of fentanyl. One of many."

"And you think he is on the island called Sotoris?" Michael asked.

"When we last spoke, that's where he was headed."

"What good is a blackbelt against automatic weapons? Huh? They're terrorists!" Karl cried out. "He may have already met his death."

Emilya's gaze had not strayed from my face. She leaned forward on her elbows. "You love him so much that you've come for him. You traveled all this way by yourself. For love."

I nodded. "Yes."

"Then you must get him back." Emilya covered Michael's hand with her smaller hand. "And you must help her."

Michael gazed into Emilya's eyes. I couldn't tell what passed between them.

Karl pushed his chair away from the table. "No thanks. I still owe a fortune for *The Dragonfly*. My insurance doesn't cover bullet holes. I have a schedule this fall. Bookings. I have paying customers." He stood and raised a curled lip at me, dashing the remaining hope that he was on my side. "I'll take you back to Athens, but you need to find someone else for your reconnaissance."

-19-

MINA

Karl stood on the curb beside the street with his phone in his hand. He was calling a cab to take us quickly back to Adamantas and back to *The Dragonfly*. I stepped outside, too, not wanting to be left on Milos with no place to stay and no transportation.

Michael followed, Emilya at his heels. "You must help her. She is clearly in love with Jonathon."

"It's too dangerous," Michael said. "He might not even be alive."

"He is alive." Saying it out loud built my confidence, even though Greg's voice beat a somber drum in my heart. *Jonathan is dead.* Or perhaps the strong espresso had given me courage.

Emilya's gaze met Michael's, and he shrugged. "I'm retired. I don't do that kind of work anymore."

Emilya jabbed him in his ribs.

"Before I go, I have one more question," I said. "Jonathon chartered a yacht with Alex Buccino. Do you know him?"

"I may have heard of him."

Emilya crossed her arms and gave Michael a look that meant business.

"Okay, I do know him," he said, giving in to her. "He stays on Kriti through the winter. Makes enough money in seasonal charters to take the time off," Michael said.

"That's not for another month," Emilya interjected.

"I don't know his routes," he said. Emilya elbowed him again and he turned to her, palms up. "I don't! I would tell her if I did."

"Karl's right," I said. "I've come on a fool's errand."

Karolos joined us with his eyes on the road. "Fool's errand? Yes.

Your man is most likely dead, and you will follow him into death if you ask me."

I slung my lightweight leather purse over my shoulder. "You're right. I'm probably in over my head, as you said, but Jonathon would do the same for me. He *has* done the same for me."

"You see!" Emilya said. She shoved Michael so hard, he stumbled. Then she lit into him with another stream of angry Greek words. Her finger pointed at his chest backed him up several paces.

"Emilya. Stop. No! I can't!" He backed away, patting the air with both hands as if trying to tamp down her emotions. "What are you saying?"

She stood taller. "I'm saying if you don't help her, I'm through with you." She spat on the dirt beside his shoe.

"Emilya, please." Michael's shoulders dropped.

Karl's taxi had rounded the turn on the curvy hillside road. When it arrived, he opened the door for me. "Coming?"

I climbed into the back seat of the small hybrid car. "Thank you for listening," I said to Emilya and Michael.

She crossed her arms and glared at Michael.

Karl slid in beside me and gave directions to the driver.

As we drove away, I heard Emilya shouting at Michael again.

Karl said, "I'm very sorry, *despoinída*. I will take you anywhere but to Sotoris. We can go to Sifnos. There are private coves to drop anchor and swim in the sea. The water is warm this time of year. Pleasant. You should try it. It will clear your head."

I could have choked on his words. I gazed out the window at the pristine, cubical homes, their clean, unsullied walls and the simple lives of people living in them. I longed to be like them.

"How about Paros? Or Sikinos? There is a beautiful place to snorkel in Antiparos. Have you seen the rainbow wrasse? Very colorful fish. I know a place where you can see dozens of tentacled blenny. I will take you there," Karl said. "They say salt water is healing. It's good for the soul."

Women in floral dresses walked along the road. Men wearing white hats seemed oblivious to their flirtations. Children playing on the hillside laughed, so carefree, and I couldn't imagine ever living like them. Not without Jonathon.

Back on *The Dragonfly*, I closed the door to my berth. Karl was right. Rory may have killed Jonathon. Trying to get to her—to Sotoris—was riskier than jumping from the seventy-foot cliffs north of Acapulco. It was more suicidal than diving from the cliffs near Dubrovnik in the dead of night.

My fingers traced the scar on my leg and the new tattoo just above it. I made up my mind. Nothing would stop me from finding Jonathon. *He is not dead,* I kept telling myself. And nothing could keep me from him.

The boat rumbled as the engines started. Karl wanted to leave this port, and since I'd paid for five days with him, he wanted to take me on the tour of the Grecian islands.

I had little time to waste. I opened my cabin door and shouted to Luna in the galley. "Don't let Karl untie the boat. Don't let him leave." I threw my things in my suitcase and zipped it closed.

Within a few minutes, I dragged my suitcase up the steps to the deck. Nathan wholeheartedly tried to talk me out of disembarking before helping me place the suitcase on the dock. Red-faced Karl argued with me. "I can't leave you here."

"You don't understand. I need to find him," I said.

"You paid for five days."

"Keep the money."

Karl let me go. "He is a lucky man. Good luck, *despoinída.*"

I watched *The Dragonfly* pull away from the dock. The eddies whipped up by the engine stirred up silt from the rocky bottom as the yacht turned slowly to exit the marina.

I dragged my suitcase to the street and dug my cell phone out of my purse. *Who would I call?*

I quickly thought of Alex Buccino and tried to dial his number, but my phone had no signal. *Crap.* Could I hitchhike? Could I catch rides to the nearest islands with fishermen and sportsmen? I sat on my rose-colored Samsonite suitcase and checked my wallet for cash. While counting out euros, a familiar sound caught my attention.

There was no such thing as coincidences. That high-pitched buzzing came from another drone.

On my feet, I spotted the black harbinger high above yachts docked at the Milos port. Its design and shape was similar to the drone that came near my hotel balcony. As it approached, I instinctively grabbed the handle of my suitcase and pulled it into a nearby patio restaurant. Peering out from behind a wall, I watched the drone scan the docks and the empty slip where Karl's *Dragonfly* had been tethered. The catamaran was headed toward the open sea but hadn't reached the outer buoys of the marina. The drone seemed to hesitate, then it zoomed off toward *The Dragonfly*. A second drone sped past the restaurant, followed by another, and another.

Horrified, I watched as, one after another, the three additional drones dove toward the Dragonfly and exploded on impact with the deck. I realized with a shock that they were weaponized. Karl ran for cover. Nathan scrambled to get away, then dropped out of sight amid the fire.

Unable to take my eyes off the scene, I stood, wishing I could do something.

Shouting and screams rose as passersby stopped to witness the burning catamaran. Some called the police on cell phones. Their gazes, like mine, were glued to the spectacle. In the marina, a number of small craft prepared to head out to the burning cat.

A little red car pulled up on the road between me and the docks. Emilya jumped out of the driver's seat and Michael exited from the passenger side. They shaded their eyes and peered out at the yachts.

"Over here!" I called. In the distance, the shouting continued.

Emilya ran to my side. "What's happening?"

"They bombed Karl's catamaran!" I gripped my useless cell phone.

"Come with us," Emilya said.

"Get in the car!" Michael reacted quickly. He grabbed my suitcase and slung it into the trunk.

The original drone circled then turned toward shore as we ducked into the car. Michael darted to the driver's side on the right and took the wheel. As we sped away, I looked back. The smoking *Dragonfly* drifting in the waves. The white flag on top of its mast moved back and forth with the sway of the boat. In surrender.

"Who do those drones belong to?" Emilya asked.

I suspected Rory Protsenko. "We can't go back to your house."

"Why not?" Emilya asked.

"She knows I'm here."

$-20-$

JONATHON

Rory finished describing the drone attack on the catamaran Mina chartered. The merciless killers operating those drones would follow any order she gave, and they did. Alex reported at least one man died. Rory had my attention now, and I was livid.

With her cell phone pressed to her ear, Rory stood in the corner of her elegant sunroom. "Did you get her?"

I sat on the edge of the couch in the middle of the room, listening to every word of Rory's phone conversation. I had confidence Mina wouldn't get caught. At least I hoped with all my heart for it to be true.

Cobalt urns the size of wine barrels bordered three arches leading out to a patio with an Olympic-sized swimming pool. Guerrillas with severe expressions and Uzis at the ready flanked each archway. One eyed me with a sneer.

"I told you we'd find Mina." Alex Buccino sat in a pillowy armchair with one ankle over a knee and his hands behind his head.

I wanted to get my hands on his neck, but Alex insisted on handcuffing me behind my back. He was afraid of me, and with good reason.

"So you can't confirm her death?" Rory yelled into the phone. "Keep searching!" Pointedly, she hung up.

"You won't find her," I said. "She's more clever than you think."

Rory slipped me the side-eye. "She thinks you're dead, Jonathon. She'll stop searching for you, but I *will* find her. I will never stop searching for her." She strode toward me. "When I do, you will watch her suffer."

I leaned forward and pulled on the handcuffs. "You have no idea who you're dealing with, do you?"

Rory took two steps forward and slapped me in the face. I didn't flinch. I didn't look away from her. She had no clue what I was capable of. "Make no mistake," she said. "I will own you, Jonathon Thomas Huen. You will beg me to be merciful. You will beg me for your life. You intercepted my shipment of fentanyl, and I am pissed. I will have your heart and soul before this is over."

I glared at her until she turned away.

Alex pushed out of the chair and moved toward the bar. "It was a good attempt, Rory. You must be close. Surveil the island. If she wasn't on the boat, she's hiding somewhere on Milos."

"Brilliant, Alex. That's brilliant. Do you have any more advice?" Rory looked like she wanted to swing at him too.

"Your sources confirmed she was with that harmless old fool, Karl Samaroulis. What you need to worry about is who he took her to meet. Who is there on Milos who can help her?" Alex chose a crystal decanter from an array of liquor on the bar.

"Find out." Rory's high heels echoed down the hallway in her wake.

"I assume you have enemies, Alex," I said.

He poured whiskey from the decanter into a highball glass and downed it. "I hear you haven't had a real drink in a long time. It shouldn't take much. You know, let's find out how loose your jaw is when you're drunk, Jon." He walked toward me with the decanter in one hand, then signaled two of the guards. The men came swiftly to my side. One gripped my head like a basketball and tipped it back as the other held my legs down. Alex pried open my mouth and poured.

-21-

MINA

Michael drove away from the marina and the burning catamaran as I watched out the rear window. Ten minutes later, he parked in a narrow alleyway and dug out his phone. He called the Harbour Corps—the equivalent to the Coast Guard in the States—to report the drone bombing, but we could already hear sirens approaching the docks.

I thumbed the password into my phone and swiped to Alex's number. As I dialed, Michael stopped me. "Is that *your* cell phone?"

I nodded before realizing what he was asking. "If someone's looking for me, they can probably track me with it." I powered it off. Tearing off the protective case, I said, "How do I get the sim-card out?"

"Sim cards aren't the problem. Do you use a Chrome browser?" Michael snatched the phone from me and got out of the car. He threw it against a wall then smashed it with a stone he found on the ground. "We'll get you a new one," he said as he climbed back into the driver's seat.

"Do you think the drone cameras spotted us?" Emilya craned her neck to gaze at the sky from her closed car window. None of us dared open them.

"I don't know anything about drones," I said.

"I do." With a grave expression, Michael peered through the top of the windshield. "The operator can see everything the drone sees, but the viewpoint from the camera is limited to a two-hundred-seventy-degree viewing area. When the drones turned toward shore, we would have been in their sites if the operator was still looking for you."

Sotto voce, Emilya asked "Do you think Karolos and his crew survived?"

I dreaded the answer. Michael pursed his lips and shook his head very slightly. "I don't know."

"If they were able to go below deck, they could be alive," I said. "I feel responsible."

"Why are they gunning for you?" she asked.

I gazed over my shoulder at Emilya in the cramped back seat of the car. She clutched her bag in her lap. Her shoulders were drawn up to her ears and a worried frown pulled the corners of her mouth downward.

"I'm not sure," I said. "Because of my association to Jonathon? Because I'm looking for him, and they don't want me to find him?"

I had many questions too. *Did Jonathon know they were looking for me? Did the drone operator think she killed me?*

Michael said, "The question is, were the drone cameras recording? If they were, someone will see those mp4 files and eventually they'll see us racing to get in the car. They'll know you're still alive."

"Authorities checked our passports at the port. They'll know I'm alive when first responders get to *The Dragonfly* and don't find me on board."

The sun began to sink behind the buildings. We waited quietly in the car for as long as we dared. Until it was time to venture out into the street again. Emilya's red car would be easy to spot if anyone was looking for us. No one chased us as we drove away. Michael drove seven miles to Voudia on the opposite side of the island. Near the shore, we parked in a parking lot.

It had been several hours since the bombing. If the drones had spotted us, they didn't follow. "I need to know if Karl, Nathan, and Luna survived," I said.

"Yes, of course." Michael dug his phone out of the cupholder and searched for the number. He handed the phone to Emilya, a native. She could communicate better than either of us. Michael and I listened intently while she was redirected to the emergency department and put on hold. For several drawn-out minutes, we silently watched airplanes and small crafts circle the channel between Milos and the island just north of it.

"Yah?" Emilya spoke to someone. She punctuated the mellifluous voice on the other end with yays and nays. Finally, she hung up.

"Karolos is in surgery. The explosion punctured his lung and shoulder. This part." She pointed.

"Rotator cuff," Michael said.

She nodded. "Yes, that. He suffered from burns, and he's in critical condition. Luna was treated for some minor injuries. I asked them to give her my number. To tell her I'm a friend of Karolos's."

I asked, "And Nathan?"

Emilya looked mournfully into my eyes. "No. He was dead when he arrived at the hospital."

Michael rubbed his palm over his forehead. His groan resonated deep inside me.

"I'm so sorry." I wanted to do something for Nathan's family, and for Karl, and planned to follow up as soon as possible.

"It's likely the drone operators are the same people who took Jonathon," Michael said.

"They must be. Who else . . ." A small plane took off from the airport and as it ascended, it doubled back and flew right over us. I didn't or couldn't take my eyes off it until I could no longer hear the motor. "They might be using me—threatening to kill me—to get Jonathon to cooperate. Those people are extortionists and criminals. In Chicago, I discovered their reach and power extends well into law enforcement and government. They are insidious and will stop at nothing in order to get their way."

"She'll kill you to get to him," he said.

She would. I thought about walking away from the car and leaving Michael and Emilya to keep them safe. But where would I go? Anyone I asked for help would be in danger. I'd come on this search and rescue mission with false hopes. Though I tried to trace Jonathon's steps, I hadn't located him or any of his friends. Greg told me the name of the hospital where emergency responders took victims of the car bombing in Poseidon Square. Javier Garrido, Jonathon's bodyguard, was lying in critical condition. Perhaps he could help me. Perhaps he had information. If I could avoid Rory's drones, it might be the best use of my time and limited resources.

"Are you going to tell her now?" Emilya tapped Michael's shoulder from behind.

Michael looked away from her and out the window.

"What?" I asked.

Emilya crossed her arms and rested her elbows on the backs of our seats. "You must help her."

I shook my head. "It's too risky. You can't put your lives in danger. Look what happened. Nathan is dead. Karl and Luna are in the hospital."

Is Jonathon dead too?

"You don't know Michael like I do." Emilya's eyes brightened. She tapped Michael's shoulder again. "You once asked for Jonathon's help and now Mina asks you," Emilya said. "That's why we need to help her."

Michael rubbed his fingers along the rim of the steering wheel. He looked out toward the sea. "Several years ago I retired from the Navy SEALs. I was stationed in Milan. Around that time I traveled to Japan and met Jonathon. Jonathon told me about the job opening with the Princess of Monaco. That's where I met my ex-wife. She was a duchess, and the princess's distant cousin."

"Yeah, yeah, we know this story." Emilya waved a circle with her hand, encouraging him to skip it.

"You were a Navy SEAL?" I breathed. I couldn't help it. My eyes grew wide. Navy SEALs were the best of the best. Trained stealth fighters, they were called upon to perform the most difficult maneuvers and tactical operations. During training, they were required to spend twenty-four hours in the ocean. Twenty-four hours floating with a life vest, facing hypothermia and other dangers. Only about a quarter of prospective SEALs made it through. It was worse than hazing in my opinion.

Michael shrugged. "Anyway, I'm familiar with terrorist cells in this area. I know what kinds of weaponry they use, and I'm familiar with their style of play. I know how to fight them. I know how to get onto the yacht without the guerrillas hearing or seeing a thing. I can figure out how to get to Rory." He nodded with his eyes closed. "After what we saw today, we'll need an RF jamming device to stop those drones from attacking us. I have pistols and semi-automatic rifles. And I can take you to Sotoris if we make damn sure Jonathon is there."

"No, Michael, you can't," I said.

"Yes he can. I can help too," Emilya said, "I'm very good at computers, and I know all about RF jamming. I'll maybe find something. Their weakness. Their vulnerability."

"You can't come with us, Em," he said.

"You listen to me." Emilya sat up tall. "I wrote my thesis on terrorism. They are brainwashed by sociopathic leaders whose ideals are skewed. They promote murder as a means to an end. They are a disease that needs to be wiped out, and I would love nothing more than to do something about it."

"Em," Michael turned toward the back of the car, "I can't let you go with us."

"No, Michael, you listen to me." She started speaking Greek at such a fast clip I thought Michael had trouble keeping up.

"Fine, but you're staying on my yacht. That's my limit," he said.

"Why stop there?" Emilya punched him in the bicep. "How far would you go for love?" she asked him. "Mina has come all this way for her true love. She is risking everything. And Jonathon loves Mina. You see? It is clear to me. Jonathon wears his heart on his sleeve. Even his enemies know how much he cares for her. That is true love."

"I know," he said. "I would do the same for you." He turned his amber gaze to meet hers.

"You would?" she asked.

"Yes, my love," he said.

"Do you love me?"

He spun in the driver's seat. "I love you with every ounce of my being. I love you from the bottom of the sea to the moon and back. I could never live a day without you."

Her expression melted and when he turned to kiss her, she leaned between the front seats and almost fell into his lap.

I was entirely too close to them. I exited the car and stretched my legs. Their post-quarrel make-up session lasted a half an hour, while I sat with my toes in the sand watching as the sun disappeared over the horizon and red spilled across the sky like a pool of blood.

I wondered again if Jonathon was a prisoner on Sotoris. Greg couldn't be right. He had to be alive.

~22~

MINA

I hadn't fully grasped what Emilya meant when she said she was good with computers. The spare bedroom of her house was a computer geek's heaven. She had multiple hard drives hooked to three screens and a laptop. The equipment and wires attached to several scanners, internet boosters, and routers. There was an expensive-looking microphone and headset, plus lighting and other features. I didn't ask what she did for a living because we didn't have time to chat.

Emilya let me borrow a smaller suitcase. While I shed the huge Samsonite and thinned my wardrobe, she packed up her elaborate computer array.

The waxing moon rose with a high wind while we carried essentials and electronics from Emilya's house to the car. We dared not turn on a light, or draw attention to her quaint home, in case Rory—or anyone else—was watching. Stealthy, like furtive raccoons scavenging scraps, we loaded towels, clean bedding, and a cooler packed with items from her fridge.

On the way to the port authority, we stopped for ice, bottled water, and several burner phones. We arrived at the marina as the wind picked up and a thick layer of clouds covered the moon. Michael unloaded our equipment and the cooler onto the docks. Emilya parked the car several blocks away in a friend's borrowed garage. If the drones had identified the car, they wouldn't be able to locate it.

I looked out past the docks to *The Dragonfly* anchored to a buoy. Yellow police tape surrounded the burnt deck and blackened sails. Guilt heated my cheeks and rested uneasily in my gut. I felt responsible for what happened to Karl and his crew. I said a silent prayer for Nathan and my need for punishment rose from its slumber.

It had been months since I thought about tombstoning. Therapy sessions and Jonathon's brand of punishment—healthier alternatives—replaced the need to dive from cliffs.

The last time I considered diving was after my best friend Traci was kidnapped. I was with her when it happened, while we were enjoying a sunny afternoon at a flea market. In the days that followed, while we brought in the FBI and searched for her, I could only blame myself for what happened. Though Traci recovered quickly once we located her, I couldn't erase the feeling of blame. I should have told her my life had been threatened. I should have kept a protective eye on her. I should have done more to keep her safe.

I had placed Traci in harm's way.

After the ordeal, I went to Lake Champlain, Vermont, and dove from a forty-five foot cliff. Diving, facing near death, was my punishment. But that sentence didn't do the crime justice. Just like then, I needed Jonathon. He could deliver punishment so sublime, so glorious . . . He had such wicked tools at his disposal. Thin biting reeds, stinging, studded paddles, burning leather whips. He knew just how to bestow excruciating pain without leaving a single mark on my skin. And when it was over, the feeling of atonement and forgiveness drew emotion from my core.

Jonathon—a self-proclaimed dominant—punished me because I asked him to. He did it because he loved me.

Here in Greece, I was closer to more cliff jumping opportunities than ever before. I had researched the places where the peaks were highest and the water deep and clear. The cliffs on Milos—the ones Nathan told me about—were nothing compared to the forty-five foot jump from Santorini cliffs on Thirasia. And even that was a molehill compared to Navagio Beach on Zycanthos.

Around midnight, Emilya returned, as silent as a mouse, from dropping off her car. We hid in the shadows cast by streetlamps and spoke only in whispers. With all our gear, Michael, Emilya, and I climbed into a small, single engine tender chained to a post on the public pier. We dared not start the engine.

Michael undid the padlock, shoved us off, and rowed out to his yacht, anchored in the bay.

He climbed aboard, efficiently untying the sleek protective cover, and rolling it away from the deck. I padlocked the dingy to the buoy where it would remain until Michael's return. Waves grew with the coming storm as Emilya climbed unsteadily onto the yacht. The boat seemed to come alive with the activity. Blond teak gleamed, even in the dark. Though I knew nothing about sailboat racing, I admired the sleek streamlining and economic elegance that was clearly designed for speed.

Michael untied ropes and prepared to launch while Emilya and I carried our coolers, backpacks, and equipment below deck.

"First things first," Emilya said. She unpacked a device with several antennae and dials, and she smiled. "The RF jamming device. It's illegal in the EU. I got it from a Ukrainian friend who fled from the war. Sadly, he needed to sell his equipment and start over after his city was attacked."

"It will keep the drones from finding us?"

"It will keep anyone from finding us."

Unlike Karl's catamaran, the long narrow monohull of the Oyster yacht had a refined lounging area and slender galley kitchen. I left our things on the low-pile carpeted floor near a royal-blue, L-shaped couch. This boat had cabinets similar to those I'd become familiar with traveling aboard the *Dragonfly*. The shelving with guardrails and other safety features kept things secure.

The increasing wind brought higher swells that hit the yacht broadside and rocked the Oyster side to side. I stumbled into the table, then secured the water bottles and Emilya's computer equipment wherever I could.

The motorized anchor lift engaged and the sound of the chain winding up the anchor indicated we were about to depart. The engine purred to life. I climbed back up the hatchway to the deck and joined Emilya in the cockpit. Michael was at the helm. Above him, jagged lightning skittered across the sky, illuminating dark clouds heavy with rain.

"We're going to hit a squall tonight," Michael announced. His words were the first spoken aloud in hours. "In autumn, the Mediterranean is very warm. Tornados are common this time of year."

"Tornados?" I was quite sure I didn't want to be caught in a tornado while at sea. Or even on land.

"In other words, prepare for rough seas," Michael said. "I usually have a crew of three men who help sail this boat. It will be rough going with only Em and me sailing."

"I'll help. What can I do?" I was willing to do anything they asked.

Deadly serious, Michael said, "Follow orders when it comes down to it."

We set course for Kriti, the largest Greek island. This yacht had two circular tillers at the stern, one on either side of the seventy-five-foot boom. He stood behind the right-side helm. The electronic navigational equipment, his barometer, and engine gauges lit his face with a greenish glow. In front of him, two huge winches—like oversized spools—were wrapped with two-inch thick rope for letting out the mast while sailing. All the operations were electronically controlled from one of those two helms. They had stabilizing platforms that remained horizontal when the boat heeled over.

Having never been on a racing boat, I was a little leery of the tilt and of the speed.

Anxious, I looked out at the white-capped, roiling waves. We headed into the wind as we exited the U-shaped bay of Milos. By the time we hit the open seas, driving rain made it impossible to see beyond the bow of the yacht. Emilya brought out rain slickers and Michael declined his. We were already soaked from warm water splashing over the hull and the sides of the boat.

Michael shouted above the rain, "Emilya, look at the weather app. I need to know how long the storm will last."

"What does your barometer say?" she asked.

He said, "Looks like it's moving pretty fast. Will we go through it?"

Under her jacket, Emilya shielded her phone from the rain. "The Meltemi winds—the summer winds—are through for the year. This is an unexpected squall. The storm's moving east at about sixty-four knots. We should be past it in an hour or two."

As we turned southward around the island of Milos, it seemed like the seas calmed. In actuality, we were riding the swells southward rather than fighting to navigate into them.

"It seems calmer," I shouted above the wind.

"We're moving with the storm," Emilya explained.

"In this weather, it's wise to keep the sails down. We'll sacrifice speed for safety," Michael shouted above the pouring rain. "I'll manage the helm until we get on the other side of this. Em, get some shut-eye so you can help me raise the sails in a few hours."

Emilya agreed to do just that.

"What can I do?" I asked.

"Help me stay awake. This lady pretty much navigates herself. It's a straight line to Kriti." Alex Buccino was in Kriti.

The bow dipped into an oncoming wave. Salty spray sluiced the deck.

Michael said, "It's going to be rough. Better rope yourself in."

In two hours we were on the other side of the storm, but my stomach hadn't weathered it as well as I hoped. I spent much of that time leaning overboard and retching into the swells.

As the storm cleared, so did my nausea. Emilya came up on deck after her nap, though I wondered how anyone could sleep through those rough seas. It was still dark. We followed the captain's orders, closed the hatch, and toweled off our faces and hair. When it was time, the two of us untied the stays securing the main sail. She and Michael hopped from task to task like expert sailors, loosening ropes and cleats, preparing the boat to make way under sail. With the push of a button, the massive sail rose and filled with wind. I stayed low in the cockpit as the boom swung outward at a forty-five degree angle to the boat, and we picked up speed.

Michael shut the engine off and we moved like a whisper with the waves, barely making any noise. As the clouds cleared, stars appeared above, and a crescent moon shone bright.

Emilya took the helm. "You sleep for a few hours, my love. We have about seventy kilometers to go. I'll wake you in two hours."

Michael kissed her and slipped below deck.

I went to my cabin to change into dry clothes but found the closed quarters exacerbated my queasiness. I dashed back up on deck to get an unobstructed view of the horizon—a pretty reliable fix for seasickness—and sat in the cockpit. As the horrible feeling passed, I dug the burner phone out of my back pocket. I longed to call Jonathon. To hear his voice. I needed his reassurance that everything would be fine.

-23-

JONATHON

A massive headache woke me, but then came the nausea. Forced out of bed by the sudden urge to vomit, I staggered to the bathroom and crouched over the toilet. When it was over, I turned on the shower—dove into the cold stream—and washed my face, scrubbing my beard with citrussy soap until the stench of alcohol was gone. Bits of what occurred last night tumbled into and out of my mind.

Alex force-fed me bourbon until I was stinking drunk. It hadn't taken much, considering I hadn't had a single drink in five years. Okay, five months. In June, I had just met Mina—again—and we'd met at Alinea restaurant. I knew the cook, and he assured me a private table. So I asked Mina to meet me there.

When we signed the Elements of Engagement contract, that very moment I handed the tablet back to her, she looked down at her iPad. When she drew her finger across the signature line and looked up at me with those dewy hazel eyes, I knew she was the one.

The One. I was smitten.

After Rory, I had never wanted to date anyone seriously ever again. Sure, I had my long-term friends with benefits, but we were too smart to take once-a-month romps between the sheets seriously. Besides, I was on the local news frequently and way too often. The local reporter called me Chicago's *most eligible bachelor.* I hated that.

That day at Alinea, I saw Mina sitting across the table from me, disguising her nervousness with sharp banter and intelligent questions. So confident and . . . beautiful. She resisted me. I could tell she wanted to keep her distance, but even she couldn't fight the attraction between us. I wanted to push her away, but I was drawn to her like a magnet to sheet metal.

After she left Alinea restaurant, Asaad drove me to a liquor store where I bought a liter bottle of the best vodka money could buy. I hadn't had a drink in years, but I had to get her off my mind. The vodka went down so easily.

For some reason I thought that by getting drunk, I'd stifle the blooming feelings I had for my criminal defense attorney. *Ha!* Hiring her had been a joke. I knew the cops would never arrest me for Kymani's murder. I hired Mina because I'd been following her career. I learned everything there was to know about her after Janko pointed her out that night in Dubrovnik. I needed to make sure she was safe.

I drank the better half of that bottle of vodka that night. I don't quite remember everything I did. Asaad drove me to a dark strip club where I watched women in sequined thongs dance to get my mind off her. Somehow I made it back to my condo. Asaad must have helped me.

The next morning, I was tagged in several posts on social media. A video of me staggering out of the strip club went viral. Assad and my bodyguard—Travis King at the time—carried me away as the cameraman took photos. An article in the Trib said I was kicked out of the bar for picking a fight with the owner. I'm pretty sure I told him he was a scumbag for providing such debaucherous entertainment. And for his treatment of his girls.

Somehow Mina caught wind of the scene. She probably saw the viral video posted on social media. She showed up at my condo looking angry. Her arms crossed and her brow furrowed. And she was stunning. "You," I said.

In that drunken state I believed it was her fault that I drank so much.

"Are you trying to get arrested?" She pushed past me into the apartment. I couldn't even stand up straight, so she almost knocked me over. She looked around the condo, getting the scope of what had happened last night. She picked up the vodka bottle, examined the meager contents, and said, "Nice work."

I snicked the bottle away from her. "Why did you come here?" I fumbled with the cap, then poured the last of it into my glass.

"Assad called me," she explained. "And I saw the video on Instagram,

Facebook, TikTok, *and* X. Your people are worried about you. They must love you very much."

"They don't love me. They love their paychecks," I remembered saying. I was trying to make her hate me. "You're here for the money too. What am I paying you for? I'm ob-vioushly innocent. Oh, did I slur? Does it offend you?"

When I lifted the glass to my lips, she gently touched my arm to stop me. I downed the booze anyway. "Why are you here, Mina?"

She took the glass from me. "It was never about the money."

"Then what? I'm not a criminal. I'm not a killer. We have no business together."

"Right. I don't think you killed Kymani Zhao. I don't think you're a sociopath like the rest of my clients. For some reason, I think you might actually be a good person. Someone who isn't insanely murderous. And I happen to like you. A lot."

Like this morning, I'd rushed for the toilet and made it just in time.

Last night's events were just as much of a blur.

"Who is helping Mina?" The bourbon and the darkness distorted Alex's face. It had been late at night by the time he started interrogating me. *"Where is she?"*

"Mayhem," I said. Then I thought of those insurance commercials on TV featuring a reckless, destructive character of the same name and burst into laughter. Alex had no idea who Stan Moorlehem was. And he wouldn't find out until it was too late.

It still brought a grin to my lips. After showering, I found a plate with a continental breakfast on the desk. The door to my room had been left open. *Has Rory had a change of heart? Did they find Mina?*

I had to find out. Though food would probably help, eating a croissant was the last thing on my mind. In my blue pajama pants and T-shirt, I walked out of the room and stopped at the top of the stairs. Sitaara's door down the hall was still closed. I placed my hand and an ear against it. "Sitaara? Are you in there?"

I heard shuffling. And the door handle rattled. "Please. I want to see my parents."

Was Rory holding her for ransom? The kid needed a hug. She needed the loving reassurance of her parents. "I'm doing everything I can. I promise." The words felt dry and useless. But I meant every word. When I got free from Rory's grip, I'd take Sitaara with me.

I hung my head on the way down the stairs past a new armed guard. "Good morning," I said.

The guerrilla didn't answer. I made my way back to the main lounge where Rory and Alex ate breakfast at a linen-covered table.

"Surprised to see you up," Alex said. His smug expression made me want to punch him.

"You can't break me with booze."

Rory set her coffee cup down and pushed her chair away from the table. "Alex doesn't know you like I do."

I'd had enough of their small talk and games. "What's going on with Sitaara? Why is she locked in a room?"

"None of your business."

"She's a child." I didn't dare tell her that Sitaara's father was a friend.

"She's my father's prisoner." Rory pursed her lips. "I don't want anything to do with her."

"At least let her out of the room."

"Sit down, Jon. It's too early for this contentious crap."

"Do I have a choice?"

"No. Father called this morning, and he wants to see you."

Artur Protsenko.

"He wants to form a partnership," she said.

"I'd never—"

"He can be persuasive."

On the white linen tablecloth, Alex's cell phone rang. He picked it up and smiled as he pushed away from the table. "Good morning, Mina."

Mina! I had to tell her Alex was untrustworthy. I lunged for him, but the guerrillas were faster. One caught my arm and the other stepped between us with his Uzi aimed at my face.

"Mina!" I roared.

"Shut up!" Rory shot daggers with her gaze.

On her orders, the guards dragged me out of the room.

"Mina, don't listen to him!" I shouted over my shoulder as they dragged me away.

I could still hear Alex's smooth, lying voice. "You don't say, Mina. Drones? That's terrifying. I'll meet you at the ruins later today. We'll figure out what to do."

"No!" I cried as they took me down a flight of stairs.

~24~

MINA

"Where are you now, Alex?" Sunny skies heralded the new day, but the night had been rough. I woke on the cockpit couch, weak-kneed and woozy. We made it through the storm, and our current heading was south-by-southeast as we sailed along the coast of Kriti.

"Me? I'm at a little bistro near the beach," Alex said.

"Is someone shouting?" I could have sworn I heard someone yelling my name in the background.

"No, it must be the seagulls."

I looked up at seagulls flying overhead and shaded my eyes from the midmorning sun.

"Are you there?" Alex asked.

"Jet lag," I said. Unlike the catamaran, stabilized by two pontoons, the Oyster had a monohull subject to side-to-side motion as well as forward and aft. No amount of Dramamine helped. I spent hours above deck leaning over the side rail and retching. "Have you heard anything from Jonathon?"

"I heard about the explosion on Mikonos. Four dead."

Jonathon's bodyguard, Javier, was hurt badly. But since I didn't hear any sincere sympathy in his tone, I trusted my gut and didn't say a word about it to Alex. "I know."

"Devastating," he said. The socially acceptable response.

"Do you think—"

"What? That Jonathon was killed?"

My throat closed. I nodded.

"Oh, no, Jonathon is alive. I'm sure of it."

My heart skipped a beat. "Have you heard from him?"

"I have. And I can take you to him."

"That's wonderful news!" Indeed, the best news I'd heard in weeks. "Where is he? Does he have a cell phone? I need to talk to him."

"Meet me at the Venetian Fortezza Castle at one o'clock today," he said.

"Do you have a phone number for him?"

"No. Trust me, *despoinída*. Meet me today."

The sun was already high, and we sailed smoothly along the coast of Kriti with Michael at the helm. I let Michael know how important this meeting was to me and he aimed the boat for a port near Rethymno. I headed downstairs to the saloon to see if food would settle my stomach.

Emilya silently unloaded the cooler she brought from home into the refrigerator. The long narrow kitchen was equipped with more streamlined features than Karl's catamaran.

"How can I help?" I eyed a box of breakfast bars on the counter.

"You can relax." She did a double take and cocked her head while looking at me. "You seem very happy this morning. Did you hear news?"

"Alex says Jonathon is alive!" I told her about the conversation with Alex.

"Perhaps our journey won't be so difficult after all." She placed fruit in a hanging basket tied to the wall.

"Have you and Michael been together long?"

She smiled. "Only two years. The most wonderful years of my life. Would you like something to drink?"

The earthy smell of brewing coffee turned my weak stomach. "Just water."

"How long have you and Jonathon been together?" She broke apart an eight-pack of water bottles, handed one to me and tucked the rest into a storage compartment beneath the sink.

"Only five months, but it feels like a lifetime," I said. I leaned against the galley wall with the yawing of the boat. Gazing at the horizon helped, so I looked out the window and searched for it.

"You love him very much to come all this way looking for him."

"Very much. I'm so grateful to you and Michael for helping. I don't know how to repay you."

"First let's find Jonathon. Then we can discuss payment." Her friendly smile warmed me.

The boat rolled with a larger wave, and I held on to the grips nearby. "Michael loves this type of adventure. It is *good* for him. Like a race. He will want to win it." She spoke of him with admiration.

"Michael seems a lot like Jonathon. I bet they get along well."

"Jonathon must be formidable. I sense that you love that about him."

The Jonathon I knew worked hard. He had lofty expectations of himself and the people around him—as did I. It was the reason we were so compatible. We both demanded excellence.

She took her coffee to a corner navigation desk where her computer and electronics were set up. Electronic devices and a computer screen were all built into the cabinetry. There were headsets, phones, and communication devices hanging from wall mounts. There were gauges and monitors, red and green lights blinking, and behind her, a circuit board. She had other bits of hardware crowding the desk beside her laptop. To me, she seemed like a tech wizard.

"Have a seat. I brought my work with me and have a few things to sort out," she said.

"What do you do?" I sat on the royal-blue bench opposite Emilya.

"I'm a journalist and true-crime podcaster. This morning I'm researching the transnational crime syndicate you spoke of. This is a great resource for my podcast. They are a wicked bunch."

"What have you found?"

"Plenty of material for my podcast, but nothing to incarcerate. They are stealthy, no? An article published this year in Germany and Croatia speculated that government officials are involved with trafficking weapons to terrorists. Those articles were removed from publication. The author seems to have stopped writing."

"Or she's dead." I cautiously nibbled a breakfast bar and sipped water.

"But I found another story about the mysterious disappearances of two investigators who connected Artur Protsenko to shootings in Montenegro. Now no one can find them."

"And that doesn't scare you?" It scared me.

Emilya's sea-green eyes lit with enthusiasm. "No way. This is the kind of story I like to highlight on my podcast." Emilya was my kind of woman, tenacious and tough.

I missed my contacts list on the phone we'd left in an alley. She helped me find Alex's number earlier. Now I wanted to call Greg. "Can you help me locate another phone number? I need to share the news that Jonathon is alive with his friend Greg."

"No problem."

I gave Emilya Greg's name, and her fingers typed a rat-a-tat on her keyboard. "A blocked number," she said. "Protected from malware, spyware, and government access. Here it is." She found his unlisted number so easily it shocked me.

"How'd you do that so fast?"

"I have skills," she said with a smile.

"Thank you." I left the granola bar and took my water bottle on deck with my cell phone in the other hand. The fresh air and blue skies were a healing tonic to my seasickness hangover.

Belled out by the wind behind us, the formidable black sail made Michael's yacht look like a pirate ship. Metal pulleys and lines that rose to the top clanged and thudded against the mast. I sat in the cockpit and dialed Greg's number. I didn't expect him to answer right away, since he wouldn't recognize my number, but he did.

"It's me."

"Jesus, Mina! I almost called the police. Where are you?" he asked.

Someone spoke in the background as if making an announcement.

"On a yacht near Crete. Greg, Jonathon's alive!"

"Wait, how did you know? Did he call you too?"

"He called you?"

"Late last night. He sounded drunk."

The news gave me a surge of hope. "When? What did he say? Where is he?"

"He didn't call from his own cell phone. I think it was a New York area code. I took the call because it rang three times in a row from the same number."

"What's his number? I need to call him."

"We didn't talk long. When I told him you were on your way, he said he expected you to follow him. But Mina, he doesn't want you there."

"Why not?" I sat on the aft deck watching our wake form behind us.

"Not sure. If I had to guess, there was something furtive about his tone," Greg said. "The conversation was very short."

"Did he find her, Greg? Did he find Rory?"

"He didn't say. But I got this weird feeling she was listening."

"It makes sense. I suspect she kidnapped him." I was in more peril than I feared. I gave him the abridged version of the past day and a half. "Greg, Alex Buccino is taking me to Jonathon later today. Do you think I can trust him? I'm afraid he's working with Rory."

"No. Don't trust anyone. First, I can't find an island called Sotoris. Most likely it's a private island . . ."

"Michael knows where it is." I felt queasy again, so I locked my gaze on the horizon.

"Wait until I get there. I'm in touch with Stan Moorlehem. He has the resources and the skills," Greg said. "We'll find Jonathon together."

"What about Alex? I promised to meet him."

"See if you can get a better read on him in person. But I wouldn't let him take you anywhere. We don't know who he's working for."

"Got it." Through the phone, I heard another announcer. I could have sworn the voice said, *"Now boarding."*

"Greg. Are you at the airport?"

"I leave for Greece in an hour."

"Are you crazy?"

"Are you?"

"How the hell will you find me? I'm on a yacht in the middle of the Mediterranean for chrissakes. I have a burner phone, and I'm being hunted by drones."

Emilya came up on deck and drew a line across her neck, a signal for me to cut it off. Even though it was a burner phone, the call could be traced.

"I have to go. Give me Stan's Moorlehem's number."

"He can't be reached. Keep in touch, Mina. I'll find you."

I hung up and silently wished him well. I admired Greg for stepping into the fire with me and hoped he remained safe.

The sunshine warmed my face. I closed my eyes for a moment and when I opened them, Emilya stood before me gazing toward Kriti where the tallest mountain in Greece rose from the sea. A dozen coastal cities populated the shores surrounding Mount Ida. High in the blue sky puffy white clouds surrounded the eight-thousand-foot snowcapped mountain.

"That's the Venetian Fortezza Castle." Emilya pointed to a rounded structure on the cliffs near the shore.

On a stony outcrop, an austere fortress wall surrounded a dome-shaped building. Beneath it, rows of white-and-blue beach umbrellas dotted a sandy stretch.

"It's where I'm meeting Alex."

~25~

MINA

That afternoon, we took a taxi to the Venetian Fortezza Castle and climbed steep stone steps to the ruins. The domed Sultan Ibrahim Han Mosque was one of three lonely structures left of the fortress. Sidewalks and sandy paths wound away from the entrance of the ancient tourist attraction to five-foot-high stone walls protecting the structure. Beyond the walls, the view of the Mediterranean Sea was breathtaking.

Although, the chance I'd soon come face-to-face with Rory was likely, Alex had given me hope with his offer to help. Jonathon was alive. Alex promised to take me to him. Greg and my gut said *be wary*. After witnessing the bombing of *The Dragonfly*, I had no other mindset. Alternatively, if I didn't find Jonathon, if he was dead, would I be able to go home? To start again? Would I be able to return to my Lincoln Park condo to a *normal* life?

I didn't know what normal meant anymore. It seemed like I'd been looking for Jonathon for months. In actuality, I arrived in Athens less than a week ago.

Michael looked at his nautical Rolex watch. "We're right on time."

It was hot this time of day, and I had my hair up. A sundress with spaghetti straps kept me cool and the smell of coconut-scented sunscreen wafted from my bare shoulders. I looked past the mosque to the smooth, pale wall about a hundred yards away. A few cactuses dotted the dry, desertlike terrain. Tourists wandered the dusty grounds in small groups of two, three, and four.

Keeping an eye out for Alex, I peered into the ancient circular mosque. The walls were made of large stones and thick white clay. The air inside the round tiled room seemed much cooler. Arches framed windows and prayer portals, and the domed ceiling was inlaid with faded tiles that must have once been vibrant and colorful. People inside whispered, their soft voices echoing in the hollow chamber.

I didn't stay long because I worried I'd miss Alex.

Heat radiated off the bare clay earth. Far beneath the fortress wall, cars drove along the coastal highway. I looked out at the sea or watched couples pushing strollers. I took photos for geriatric travelers with the scenery behind them, while we waited for nearly an hour. Michael and Emilya leaned into each other, their elbows on the fortress wall, talking quietly about private matters with their backs to me. Sweat dripped down my neck and I fanned myself with a brochure and sipped a bottle of water.

Through the dust and glare, I saw two men strolling our way. The mirage effect rising off the hot terrain distorted them, so I couldn't make out their features. The first had a confident stride and wide shoulders. As he drew closer, I made out he was burly and bald. He wore black slacks and a bright red short-sleeved shirt.

The muscular Black man behind him stopped about ten yards away and assumed an at-ease stance. Dressed in camo cargo pants and a fitted black T-shirt, he appeared to be military, but something about him made the hairs on the back of my neck stand at attention.

Something was wrong.

I raised my hand to shade the glare.

As the man approached, he tucked his hand behind his back. Prickles scattered up and down the back of my neck as he looked right at me.

"Mina?"

"Alex?" *Be wary.* Greg's voice echoed in my mind.

He was right in front of me, and as I went to shake his hand, I saw his gun pointed at my chest. "I'm Alex Buccino. Jonathon was right. You are easy on the eyes."

I took a breath. "Where's Jonathon? You promised to take me to him." I suspected he was with Rory, but the hope he would lead me to Jonathon blinded me. He didn't know we were ready for this.

Alex was about to answer, but his gaze flicked to my left.

"What's going on here?" Michael was at my side with Emilya behind him. "Are you Alex?"

"Who's this?" Alex asked.

Michael pushed away the barrel of the gun and stepped between me and Alex. He spun swiftly and using a martial arts move I recognized, he slipped underneath Alex's arm. He gripped the hand holding the gun. As they struggled for control of the weapon, Emilya grabbed my arm. The military dude lunged forward at a frightening speed.

"Run!" Emilya shouted.

Michael knocked Alex's weapon high into the air and it landed on the ground in a cloud of dust as Emilya and I took off across the rock-strewn field, through the ruins, and past the temple.

I looked back and saw Michael shove Alex to the ground. The military guy raced after me and Emilya. I ducked beneath a few straggly pines, and we fled downhill toward an amphitheater where a group was setting up band equipment on the stage. The rapid-fire gunshots behind me sprayed the ground nearby with bullets. I kept running.

"What about Michael?" I shouted to Emilya.

"Don't worry about him!" Several paces ahead of me, she maneuvered the amphitheater steps with speed and agility. She darted between tourists and headed toward the parking lot.

When we reached the bottom of the hill, we ran with traffic along the coastal road. I glanced over my shoulder just as Michael emerged from the stone walkway to our right. "This way!" He pointed toward an intersection a few hundred yards away.

The Black man closed quickly as we ran past cars parked in the street and toward the populated avenue. The covered sidewalk near the beach was packed with tables and chairs belonging to local eateries. Slow traffic blocked our escape as we ducked between tourists and pedestrians. The man was gaining on us.

The oceanside straightaway had no turnoffs, no side streets that I could tell. Emilya quickly took the lead and Michael stayed behind me. "Keep running!"

We zigzagged between cars, and at the end of the strip we crossed a courtyard and slipped down an alley. Emilya ran into a tourist shop where postcards and chachkas lined the shelves. I knocked over a spinning sunglasses display and stooped to stand it back up.

Michael took me by the arms and pushed me forward. "Don't stop!"

Emilya held the back door open for us and closed it after we burst through.

"Wait!" Michael held the door closed.

I saw what he was looking at and picked up a broom. Black wrought iron security bars covered windows on either side of the alley door. I jammed the handle of the broom behind the bars and across the door. Someone on the other side tried to open the door and we ran.

"I know where we can hide for a few hours," Emilya said over her shoulder.

As we came through the alley and stepped back into the sun, a man yelled, "Stop them!"

"It's Alex. Keep going!" Michael pushed me forward. We dashed between scooters and bicycles where tourists crowded the one-way road. We ran against traffic and ducked between buildings. Emilya led the way down a brick, one-way alley.

My legs and lungs burned as I inhaled the scent of grilled seafood and savory dishes along the way. But I became winded. Alex was right on our heels.

"This way." Emilya waved us onward. We slipped down another alleyway lined with fig trees and palms, and she took a sharp left into a small grocery store. She ran all the way through, pushing shoppers out of the way until she reached a swinging door at the back of the produce section.

"Theítsa?" she called. "Catherine?"

A woman emerged from the back room carrying a crate of red ripe persimmons. "Emilya?"

I have no idea what Emilya said, but she quickly conveyed our situation.

Michael kept looking over his shoulder. Someone at the front of the store yelled, "Where did they go?"

"Hurry!" I said.

"This way." Catherine set the crate down and lead us to a trapdoor. She pulled it open, and we scrambled down to the cool basement. She shut the door and locked it. A moment later, Catherine yelled at someone. Their argument grew in volume as we looked up at the ceiling and trapdoor. Footsteps stomped overhead then it all became quiet.

My heart pounded against my rib cage as I tried to catch my breath.

"She told him no one came through. She told him to get out of her store." The whites of Emilya's eyes shone in the dark. "She told him she's calling *astynomía*. Sorry. The police."

After several tense minutes in the dark, we all relaxed.

Emilya pulled the chain on a single bulb and smiled.

-26-

JONATHON

The guerilla's led me down a hall in Rory's Mediterranean mansion. I looked out the windows to try and find landmarks. As long as we were on ground level, my height phobia remained asleep. Like a hibernating grizzly bear.

Rory's villa was built on an island high above the sea. This, I knew, was Sotoris. The island I'd been searching for. Since arriving, I'd watched the sun rise and set. Mount Ida on Kriti was situated far to the southwest. On very clear evenings, the peak was visible in the distance. The mountain of the gods. But because of the curvature of the earth, no other land masses were visible except one small island directly west. If my theory about the location was correct, Sotoris was somewhere between Karpathos and the Dodecanese Islands.

Ahead of me and the guards, Rory's spike-heeled sandals hit the tile floor like gunfire. She stopped to unlock the door. "This is where you'll stay from now on. Under *my* watch. Father will be here soon. He wants to speak with you." She threw the door open.

I immediately recognized similarities to the dungeon at my Lake Forest home. A four-poster bed with top rails. A rack of whips and similar devices. I quickly took in my surroundings and the devices she chose to display in her bondage and discipline room. I'd heard Rory became a dominatrix, but that label meant nothing to me. She was a vindictive bitch in my book. This was her sick way of exacting revenge for a broken heart.

"Padded cuffs?" They hung beside other gear on the wall. I smirked. "You've gone soft in your old age."

She stepped forward and slapped my face. "I haven't softened. You'll see."

"You don't scare me, Rory."

She waved her arm, pointing toward the bed. "Move him over there."

The guards forced me into the room. I stopped after a few steps and the barrels of their Uzi's rammed into my back. "What happened to you?" I asked.

"What happened to me? What happened to *me*?" She moved toward the wall and pulled a pair of handcuffs from a hook. "*You* happened to me, Jonathon. You and your empty promises."

"I promised nothing."

She threw her head back and laughed. "You're right. Now that I think about it."

I narrowed my gaze. "I delivered what you asked for."

"You stopped giving me what I needed!"

"I couldn't give you *enough*. Nothing was ever enough!"

"Shut up," she said. Anger seethed from her pores. Had I done that to her? "You'll give Father what he asks for, or your precious Mina will die." She took a threatening stance. "That's what this little game of yours has come to. Alex is meeting her today. He's bringing her to Sotoris. To Father."

Three more guards entered the room with enough firepower to shred me. "Rory, this is a mistake." Her men pushed me toward the bed. I pretended to stumble and fell to the floor. From there, I looked up at Rory.

Rory lowered her chin and looked down at me. "Did you ever love me, Jonathon? Did you love me as much as you love her?"

The question was a double-edged sword. One I would never answer.

"It doesn't matter," she said. "We had fun together. Remember that Japanese rope tying class? I could never get those knots right. You were brilliant. I loved watching your hands while you tied me up. Your fingers moved like a piano player. The way you stroked my tender skin after slapping it raw—"

"What do you want from me, Rory?" I sat back on my heels and rested my hands on my thighs. To a dom like Rory, it was a submissive pose. In yoga, it's called Hero's Pose.

"I already have it. I have you. How does it feel to be defeated, Jonathon?"

I was not defeated, yet.

"The longer you resist, the stronger I become. It doesn't matter how many guerillas you kill. I can always get more. And once Father gets her...Let's just say he doesn't care for you like I once did."

"You can't keep me a prisoner forever." I wasn't picking a fight, just being honest.

"No?" She laughed. "I'm no different than you. I have money and power and I use my advantage to make changes in the world."

I turned my head to get a better look at her face. "Is that what you think?"

"It seems like we're on opposite sides of the drug war, but really we're fighting the same battle."

"How's that?" The twisted statement made my head hurt. "If I'd known I would wake to an existential debate about big pharma—"

"Big corporations are just as corrupt as street dealers, selling their products with infomercials and buying doctors with payouts. They don't care about improving people's lives, they're just trying to make bank. I realized I could make far more money by being on the other side. By selling illegal drugs. It's simple supply and demand."

"You're killing people." I stood and suddenly we were eye to eye. I was barefoot, but not threatened by her. Her high heels gave her six inches.

"And you're not?" Rory looked into my eyes.

"I own a software company. I'm not feeding addicts with deadly painkillers."

"No. You just make access easier for them to get it."

"The software is for doctors and pharmacists."

"Logistics. When will you see the light, Jonathon?" She turned away and took a step back.

"What light?"

"There is power in control. With your help, with your influence, we could control the market. We could beat out the Chinese and become the world leader in manufacturing and distributing fentanyl."

I took a step toward her, and the guards raised their weapons. "That's what you want?"

She signaled to them to back off. "Father wants it. You'll work for him, or he'll make your life miserable. He'll strip you of everything and everyone you love."

"And that's what you want?" I asked.

"You're still the most handsome man I've ever known." She put her cold hand on my arm.

I cringed and tried not to pull away because she dared to show her vulnerable side. "Rory. If you think flattery—"

"Of course not." Her gaze met mine and her mouth softened. The hard lines disappeared from her forehead. "We were good together. We really had something."

"It was a long time ago," I said. Arguing with a narcissistic dictator was getting me nowhere. I anticipated what was coming and on the fly, came up with a plan.

"Perhaps. It doesn't have to be over," she said. "I miss you, Jon. I miss the way you made me feel. You never put up with my bullshit. No one else has ever come close to that. They all cower."

I shook my head. "Rory, I—"

"I still love you."

And there it was. Rory's weakness. I knew exactly what to do to get out of this mess.

I pried her fingers from my arm and turned my back on her. I didn't want her to see my face or have a chance to see through the lie I was about to tell her. "Mina means nothing to me. She's a submissive. She's my slave."

Her heels clicked on the floor. "Then why has she traveled all this way to rescue you?" Rory sat on the bed.

"She craves punishment."

"Perfect. Alex will be happy to oblige."

It took every ounce of control not to cringe. I turned to face her but before I could reply, Rory's cell phone rang. She pulled it from the pocket of her white slacks.

"Yes." A look of anger tightened her lips. "You lost her?" She caught my gaze and turned around.

"I know how to reach her," I said.

"Who was the man with her?"

"Let me help you find her," I said. "She'll come to me if you'd just let me talk to her." It was the only chance I had to save Mina. If I could get Rory on my side . . .

Rory turned and her gaze fell on me. "Come back to the villa. There's been a development." She hung up.

I turned and gave her the most sincere smile I could muster. "She means nothing to me." In order to protect Mina, I had to minimize her importance to me. "I'll help you find her. I'll even help you find a high bidder. Someone who will punish Mina the way she wants. The way she needs. You and Janko were right. Mina is a true submissive. She's a rare find. In a lot of ways, she's like you. Strong willed and intelligent. Powerful in her own right." I took a step toward her.

"Careful. That smacks of love, Jonathon."

"How could I love a slave?" I clenched my fists. I almost had her. "Rory." I looked into her cold blue eyes. "It's been so long since I've seen you. I didn't realize I still had feelings for you until I saw you." It was a lie. Inside, my heart burned with betrayal.

Rory examined me. She took her time. Finally she crossed her arms. "Go on."

"You and I were made for each other. I've been thinking about your offer. We could work together. I'll tell you everything. I'll share my resources. I want to be on your side."

Rory stared at me with her lips parted.

I sat on the bed beside her and placed my hand on her back.

She immediately shrugged me off. "Don't—"

I rested my hand in my lap. "You're right. We made a great team, once. Remember that time we drove to Chicago? It was right around the time Darren and Jack and I were forming our first ideas about the medical software and PPS. We met with the director of one of the hospitals."

"In Belvedere."

"Right." I chuckled at the memory. "You walked right up to him and shook his hand."

"He liked me." Rory looked down at her lap. "He liked you too..."

"I'm certain you helped secure the deal."

"He agreed to test your initial software." Rory looked up at me. "Jon—"

"I want to help you find Mina." That much was true. "Can you trust me?"

"We'll see."

-27-

MINA

We rested for hours in the cellar of the Greek grocery. After dark that evening we thanked Emilya's Aunt Catherine and bought provisions. We took a cab back to the marina and a water-taxi out to Michael's yacht, which was anchored to a buoy. Onboard, we stayed below deck in the spacious saloon. Though Emilya made sure the RF blockers were running, we remained out of sight in case Alex and Rory had sent drones.

Michael prepared a scrumptious Greek meal in the gally kitchen where cooking knives hung on a magnetic wall-mount near the deep stainless steel sink. The kitchen had an air fryer, microwave, convection oven, and Cuisinart blender. He served creamy cucumber tzatziki, fresh peppers, and toasted pita points while we discussed our next move.

Now that I knew Alex was working with Rory, I thought back to our conversation on the phone. I was almost sure I heard someone shouting my name. Alex said it was seagulls but that wasn't what I heard. I thought—and maybe it was my imagination—I thought it sounded like Jonathon's voice. "I'm going back to square one. What if Rory took Jonathon to the island?"

"It would have to be close to Kriti," Michael said.

"Close enough for Alex to meet us today at the Fortezza." Emilya poured red wine into three glasses while a casserole heated in the air fryer.

"Remember the terrorist superyacht I told you about?" Michael said. "The one I keep track of so I can avoid it? The ship's name is *Ivan*. People in the area call it *The Crazy Ivan*. It's anchored near a restricted island northeast of here."

Emilya handed us glasses of Agiorgitiko, a Greek red wine.

"Do we think the island is Sotoris?" I asked.

"After what happened today, I believe it could be." Michael sipped wine.

Emilya took her wine glass and dropped into the bench near her computer. "Alex could have flown to Chania International Airport in Rethymno. It's the nearest airport, and only about forty miles from the ruins where we met him today. I'll check the air traffic logs."

"Good plan," Michael said. "Look for any helicopter landings, as well as small privately owned crafts."

Emilya's fingers played staccato rhythms on the keyboard. "I like this idea. The Protsenkos have enough money to buy an island. If Jonathon is alive, they would have taken him to a secured facility."

"We need to narrow the possibilities." The red wine warmed me from the inside. "If you're sure the *Ivan* is anchored near Sotoris Island, then that's where they've taken Jonathon."

"The *Ivan*'s well protected, but I think we can get past their scanners and drones." Michael picked up a pen and paper. "While you were cleaning up, I called Greyson Andrews, a local friend who has connections in Interpol. He's not a policeman, but an informant. He could be helpful if we need reinforcements."

"My friend Greg flies into Athens tonight too. He's been in contact with Stan Moorlehem, the man Jonathan hired. I need to get in touch with him after he lands."

"I found something." Emilya tapped a pen on the table. "Social media went viral today when an unidentified amphibious plane landed near Georgioupolis Beach around noon. The pilot drove right up to the dock. Someone took a photo of the plane as the passengers deboarded. Here." She turned her screen and zoomed in on a photo of Alex and the soldier who had chased us through Rethymno.

Michael and I peered at the computer. "You're brilliant, my love," he said.

"Landing a small plane at a public pier is illegal. I wonder if police questioned bystanders after the plane flew off." Emilya leaned forward with her hands on her laptop.

"Is there a way to find out who owns the plane?" I asked.

"Simple. Give me a second." Emilya opened a new tab. "Look. I zoomed in on this photo of the plane. All small planes have an identifying number on the tail. It's like a license plate. I can look it up and tell you who owns the plane."

I smiled. "You're good!"

"Yes." she said. "The alphabetic number at the beginning of the series indicates the country of origin. This means the plane came from Croatia. I'll enter the number into a database. The pilot is required to report his flight plan every time he flies into Grecian airspace."

Michael smiled. "When we find the owner, I suspect we'll find an address."

"Unless it's illegally owned," I said.

Michael frowned.

I shrugged. "I'm a lawyer. I'm always questioning the truth."

Emilya turned her computer toward us. "Vedran Kolak owns the craft. When I search his name here"—she typed his name into a search engine—"he appears on a wanted list. I suspect he's been working for your TOC group for years."

"If we find out where he keeps the plane, we'll find Jonathon," I said.

The buzzer went off and our casserole was done baking. "I'll get it." I didn't cook, but I could handle pulling something out of the air fryer.

"I'll keep looking," Emilya said.

Michael sat at the table next to Emilya. "I know how to get onto the yacht without the guerrillas hearing or seeing a thing. I'm familiar with terrorist cells in this area. I know what kinds of weaponry they use, and I'm familiar with their style of play."

"You'll need an arsenal. Do you have any weapons?" I set the hot dish on a trivet.

A smile lit Michael's face. "I have a few pistols and semi-automatic rifles. But my friend Greyson is bringing the supplies we'll need: scuba gear, bullet-proof vests, harpoons, and climbing cups to help us board the yacht. I'll take you to the *Ivan* if we make damn sure Jonathon is there."

"I found it!" Emilya said. "Vedran Kolak didn't register his flight plan with AOPA, the Aircraft Owners and Pilots Association of Hellas, but I found where he last fueled, Heraklion airport. Airplane fuel is regulated and only available in specified, licensed facilities. He flew to Heraklion after dropping off his passengers. There, he had to file a flight plan in order to leave the airport."

"If he's a wanted fugitive, why didn't they arrest him on the spot?" I asked.

"The pilot name is wrong. I wonder if it's an alias."

My wheels were turning. "I'll bet Rory has her hooks in people everywhere. Just like in Chicago where some law enforcement and government officials are corrupted by the organization, maybe there's a payoff. Someone at the airport could have been told to look the other way."

"Where did Vedran Kolak fly off to after fueling?" Michael seemed just as anxious to learn more as I was.

"First he picked up our friends, Alex and his goon, at a private pier near Rethymno. Then . . ." Emilya turned her laptop screen toward us. She zoomed in on a map of islands northeast of Kriti. The largest were Kasos and Karpathos. West of those were the Karpathos Pelages, a handful of microdots on the screen. Emilya zoomed in on one tiny dot.

"Voila! Here is where the airplane landed this evening. And this is interesting." She clicked Google Layers to show satellite photography of the island and the photo was chunky, blurred out, and pixelated.

"Someone didn't want Google sharing photos of their island," she said.

I cleaned up the dinner plates while Michael and Emilya weighed anchor and started the engine. Michael set the GPS Chartplotter for Karpathos, and the electronic device set the course. He navigated out of Rethymno Bay, and Emilya unwrapped the stays and loosened the halyard to prepare the sails.

We motored north eastward as city lights illuminated the shore at dusk. Michael said, "The barometer shows smooth sailing this evening. No storms."

I sipped a soda water, anticipating the return of my seasickness. "My stomach and I are happy about that."

"Have you never sailed before?" Emilya asked.

"Nothing like this. My aunt owns a house in Lake Geneva, Wisconsin, where my brothers and I used to spend summers with her and my cousins. We water-skied more than anything. For a few years, my cousins had a small catamaran, and I rode along. It was a long time ago."

"If you're up for it, it's a beautiful evening to show you what this boat is capable of," Emilya said. "And I have extra Dramamine, just in case."

"I'd be delighted." Indeed, I loved watching the Australia Sailing Grand Prix. Those racing boats literally flew across the water at speeds up to forty-five kph.

Michael smiled and looked out at the seas ahead. He shut off the engine several miles from Rethymno with no other boaters nearby. The salty wind blew my hair into my eyes. I pushed the strands behind one ear. Waves lapped the sides of the boat and rocked us back and forth. The lines flapped, fluttered in the breeze, clanging against the metal mast.

"All-hands-on-deck!" Michael cried out. "I love saying that." His smile deepened his crow's feet.

The couple danced around the equipment and the twin helms. They brought the sailboat to life. Michael stood at the navigation helm on the port side—on the left—and hit a few buttons. "Are you ready, Em?"

"All ready," she said.

"I'm raising the main." The electronic halyard unfurled the black sail, raising the tip to the top of the seventy-five-foot mast. The sail fluttered loudly, as Michael steered into the wind and Emilya guided the main sheet attached to the boom.

Michael shouted, "Mina, go to the bow and loosen the sheet for the ancillary sail."

I walked to the bow with one hand on the guardrail and one hand ready to catch me if I stumbled. Without propulsion, the ship tipped to-and-fro, at the mercy of the waves. Thankfully, my Sorel all-terrain shoes had good traction on the smooth teak deck.

Emilya raised the ancillary sail at the bow. "Now, sit your butt down and prepare for some speed."

I dropped to my knees and got comfortable in a cross-legged, sukhasana position. Easy pose in yoga. I looked back at the cockpit, where Michael stood at the helm manning the navigational wheel.

Emilya sat next to me. "This is exciting, no?"

"It's amazing."

As the wind caught the sails, they filled and tightened. The boat yawed to the right and shooshed through the water. We picked up speed and the wind blew my hair back. With the last red rays of sunset in our wake and the dark night sky ahead, I felt the rush of being small and human compared to the forces of the planet.

-28-

JONATHON

"Four men. They believe I'm dead. My orders were to dissolve the team, should anything happen to me. I ordered them to burn any generated documents and purge their computers of all traces. I ordered them to go home. You won't find them. They are very good at blending into the common crowd."

Rory's eyelashes fluttered. "How can I trust you?"

She invited me to sit with her on the patio overlooking the Aegean. Her guards surrounded us with their weapons ready, but this time, I had no desire to run.

"Do you have an alternative?" I asked.

She set her espresso cup down and her gaze seemed lost somewhere between the cup and the linen tablecloth.

"I've told you; I'll help you find her," I said.

"You'll help regardless. When Father comes, you'll no longer have a choice." As if Rory belonged in the Chicago business district, today she wore a white blouse and pencil skirt with a pair of blood-red stiletto heels.

"He sounds like a man I can respect." I almost choked on the words. Artur Protsenko used threats and violence to control his people. His daughter did the same.

Did she know how much sway I had over my people? Did she know they would give their lives for me because I cultivated camaraderie and friendship with the people I worked with? It was especially important to me when their lives were in danger. It was especially important on a mission like this, where I was driven by personal desires. Now I needed to convince Rory that my team would do exactly as I asked.

"But you admit to orchestrating the attack and helping Interpol and the European DEA confiscate my shipment."

I looked away. "Can you blame me? I was angry."

"Fair enough." Her features hardened. "Father wants to form a partnership with you. To ensure that you never cross us again. And to prove your worth, you'll help me find and capture your *slave*. Because he won't trust you until the one you love the most is dead. And I won't trust you until you help me sell her to the highest bidder. Or you help me kill her."

Every muscle in my body wanted to tighten, to fight against this. I needed to bring Mina here to destroy Rory. "Whatever you wish. Let me talk to her. She'll come to me." I sipped my espresso. "What has Alex done with her?"

"Alex failed. Your precious Mina got away."

I tried to keep the elation out of my voice. "What do you mean? Where did she go?"

"If I knew, she'd be dead."

Cool relief flooded my veins. I let go of the breath I'd been holding.

"Vaolym." She called the guard near the patio door. He was the burly Black man I'd pick-pocketed. "Fetch Alex for me. He must be awake by now."

Vaolym nodded and exited.

"I'll trust you for now, Jonathon. If you make one mistake, I'll lock you back in that tower room for the rest of your life."

I made direct eye contact with her. "I understand." Trust was one thing. I needed to rekindle her desire for me in such a way that she would bring me into her fold. From that position, it would be easier to destroy her.

~29~

MINA

The Oyster swayed gently with the sea swells. The soothing motion helped me sleep for a few hours and during the night. I dreamed of Jonathon.

Low red lighting burned through the dark in the dungeon in his Lake Forest mansion. The room was more cavernous than I remembered. The walls seemed far, far away, and the room extended for miles with tunnels and hallways disappearing into the darkness underground. Like a museum I'd been to many years before, with torture devices from medieval days and his katana swords hung on racks and mounted behind glass. Displayed and labeled sexual devices, like stone and jade dildos, barbed paddles, and an iron chastity belt brought to mind torturous acts of the past.

Jonathon and I talked while we walked. "Tell me what you want."

"I feel guilty. Like the criminals I've represented." Nylah Wallace, the heiress who came to mind, kept her husband tied to a bed. She fed him so sparingly that he was weak and ill. She forced herself on him and punished him when he didn't please her. They lived in an older penthouse and the walls weren't entirely soundproof. A neighbor became suspicious when he heard noises. The poor husband managed to free one arm and use his shackles to make noise. Nylah didn't know. The neighbor called the police.

She was acquitted like the rest of my clients. I made the jury believe her husband's fetish for self-mutilation drove him insane. Nylah was victimized by his weird ways and forced to care for him. It was partially true. It started as a sexual game and got out of control. Nylah became codependent on the relationship. She needed to feel important. Though she was never diagnosed, I believed she had a form of Munchausen by Proxy.

I should have insisted she get evaluated before she found another victim.

Jonathon walked beside me and as we gazed at his collection, he asked, "What do you want?"

"I need punishment." Even as I said it, I cringed at the cruel devices in the displays. A vaginal spreader with sharp tips would tear a woman to shreds. Beside it, a penis cage with spikes to discourage masturbation would have left the user with worse problems.

"What do you want me to do?" Jonathon's voice was a smooth, gentle caress.

"I need . . ." I understood how perverse my desire was now. I turned away from the iron maiden and covered my eyes.

"I need your forgiveness. I need your tender kisses. I need you."

Jonathon wrapped his arms around me. His blood red shirt was unbuttoned to mid chest. I wrapped my arms around his neck and pulled him down. My lips met his warm mouth, and we kissed as his strong hands smoothed across my waist and low back.

"I need you," he said.

I woke to the sound of the anchor dropping. By the angle of the sun through my narrow window, I guessed it was late morning. I'd made it through the night without any sea sickness. Now, the lingering feeling from the dream made me queasy. If I were home, I'd schedule an appointment with my therapist to talk about the dream.

I sat up and looked at my burner phone. No messages. God, I missed Jonathon. I longed for a sign he was okay. Alex's betrayal hurt. Would he have taken me to Jonathon? I believed he would have, but then we would both be prisoners.

Someone knocked on my cabin door. "Mina?" Emilya called.

"I'm awake."

"We dropped anchor near Kasos. I made coffee, if you like."

"Thanks, Emilya. I'll be out in a few minutes."

Since I committed Greg's number to memory, I texted him and gave him an update. He responded almost immediately.

I'm south of Athens in . . . I can't spell it. Sitting here with Mayhem. What's the plan? I asked.

Mayhem thought Jonathon was dead, Greg responded. *The group disbanded.*

I thumbed my reply, *We know where Jonathon is, but it's dangerous. Danger is my middle name.*

I let Greg know our location. Time was ticking. I climbed the steps to the deck with a coffee cup in my hand. On the horizon, another rocky island jutted out of the sea. Out of habit, I looked up and scanned the skies.

"Don't worry, the RF blockers are working. Also, I'm tracking all scanning devices aimed toward us." Emilya turned her laptop toward me. A variety of graphs moved in real time, levels spiked and dropped in zigzag lines.

Across from her, Michael sat on the couch. A map was spread out on the table held down by their coffee cups. Michael shoveled granola into his mouth. "Good morning," he said with his mouth full.

"Morning." I pulled a green wrap around my midsection. The air had cooled overnight.

He chewed and swallowed. "My old friend Greyson arrives today. He flew into Kasos last night. We'll meet him at the port authority."

-30-

MINA

Greyson, a fit, middle-aged man with graying temples and a cleft chin, arrived around noon by water taxi. He carried two heavy duffel bags and dropped them on the aft deck.

"Thanks for coming." Michael gave Greyson a hearty handshake.

Greyson pulled him in for a man-hug. "Good to see you, old man. Good to see you." He let go of Michael and reached for Emilya. "How are you, sweetheart?"

I couldn't place his accent.

"Hello, Grey." Emilya introduced me and I shook his hand.

He stepped back to look at us. "Tell me everything."

Michael took one of the bags to the hatch. "Let's go below deck. I'll explain everything once the others arrive."

Later that day Greg and Stan "Mayhem" arrived. Introductions were made all around. Now we were six.

Wearing lime green shorts and an orange Hawaiian shirt, Greg limped onboard. "I hate flying commercial."

I'd forgotten I had POA of Jonathon's finances and control of all his assets. Including the plane. I could have asked Leo Thibodeau to bring Greg and Mayhem here. However . . . "I wouldn't have risked the phone call. Rory's people could be listening. They might have followed you here."

"You're right." Greg leaned into his cane. His bright orange and yellow shirt with marijuana leaves fluttered in the breeze. "I'll stop my whining now."

"Let's show our new guests to their berths." Emilya led the way. "We're maxing out capacity with six on board. Greg, you'll share a berth with Grey. Stan, I'm afraid you get the sofa in the saloon."

"That's fine with me. I don't sleep much anyway." Stan towered above Emilya and Greyson. His shoulder muscles bulged under a pale green short-sleeve shirt. The color looked brilliant against his black skin. He followed Emilya down the hatch into the saloon.

"Are you kidding? You snore like an ox," Greg said.

Their lighthearted banter bounced off me. "It's best we don't forget how dangerous this situation is. Rory won't stop until she gets what she wants."

"She's after you," Greg said. "By sinking her claws into you, she ensures Jonathon's allegiance."

"That's what I'm afraid of."

"And that's why we have to stop her." Greg pinned me with his soft gaze.

I looked away.

Once we settled into the cockpit with beers and sparkling waters. Greg sat next to me and yawned. He changed out of the orange shirt and into a lime green athletic shirt matching his pants. He stretched his healing knee and rested his foot with a red Nike shoe on the bench. Jet lag seemed to be catching up to him.

Stan said, "We thought Jonathan was dead. How did you find out Rory Protsenko has captured him?"

We explained everything we knew and updated them with our latest findings.

Stan sipped from a can of sparkling water then set it down. "Jonathon's plan was to meet one of the biggest fentanyl dealers in Croatia. We heard he works directly with Rory and distributes her poison all around the Mediterranean. I was going to pose as a dealer from England—since I can't hide the accent—and I was going to make a large purchase from him."

"Why not buy directly from Rory?" I asked.

"She really has no hand in selling the product. She won't go near the factory because she knows how deadly fentanyl is." Stan said, "The dealer's name was Raman Bishura."

"That name sounds familiar," I said. Then it occurred to me. "Before I left Chicago, Janko Vorobiev asked me to reach out to Bishura. He wanted me to let him know he was arrested. I ignored the request."

"Bishura's been working with Rory for about a decade," Stan said. "He told us about a container ship coming into Athens. We were to meet his contact at the docks and take fifty pounds to England."

"Fifty pounds?" Michael gaped.

I shook my head.

"We informed Interpol and DEA Europe. They intercepted the shipment." Stan sipped his beer. "From what I've been able to gather, it was the reason Rory sent a car bomb to explode near Jon."

"We believe she captured him during the chaos that ensued." Greg rubbed the scars on his bad knee.

I'd worked with murderers and knew the majority had no qualms about hurting others. "How is Javier?"

Stan smiled. "Javier was released from the hospital last week and he's doing well. He had a few broken ribs, a broken arm, and the hair burned off the back of his head. The burns are healing and he's in very good spirits. I spoke to him shortly after the explosion and he asked about Jonathon. He's eager to go back to work for him."

"That's fantastic news," I said. "Jonathon will be so happy to hear."

"Do you and Greg have a plan?" Michael asked.

"Plan?" Stan shook his head. "I have an idea. I need to get the layout of Sotoris, first."

"Before we talk about that"—all eyes shifted to me—"I need to know why you're here. How far are each of you willing to go to save Jonathon and stop Rory Protsenko?"

Michael nodded. "I owe Jonathon my lifestyle. He introduced me to the duchess."

Emilya frowned. "That woman . . ."

He shrugged. "What can I do? I wouldn't have been able to retire so young if she hadn't divorced me. Anyway, I'm here for Jon. I'll do whatever it takes to rescue him and stop Rory."

Greyson's short salt-and-pepper hair glistened in the sunset as he looked out over the sea.

"Tell them about your nephew," Michael said to him.

Greyson leaned forward and put his elbows on his knees. His lips tightened. "My sister's son was in high school. He was a smart boy. Brilliant, really. He earned a scholarship to Cambridge University for his writing and wanted someday to become a professor. He was celebrating high school graduation with his closest friends and one of them brought cocaine. They didn't know it was cut with fentanyl. My nephew and one of the girls died right away.""""

His story gave me chills. "I'm so sorry, Greyson." I said. The news was littered with stories like his. His tragedy brought dangers of the fentanyl epidemic closer to home.

"I'm dedicated to stopping this mass murder," he said. "I have contacts at Interpol and DEA Europe. Fentanyl distributors are like Nazis with the sole focus of wiping out a generation. I'll do anything you ask me to. I'm committed to Jonathon's mission and once we find them, I'll notify law enforcement."

"Two young people. Dead." Emilya put a hand on Greyson's back. "It's terrible. I know how hard this is for Greyson and others. I've highlighted stories of drug dealers on my true-crime podcast. I, too, have assisted law enforcement in catching these criminals. But the guilty are often people in power. People like Rory think they are above the law, but they must pay. I'm willing to do whatever it takes to help you, Mina. I hope we can at least send a message to others like her."

Greg's gaze landed on me. "Jon and I have been friends for about ten years. We have trained in martial arts together and he's helped me in so many ways. I was married once. I didn't know my wife had a shopping addiction. She mortgaged the house a second time to pay her credit cards and took absolutely everything I had. Debt swallowed me. When I filed for divorce and bankruptcy, Jon was there for me. He helped me climb out of the debt hole. I'm with you all the way, Mina. I owe him big time." He softly stared into my eyes, and my face heated. There was more to his reason for being here.

Stan was the last to speak. "Jonathon and I met about four years ago. It was around the time I was injured while on duty. He has given me ways to use my knowledge and training for good. Do you want my protection? I can do that. Do you need a killer? I can do that too." His dark skin glistened in the late afternoon sun. "What about you, Mina? How did you meet Jonathon?"

"Well, that's another novel." I nodded and smiled. "But the truth is, I love him. I would go to the ends of the earth to find him."

"Hear, hear." Stan held up his beer. We clinked our bottles of beer and cans of sparkling water together and toasted. "To Jonathon."

"To Jonathon," I said.

"Impressive ship," Greg said to Michael. "I'd love to be on deck with those black sails full and the wind at our backs."

"Soon enough. The Oyster's fast. That's what I love about her." Michael beamed with pride.

Greyson looked puzzled. "Oyster is the yachting company's brand name. Didn't you personalize your yacht?"

"I couldn't come up with one. For now, she's just the Oyster. My Pearl, on special occasions. Someday, I will give her a worthy name." Michael smiled.

Stan leaned over Emilya's navigation panel. "What kind of electronics have you got?"

Michael said, "She has satellite boosters for smoother internet streaming. I've got scanners and blockers to protect us from terrorists and pirates."

Emilia had launched into a show-and-tell of her computers and the equipment in the navigation center behind the saloon. She pointed to two black devices with blinking red lights. "These systems target nearby boaters. I can access their IP addresses and access their online accounts if needed." She grinned. "And in case we're being threatened, I can scramble their internet signals and alter their IP addresses. It would take them weeks to get their systems going again."

"Pirating the pirates." Greyson ran a hand through his short hair. "Nice."

Michael peered through the skylights in the ceiling. My gaze followed his to small clouds freckling the rosy sky. "Rory Protsenko has a fleet of weaponized drones," he said. "We've seen those devices kill someone. We'll need to be vigilant."

"I can set up a signal to block any radar. Unless their drones scout the area with video, they won't know we're coming," Emilya said. Her fingers fluttered over the keyboard.

"What about weapons?" Greg asked.

Michael said, "When I moved into the Oyster, I invested in anti-piracy weapons. Pirates are a normal part of life on the Mediterranean and the Aegean." He launched into a description of all the devices he and Emilya had installed.

Greyson said, "You have an LRAD."

"Yes," Michael explained. "It's a long range acoustic device to ward off pirates."

"I can help you set it up. You know it emits a sonic blast. Do you need noise canceling headphones?" Greyson said.

"No." Michael showed us four pairs of headphones. "The LRAD sends the deafening blast along a tight beam to the target. Neither the user, nor the people nearby can hear it."

Alex asked, "What else do you have?"

"I wanted to install a ship borne shore launcher, but they're too big for a ship this size. But I do have a manual launcher. And I mounted a laser on the stern." Michael explained that on the bow he affixed a black metal light box to the deck. "This boat could potentially outrun most speedboats. The laser shines a bright beam at the oncoming vessels. It can temporarily blind the ship captain and crew. It makes it impossible for them to focus their weapons at our ship."

"Have you used it?" Alex asked.

"Not yet."

"Wouldn't a gun be easier? I brought my dad's Browning." Just in case. I carried the permit too.

"The manual shore launcher fires projectiles at enemy boats. I can sink a small boat, like a dinghy or canoe if I need to," Michael said.

"When I retired, I took my Ruger EC9S and a Sig 45," Stan said. "They're in my bag right now, but when used properly, those weapons will sink a small boat too."

"A Ruger?" Greyson asked.

"Let me show you. I also have an . . ." Michael took the men into the master berth.

I backed away and closed the door to my berth. If only we knew for certain Jonathon was on Sotoris. My finger hovered over the number and before I knew it, he answered.

"This is Alex."

"Do you always answer unidentified numbers?"

"Who is this?"

I gave him a moment to think it through.

"Mina?"

"Let me speak with Jonathon."

"It is you, you slippery little—"

"I said, I want to speak with Jonathon."

Alex laughed. "Who do you think you are? You don't get to call the shots."

"Really? And yet, here I am. I'll bet Rory isn't too happy that you let me get away." I couldn't keep the smug tone from my voice. The score was even. Rory had attacked Karl and *The Dragonfly*, but I escaped capture.

Alex huffed into the receiver. "It isn't over."

"Let me speak to Jonathon."

His silence lingered for too long. I grew impatient. I needed to get off the line. "Alex. You don't even know where he is, do you?"

"Oh, I know where he is, Mina. And now I know where you are too."

I hung up. *Shit!* What had I done?

-31-

MINA

Without a plan, I'd stupidly called Alex thinking he'd let me speak to Jonathon. I'd inadvertently set the wheels in motion, but I hadn't told the others. Whatever happened now, good or bad, was my doing. Alex traced the call and discovered our location.

We motored toward what we believed to be Rory's island. The island we identified by tracking Alex's flight. If Rory held Jonathon captive, this was likely the place.

As we approached, Michael kept the sails lowered to decrease our visibility. Regardless, they'd eventually spot us, even with the RF blockers and scanner detection software running. We faced huge risks based on accounts of other sailors in the area. A number of people had posted frightening encounters online.

"They shot missile launchers at my wife and me. We were just swimming off the back of the boat." —Stefan Sauerbrunn

"Whoever owns that island is messed up. We were on a day sail with paying French tourists, and they fired on us. We scrambled to get those people to safety." —Captain Rohrbach

"I always use RF blockers and state-of-the-art scanners. I don't know what tech they're using, but they got through the blockers. They locked on to my vessel and chased us from Avgo with weaponized drones." —Captain of the *Dragon Queen*

Michael followed the trade routes and kept a distance from the island, knowing Rory and her radical insurgents would try to scare us away. We just needed to use our limited time wisely. He didn't know how narrow that window really was. None of us did.

Greyson zoomed in on the island with a pair of military-grade binoculars. "The mansion's on a cliff. It looks like it's about sixty to one hundred meters above the water. A steep climb." He handed Greg the binoculars.

We stood on the starboard side of the deck with a brisk cool wind in our faces. Clouds covered much of the sky today, but they moved swiftly. The black sea was choppy, flecked with whitecaps. Some larger swells rocked the yacht and when they did, I braced myself. In the distance the tall, rocky island jutted out of the sea. With my naked eye, I made out the white mansion, more like a villa, on the top of the cliff. Alex was there. And Jonathon. But that wasn't what my eye focused on.

The tall cliff rising from the Aegean Sea was magnificent. I wondered how deep the water surrounding the island was. Oddly, the sight didn't draw out my need to jump. I felt strangely calm, and a bit unsettled that my normal reaction—my desire to dive—had gone into hibernation. I wondered if it was because I'd jumped off a metaphorical cliff by making that call last night.

Greg was still focused on the island. "I could make that climb in a couple hours."

"No, you don't, old man," Stan said, taking the field glasses from Greyson and getting a look. "It's secured by barbed wire, and I count three, four, five armed insurgents in the yard."

I took the binocs from him. "I agree with Stan. You're not going anywhere, Greg. You stay here on tech with Emilya." I hoped that when the shit hit the fan, Greg wouldn't do something stupid and get himself shot again. I pressed the goggles up to my eyes, adjusted the spread of the ocular and turned the focus wheel.

The steep cliff rose sharply from the sea. Jagged white limestone reminded me of the islands near Croatia that I climbed without equipment during my visit to Dubrovnik. Squared off pale stones made up those islands in the Pile Sea and facilitated scaling them. The route up to Rory's villa looked clean. The crux of the climb, the most difficult part seemed to be at the bottom. Stones worn smooth by the sea appeared to have no grips or crags. Past that, there were easy toeholds and plenty of cracks and fissures. Toward the top of the route, a chimney, a narrow passage between two vertical stones looked wide enough for a body. My body, anyway. But it was hard to tell from this distance.

Neatly mowed grass spread to the edge of the cliff. I imagined standing on the carpet of thick green grass with my toes curled over the edge. What did the sea look like from there? Was the water shallow at the base of the cliff? Was it dark and deep? Or clear with a sandy bottom like the Pile Sea in the summer?

Disturbingly, my usual craving, my need to fly off that cliff and my addiction to diving were strangely MIA. And yet adrenaline raced through my veins as if I'd done a shot of crack cocaine.

Movement off to the left of the island caught my attention. I jerked and pointed the objective lens toward it. "There's a ship—a yacht—to the north of the island."

"Let me see."

I handed Stan the binoculars. "Could that be the *Ivan*?" I asked.

"That's a superyacht like I've heard about on the news," Stan said. "It's well guarded. There are launchers mounted to the stern, and militia on deck armed with machine guns. It could be Artur Protsenko's yacht, *The Crazy Ivan*. There's a satellite dish in the crow's nest and though I'm no sailor, looks like it's equipped with an extensive array of radio equipment." Stan lowered the binocs.

"Someone's locked radar onto us." Sitting in the cockpit under the canopy, Emilya frowned, then typed something on her laptop. "Michael, it's time to get out of here."

"How did they . . ?" Michael stood at the helm.

My heartbeat accelerated. No matter how I looked at it, I stood on top of that proverbial cliff.

"They must be using infrared scanners. I should have anticipated that," she said.

In the distance, several black objects zoomed across the water toward us. "Look!" I pointed.

Greyson put the field glasses up to his brow. "Sea Eagles. Manned with armed soldiers. They're heading straight for us."

"Get us out of here, Michael!" Emilya folded her laptop closed and dipped down the hatch.

"Places everyone!" Michael seemed calm as he turned the wheel and accelerated from the starboard helm. The yacht didn't exactly turn on a dime, but we all knew our jobs. Michael and Emilya had taken time to show me the *ropes*. And then they told me, there are no ropes on sailing vessels, only lines. I released the cleats holding the main sail.

The rest darted to their assigned positions on deck. Greyson released the primary winch as I unwrapped the sheet attached to the boom.

Stan picked up the LRAD and positioned himself near the bow. He aimed and fired. "Too far away," he called over his shoulder.

"Greg, take the helm and keep turning," Michael scooted out of one of the captain's chairs and Greg sat at the twin helm on the port side.

"I'm no sailor, Mike."

"You are now." Michael darted to the bow of the boat and began to unfurl the jib. The triangular sail at the front of the yacht bloomed like a black balloon with the wind. It helped pull the bow around and turn us away from the wind.

I finished with the last of the stays and yelled, "Okay! Raise the sail!"

"They're gaining on us. Hurry!" Greg stood at the stern with the binoculars.

Greyson shouted, "Raise the main!" When he was done there, he moved to Stan's side and picked up a missile launcher.

Greg pushed a button in the helm—Michael had given him a long lesson last night in anticipation of today—and the mainsail began to climb the seventy-five foot mast. The boom lifted off the deck as the rope tightened. When the massive black sail reached its full extension, Michael took over at the helm.

I sank into the cockpit, with guilt closing my throat for bringing this upon us. I loaded nine millimeter shells into my Browning. Having only used my dad's service weapon in self-defense once before, I wondered—would I use it on Rory? If I were taken prisoner, they would quickly disarm me. The myriad of possibilities from this moment forward swarmed my mind as Greg—in red shorts and a bright yellow

T-shirt—staggered into the cockpit. The boat was moving now. He picked up a rifle with a laser site on it. "It's go-time," he said.

He didn't know how right he was.

As the wind filled the sail, Michael yelled, "North, northeast. We're on heading!"

"Good, because they're gaining on us!" Stan had moved to the stern and crouched down low with the LRAD perched on his shoulder. He fired again, and a splashy explosion in the distance indicated a direct hit. "Now there are four," Stan said.

I shuddered and watched the team defend Michael's Oyster.

Beside him, Greyson fired the missile launcher. The ear-splitting blast made my ears ring. My Browning loaded and ready, I took a position near the stern. I raised my gun and aimed at the nearest Sea Eagle. Too far for a clean shot, but the unmistakable high-pitched buzz rode over the wind as the four boats sped toward us. I made out eight armed insurgents—two per boat. One skiff had a scaffolding for a launcher mounted to the center.

Greyson fired again and one man fell into the sea.

Michael shut off the engine. "We have a strong wind today, and the Oyster is dying to show you what she's made of. Hang on everyone!"

The guerillas began firing on us. Greg and Stan fired back. I crawled into position beside Greyson near the rudder. The Oyster heeled away from the wind, and I could feel her accelerating.

"Everyone to port side!" Michael shouted.

I climbed the deck to a higher point near the rail and hooked my heels on the nearest ledge. Greyson came to my side, and we looked back at our attackers. One pulled away from the rest and raced alongside the Oyster. Greyson fired and another man fell into the water. The remaining guerillas fired back. A missile exploded in the water near the hull. I ducked and fired over the edge of the boat.

The Oyster sped onward. Greg and Stan kept firing, and one of the Sea Eagles flipped. The men on it were thrown into the sea. The remaining two Eagles dropped back and launched another missile. It exploded in our wake. We were making headway and gaining the lead.

The remaining terrorist maintained a close distance to the port side. He fired his Uzi over my head, putting several holes in the mainsail.

"Someone do something about that guy!" Michael sounded furious.

The deck was at a forty-five degree angle to the water now as we raced the Sea Eagle.

Stan crawled to my other side and hung on. "I wasn't made for this kind of travel," he said.

"You're doing fine!"

They were all handling the attack far better than I was.

Stan gripped the edge of the boat and peered over the side. Another machine-gun shot was fired. Stan took aim with his Sig and fired once. I heard a splash. The last unmanned Sea Eagle fell behind.

Relief and guilt flooded my body. Awash in a sense of failure, I tried to smile as the crew raised their fists and cheered.

-32-

JONATHON

Artur Protsenko's superyacht arrived. It was anchored near Sotoris, like a coyote pacing the chicken coop, but he hadn't come onto the island yet. I promised Rory to help capture Mina. After all that had come between us, I was surprised to gain her trust, however minute the amount.

This time, when Vaolym opened my door, Sitaara brought me folded clothes and a heavy fabric shopping bag.

"Thank you, Sitaara. I appreciate your help," I said in English, hoping she understood.

She looked at the floor. Today she wore a purple and pink head scarf and a pink dress with daisies on it. She could not have been more than eleven or twelve. I wondered if she was in school. And as she briefly caught my eye—with so much fear—I saw an unspoken cry for help. My heart ached for her.

I placed a hand on her bony shoulder. I wanted to reassure her everything would be okay. I whispered, "It's going to be okay. I promise." *Would it?*

She looked up at me with pleading eyes.

Vaolym barked a command in an Arabic dialect I didn't recognize, and she spun away. His hard gaze told me I may have crossed a line. I didn't care. She was just a child.

"Ms. Protsenko waits on the patio," he said.

Though Rory insisted I stay in the locked room overnight, Vaolym left the door open when he took Sitaara away. I considered it a step toward freedom. .

I emptied the bag. Rory sent black slacks and a pressed white polo golf shirt, along with an electric shaver. I got to work trimming my ragged beard.

In an hour, I was standing near the wall of the patio—far from the stone guardrail—sipping coffee, waiting for Rory. Over the railing I could see Artur's yacht anchored about the length of a football field from shore. It was well-equipped with satellite dishes and antennae. Four military-grade launchers mounted on the stern would scare off any potential pirates. Law enforcement would certainly pause before launching an attack.

Alex came outside and looked me over. "Well, well, well. You clean up nice, Jon. You almost look like a member of society."

I gripped the coffee cup tighter. It was all I could do to keep from lunging at him. "Alex."

"What did you do to gain Rory's trust? What did you say?" The smug smile suited him and made me hate him even more.

"Nothing that you wouldn't have done," I said through clenched teeth. *You two-faced, lying son of a bitch.*

Alex stared without blinking as if trying to provoke me.

Rory sauntered out onto the patio with a legal-sized leather pouch and a cell phone in a diamond-crusted case in her hand. Her entourage of guerrillas followed like a pack of hyenas. She eyed us briefly. "What did I walk into?"

She moved between Alex and me and sat at the glass-topped table. She set the zippered pouch down and poured coffee from a silver carafe. "Be civil, gentlemen. You're going to be working together."

Alex and I remained with gazes locked. The clink of china and the cry of seagulls started to set my nerves on edge. I took slow deep breaths and counted through the inhale. The exhale. I refused to release Alex from my gaze.

"Have a seat," she said. "You're like a couple schoolboys on the playground."

Alex laughed and finally lowered his gaze. He pulled out my chair for me and said, "Nonsense. We're old friends, eh, Jon?"

I yanked the chair away from him and sat. "Let's get on with business," I said.

"Yes." She looked sideways at me. "I'm glad you kept the beard. It makes you look more distinguished."

I ran a hand across the trimmed cut. I'd kept it because I'd grown used to it. Certainly not to please her.

Rory unzipped the pouch and removed a stack of photos. The top eight-by-ten glossy was a close-up of Mina standing on a sailboat. "We caught up with her outside of Kasos. We tracked a water taxi carrying two men with luggage to a yacht. Here. It was anchored a few miles from the airport." She spread the photos out and lifted the corner of one with her long fuchsia thumbnail. She put it on top of the others.

The photo was pixelated, as if it had been greatly enlarged. But I recognized Greg's bright-colored shirt, and Stan "Mayhem's" muscular shoulders at the front of a small motorboat. Both wore dark glasses.

"You know them?"

There was no point in lying. Rory would find out one way or another. "This is Greg Hauser, and this man is Stan Moorlehem." I explained who they were and what they were probably doing here.

She pulled another photo of a fine craft with black sails. "We followed them to this yacht, owned by Michael Bettencourt."

"I thought so," Alex said.

"What do you mean?" Rory asked.

"He was with Mina on Rethymno." Something flashed in Alex's eyes. He blanched then recovered quickly.

Mina's in very good hands. I kept my smile to myself.

"Michael Bettencourt was a bodyguard for the princess of Monaco's cousin—the duchess," Alex said. "I believe he married her. Although I have no idea why she'd want someone like him."

"They're divorced," I said. "She made him a very wealthy man."

"It's irrelevant." Rory sipped her black coffee and left a red lipstick smudge on the cup. "They sailed near this island yesterday. We have reason to believe they're staging a rescue, Jonathon. Why would they do that? Specifically, why would your *slave* care enough to come all the way to Greece to rescue you?" She pinned me with her blue-green eyes.

In the past—in our past—the only way to get through to Rory was through sex. Power dynamics, control, domination, and force were the only things she understood. That's why I went down this rabbit hole without faltering. "Mina is unique. She craves punishment in ways you'd never understand, Rory."

A breath caught in her throat. I had touched a nerve.

"She is a submissive woman to her core," I said. "I gave her something no one else was able to give."

Rory softened for a moment. Her shoulders relaxed and her lips parted as if she was aroused.

I continued, "Perhaps I went too far with her. She gave herself to me, and when I left, she had no one to turn to. Without me, she probably felt out of control. The only way for her to gain back stability and normalcy in her life was to find me." It was a partial truth. Mina was far from helpless though.

At one point in my life, I would have been thrilled if a woman wanted me like that. Rory changed me. I could never treat anyone badly or claim ownership of anyone ever again. And knowing Mina softened my heart.

Something shifted in Rory. She stiffened again. "Impossible. I don't believe this is a dominance and submission issue. She is in *love* with you." She spit out the L-word like it contained poison.

"That's where you're wrong. You see, unlike our relationship, Mina and I signed a contract. We defined the dominant and submissive roles clearly on the page. And as a criminal lawyer, Mina has profound respect for the written word. She signed the document knowing full well what she was getting into."

Alex's mouth hung open in disbelief. He could have caught flies.

"Don't believe me. I don't care. But she *was* just another submissive to me. I don't care about her. She was a plaything. A toy." I had to be convincing, or Rory would know it was a lie.

She shook her head. "Whatever. We're going to bring her in. You're going to help me." She set the diamond-crusted cell phone on the table. "Do you have the number, Alex?"

Alex dug an iPhone out of his back pants' pocket. "Sure. She called me yesterday. We chatted about you, Jon. She's desperate to find you—like you said. She wanted to talk to you. She wants to know you're alive. Isn't that sweet?"

"The number?" Rory seemed to grow impatient.

"It's right here."

"Call her. Bring her here so we can get on with this." Rory tapped her long red nails on the table.

-33-

MINA

After our close call with the insurgents, I went to the head and splashed cold water on my face. *What have I done?* I put these kind people—*my friends!*—in danger. The Oyster had taken gunfire. The sail was torn and needed repairs. The teak steps on the aft face were essentially ruined and hydraulics for the bathing platform at the stern weren't working correctly. Thank the heavens no one was injured.

I'd made a bad choice. Now I owed them my life.

I patted my face dry with a hand towel and took several deep breaths. No more secrets. I vowed to tell Michael and Emilya I'd called Alex—to see if Jonathon was with him—and gave him enough time to trace our location. My mistake almost cost someone's life.

I was just about to exit my berth when a buzzing ringtone halted me. I dug underneath the bed covers and answered the burner phone tentatively. "Hello?"

"Mina. I'm glad I reached you."

Alex. I didn't respond.

"Someone here wants to talk to you."

Who? Rory? Was she upset that her thugs hadn't caught me?

"Mina." Jonathon's voice was like salve on an open burn.

"Jonathon!" I gasped. "Are you okay?"

It had been forever since we'd spoken. A lifetime. My legs went weak, and I sat down hard on the unmade bed.

"I'm fine," he said.

He sounded calm—more composed than I was at this very moment. But then, he always had that quality of serenity. It was one of many attributes I loved about him. "Why did you come here? Why did you come to Greece?"

"You know why." *Had he forgotten?* "You went missing and I . . ." Under no circumstances would I discuss this over the phone. I reined myself back. "It's good to hear your voice. I've been looking everywhere for you."

"I'm with Rory."

"I know. I mean, I could only assume that . . . After the car explosion we thought you were dead."

"I'm saying, I'm *with* Rory. We're working together now."

"What?" It had to be a lie. I hated not being able to see his face.

"You heard me. We're together now."

My heart clenched. Though it came directly from Jonathon's mouth, I couldn't believe it. *Was it true?* Months ago he professed his love for me. He signed over his finances to me so I could search for him. He'd planned for this.

"I want to see you," he said.

"Is Rory there? Is she with you now?"

Something scraped the surface of his receiver. I heard muffled talking and a pause that seemed to last forever. I checked the time on my watch. The burner originally had one hour of call time. Yesterday I used twenty-eight minutes talking to Alex. This call had already taken seven minutes. Twenty five to go. Could I hold him on the line long enough for Emilya to get a trace?

"Jonathon?"

"Yes. Rory's here. She wants to meet you. And I . . . I want to see you too."

Something was wrong. Whatever was happening, it wasn't going as smoothly as he made it seem. He said he was with Rory, but he wasn't *with* her. He was lying. I rushed out of my berth and burst into the saloon where Emilya sat at the navigation desk. I said, "Oh my God, Jonathon. You have no idea how much I've wanted to talk to you. How much I needed to hear your voice. Are you okay?"

Emilya looked up. "Mina?"

I put a finger to my lips and signaled that I needed a pen and paper. I put the call on speaker and set it on her desk.

"I'm fine. Listen. Tell Michael to turn the yacht around," Jonathan said.

He knows who I'm with.

Emilya shoved a blue Post-it Note pad in front of me. Her big brown eyes like question marks on her round face.

"Rory promises not to attack the crew. She'll provide transportation to the island. Come with her armed guard. He'll bring you to me." His sentences were disjointed, as if someone was writing out the plan as he spoke to me. This wasn't his idea. Alex or Rory forced Jonathon to go along with this crazy scheme.

I scribbled on the notepad, *Trace the call?*

Emilya nodded and got to work.

"Do you understand, Mina?" Jonathon asked. "I'll be here on the island when you arrive."

I shook my head. "No. I'm not doing this her way."

"What are you saying?"

"We'll do this my way," I said, "or I'm going back to Chicago."

"No, Mina," Jonathon said. "The safest thing to do is to come to me."

"I know what she's capable of. Believe me. I've been living with her frequent drone attacks and Alex's lies for the last few weeks. I refuse to believe she doesn't intend to kill me."

"I won't allow that to happen," he said. Something told me that he might not have any control over the matter. He would never willingly go along unless his life were threatened. Rory was behind this.

"We'll do this my way, or no way." I looked at my watch. Sixteen minutes had passed.

Emilya tried to lock on to the call. Her fingers played an etude on the keyboard. I took my time—as much time as she needed. "How is she, Jonathon? How is Rory?"

"She's as beautiful as ever."

"Fuck you."

"I thought you wanted to see me. I thought you came here because you needed me."

"Yes. But if you're with Rory now, I don't know if I can trust you."

"Of course you can trust me. No one will hurt you unless. . . I know how you feel about punishment. I can give you what you need. As per our contract, you need to do what I say, Mina. You need to follow my orders."

What was he saying? He'd ripped up the contract before he left.

"I want you to come to the villa," he said. "Rory and I both want you to come here."

"No." I wrote on the pad, *Someplace safe to meet Rory.*

Emilya wrote. *A crowded city? Athens?*

"You're my submissive. I'm telling you to come to the island. We'll meet you at the docks. I promise no one will be harmed."

I wasn't Jonathon's sub. Before he left Chicago, he'd destroyed our contract. What was his angle? *It was a signal. Before he left, Jonathon said, the submissive has all the control.*

I looked at the clock. Nine minutes left.

Emilya raised her arms up in a silent cheer. "I have a lock," she whispered. "I know where he is."

I gave her a thumbs-up and took a breath. I would do this my way or no way. I refused to put anyone on the Oyster in danger again. "Meet me in Dubrovnik, Jonathon. Alone," I said.

~34~

MINA

Jonathon was alive! The sound of his voice settled my nerves in un-imaginable ways. I longed to see him. To touch his shoulders. His strong arms. To hold his hand. The urge to go to him—to run to his arms—was so strong, I could hardly fight the impulse. Emilya poured me a whiskey, and I drank it in one gulp.

"She's behind this," I said. "I have to stop her."

"I know." Emilya squeezed my hand. "Follow your heart, Mina. I'm behind you. Let's free him from that evil bitch."

I took my refilled glass up on deck and scanned the horizon. I needed a moment. I stood on the bow of the Oyster, letting the wind hit me. The torn black sail fluttered in the wind. With Greyson's help, Michael worked on the swim platform repairing damage.

The damage was my fault. For being ignorant. For letting my feelings get the better of me and giving Alex enough time to trace my call. It was an accident—an honest one—but I felt raw. Sunburned and ex-hausted. Stripped of my strength and flayed.

The stilted conversation with Jonathon was peppered with angst, both mine and his. I had no idea how much worse it would get before seeing him in person again. Now I thought about that cliff below Rory's villa. I imagined myself flying over the edge and hitting the water.

I needed Jonathon's forgiveness.

The night before Jonathon left Chicago, we lay in my bed with our legs entangled. Ropes lay in a heap on the floor. A crop had been flung to the corner. My ass and my sex were still warm as I rested my head on his bicep.

Chicago's city lights coming through my blinds outlined Jonathon's soft and wavy black hair. His strong jaw. "I'll miss you so much," he said. His fingers twined through strands of my hair.

"I'll miss you too, but I support your decision. You're doing the right thing."

"She has to be stopped."

I thought about all the stories Jonathon had told me about Rory. About sex with her. My friends would have been appalled that he shared so much about his ex with me. Honestly, I'd dragged it out of him. It was a painful time in his life. Hearing about it helped me understand who he was.

My fingers caressed his warm, sculpted chest. "Tell me again, what will we do if she captures you?"

"I'd tell you to stay in Chicago, but I know you won't listen." His chest moved with a laugh that never reached his vocal chords. "You're strong-willed, Mina, and that's what I love best about you."

"So what's the plan? If Rory—by some stroke of luck—is holding you captive. What do I do?"

He stared up at the ceiling fan turning slow circles. "She will want to hurt me. I don't care about the physical shit. That doesn't bother me."

"It bothers me!" I raised my head to see him more clearly.

A muscle in his jaw pulsed. "She's going to go deeper than the flesh, and she'll want to strip me of everything I care about. The thing is, there's only one thing. One thing that she can take from me that will truly crush me."

"What's that?"

He pulled his arm out from under my head and pushed himself up to an elbow. His free hand touched my face with tender, loving strokes. "You." His voice cracked. "You, Mina."

"Oh, Jonathon. I-I love you so much." My lips met his with renewed passion. I twirled my fingers through his hair as my mouth opened for him as he stroked my teeth with his tongue.

His hand slid beneath the small of my back, as I pulled him on top of me. He straddled me and his engorged sex brushed my vulva. Our mouths remained connected as I eased him inside me.

He thrust his hips into mine, and I arched my body to meet him, thrilled and so willing. As our bodies became slick with sweat, I inhaled his intoxicating aroma, aroused by our mingled scents, and then tugged his hips toward me. His strong arms supported his weight as his passionate thrusts sundered me, and his soothing voice enchanted and captivated me. I pulsed my hips to match his intensity. We breathed as one.

He filled me deeply, and my body shuddered with the exquisite spasms of orgasm. He slowed, lowered to his elbows, and whispered in my ear, "I love you, Mina."

My explosive contractions triggered release for him. He began to speed up, thrusting faster and more vigorously until he burst inside me. "Oh!" he cried. "Mina!"

When it was over, I held him and stroked his back.

A little while later, we stood entwined in the shower. Jets of warm water poured over our heads and down our legs. "Promise me something," he said.

"Anything."

"I'll do everything in my power to keep you safe. But stay away from Greece. That's her territory. You'll be walking right into a trap."

"I don't know if I can. If she—"

He put a finger to my lips. "If she kidnaps me, then I've staged the ultimate coupe. I've infiltrated her organization from the top, and I have it under control."

His damp, black curls framed stormy blue eyes. Water cascaded down from his jaw.

"How will I know?"

"The resources will be there for you. My people will be there. Trust me. You can't fight her."

"Then what do you want me to do?

"Stay in Chicago."

"Come on." I held him at arm's length.

"You're smart, Mina. Do what you do best."

"That's extremely vague."

"The submissive has all the power."

"What does that have to do with—"

He spun me under the showerhead. "If anything happens, I want you to know I'm still yours."

Before Jonathan left Chicago, he'd said, "I love you."

But not today. Time had not changed his feelings for me. He was under duress.

I needed to tell the crew the new plan. I swallowed the rest of the whiskey and looked at the clouds. High up in the sky, something that could have been a black bird hovered above the yacht. I thought I heard the buzzing of a drone engine.

-35-

JONATHON

*D*ubrovnik. Where it all started. They say there's no such thing as love at first sight. I disagree. I fondly recalled the image of Mina sitting at the linen-covered table overlooking the Pile Sea. She looked so beautiful in the evening light. On Janko's suggestion, we sent her a bottle of champagne. When I introduced myself, I wanted to stay. To learn more about her. Because in a freakish way Janko seemed fixated with her, I kept a distant eye on her. When the opportunity finally came, I hired Mina only because I had to get to know her better.

"Dubrovnik? Not a chance! Father won't allow it." Rory pushed back her chair. "She's not calling the shots, I am." She flipped open a silver cigarette box and dug out a cigarette. Alex lit it for her.

"Get my pilot on the phone, now," she said with her exhale.

Obsequious Alex dialed a number. "Kolak? Alex here." He walked to the patio railing as he explained the situation. Rory followed him, her wide-legged pants sweeping the black marble floor.

I locked my gaze on them and stood slowly. On the phone, I let Mina believe she would meet me in Dubrovnik, though I knew Rory had no intention of letting that happen. The trick now was to keep Rory on the hook.

Alex handed Rory the phone and she paced with it while conversing with her pilot. I walked to the archway leading onto the patio but stayed back, avoiding the rail. I didn't need the sleeping bear—my fear of heights—to awaken now. Snippets of the conversation reached my ears. "Nearest airport . . . How long? . . . Bring her here." When she hung up, Rory gave the phone back to Alex.

He placed a hand on her back. "She'll be here before you know it."

She shrugged him off. "Lay off, Alex. You and Vaolym should have caught her in Rethymno."

"We're all doing the best we can," he said.

"Ha!" She walked to the stone railing and looked over the side. "Send a drone to follow that yacht. We need to know where she's going next. Where she's flying from to Dubrovnik."

"I'm on it." Alex backed away and dialed another number. *What a tool.* He would crawl on his knees for Rory—he probably already had—and it was the reason she didn't respect him.

Rory turned to me again. "You said Mina was the submissive. I'm beginning to doubt it. You haven't changed, have you, Jon? You're the complacent one. Your obliging, puppyish devotion is written all over your face. You let her walk all over you, just like I used to do. When will you learn?"

"I set this meeting up for you. Mina manipulated the conversation. That's all." *Because I let her.* "I let Mina think she had power, but you and I know she doesn't have any footing. She needs motivation to come into the spider's web. I can spout the clichés, but you already know you can't win people over with threats."

"I think you are the sub, Jon."

She was wrong. I wasn't weak. I drew strength from Mina. I was stronger with her than I'd ever been alone.

I had to make Rory believe in me, or Mina and I would both die. "Teach me how to be stronger. Teach me how to be a better man."

"I'll consider it if you can prove to me you don't love her."

I sucked in a breath. That was the test? I kept my gaze locked on her dark blue eyes. It would take all my strength to keep from melting at Mina's feet when she arrived.

Rory turned away first, and I took a deep breath. She walked to the railing and looked out over the sea at the *Ivan* anchored in the distance. "Where's my phone?" she asked, spinning in my direction.

After the call, I slid the jewel-encrusted iPhone into my pants pocket. She snatched it from me and walked away, dialing a number. As she moved past the staff cleaning up after breakfast, she said, "Papa? How was your trip?"

$-36-$

MINA

Clouds raced across the sky as if running from something. My heart raced right along with them. The six of us sat around the cockpit, a tighter group than yesterday as the October winds blew a chilly breeze from the north.

"It's a crazy idea, Mina." Greg stared at me with a gaping mouth.

Stan and Grey debunked Michael's ambitious plan to climb aboard the *Ivan*. It was far too dangerous. I came up with an alternative.

"It's a brilliant idea." With her chin tucked to her chest, Emilya looked up from her laptop. She had a yellow cotton or rayon scarf with flowers on it wrapped loosely around her neck. "I like it. It's what I would do for you, my love." She slid her hand over Michael's leg.

He nodded. "I think I see a way to make it work." He started drawing a diagram on a spiral notebook in his lap. Several pages later, he had a solid plan. At most, it would take a week to get Jonathon out of there. If everything went by the books, I would meet Jonathon in Dubrovnik and we would fly back to Thera, Greece to meet Michael and the rest. With Jonathon on board, we planned to enlist Greyson's connections at Interpol. Together we could form an army.

If plans didn't work out . . .

I shivered and warmed my fingers between my thighs. I was charged and ready for this. "I don't want to lose any of you," I said.

"We're not the ones in danger," Stan leaned forward, his elbows on knees. His black windbreaker rustled with the wind. "Recite the plan again. I want to make sure you know exactly what to do once we put this in motion."

"We're all aware how dangerous this is." Michael's amber eyes sparkled, as if this was the most exciting thing that had happened to him in years.

We ran through the details again. The success of this reconnaissance depended on meeting Jonathon in Dubrovnik.

Emilya radioed ahead to reserve a docking space at the Vlychada Marina on the southern tip of Thera, Greece, the closest island with an airport. I needed to call Leo Thibodeaux, Jonathon's pilot, who'd flown me to Athens, but I no longer had his number. That cell phone was long gone. Emilya located Leo's number with her unlimited resources, and I called him from a new burner.

"Meet me at the Santorini Airport on Thera in two days," I said.

"I am at your beck and call. And where are we flying to?"

"Dubrovnik."

"An excellent choice."

I had no idea how much money he made working for Jonathan but wasn't about to tell him I was meeting terrorists.

During the trip to Thera, Emilya and Stan prepared me for meeting with Rory. We sat near her navigation desk below deck.

Stan sterilized a tiny GPS tracking device in a dish of rubbing alcohol. "In the UK you need special authority to buy a GPS locator and get the training," he said. "It requires police or a military background. Emilya, what channels did you go through to get this equipment?"

"Michael's full of surprises," she said with a wink.

"I don't want to know then." A smile brightened Stan's dark eyes.

"Don't worry. I won't tell if you don't." Emilya smiled and put on a pair of black latex gloves. The tracking device was about a centimeter long and looked somewhat like the small fuses that come with a string of Christmas lights.

"How does this work?" I asked.

"Usually the GPS trackers are injected into one's neck." Emilya loaded the tracker into the gun. "Since you'll need to wear a bandage for a few days, I don't want to put it on you where it will show."

"We expect them to pat you down. They may even scan you for metal implants. The tracker is made of titanium and is about the size of a medical device. It shouldn't show up on a metal detector." Stan said. "Where do you want it, Mina?"

"My tattoo starts here on my hip." I pointed to my right hip bone. "If we bury it under the ink, the scar will be hidden to the naked eye." I lifted my shirt bottom and pulled my shorts down a few inches. "How about in the muscle there?"

"If someone sees your naked hip, you're in big trouble." Stan laughed, but I didn't.

"They won't," I said. And meant it. I didn't want to imagine scenarios with Rory where that might occur.

"Perfect." Stan readied the alcohol swabs.

I unzipped my cargo shorts and pulled them down just enough to expose the flesh behind my hip bone. I swabbed the area with alcohol and turned to face her. "Ready."

Emilya didn't pull punches. She aimed and fired without giving me a second glance. It stung no worse than I expected. And no less. "Ow."

"There you go," she said. "Now we can send you off safely into the arms of the terrorists."

"When you put it that way . . ."

"You'll be fine," Stan said.

Stan handed me a dry gauze bandage. "Hold it on there until the bleeding stops."

Emilya set the gun down. "This GPS tracker will give us real-time tracking. We'll know your location by following you on this live satellite map." She pulled up the app on her computer and zeroed in on the blinking cursor out in the middle of the Aegean Sea. "We'll have twenty-four-hour monitoring and—" The image flickered and locked. "As long as I have internet..." She adjusted the feed on her internet modem. The image recovered and the timestamp updated. "We'll be able to track you."

"In the best-case scenario, you'll meet Jonathon in Dubrovnik and fly back to Thera." Stan sat on the edge of the sofa in the saloon. He put his hands on his meaty thighs and leaned toward me. "I anticipate that Jonathon will take you to Rory."

"I know," I said. "It's why I wanted the tracking device."

"And that's where we come in."

Emilya pulled up a map on her navigational screen. "If things go awry in Dubrovnik, Michael will head back to the Karpathio Pelagos islands. We expect Jonathon—or someone—will take you back to Sotoris. No matter what, we'll be nearby."

"Good to know." I peeked under the gauze at the hole in my skin and pressed down to stop the bleeding. "But what if they take me to her father, Artur Protsenko, instead?"

"Let's hope that doesn't happen," Stan said.

"Just in case—if Rory does something unexpected— the tracker has a two-way panic button."

"Great. How does it work?" I asked.

Emilya dragged a small box to the front of her desk and opened it. Inside, a silver ring rested on tissue. "Since I don't believe they'll allow you to have a cell phone, we set up the two-way panic button on this ring." She handed it to me. The ring had a quarter inch round sparkling jewel in the center. When you depress the button, we'll notify Interpol. We'll tell them how to find you."

"It's beautiful." I tried it on.

"It's Austrian crystal. Nothing too fancy," Emilya said.

"Push the button." Stan leaned forward.

I slipped the ring on my right ring finger and pushed the jewel. The tracking device vibrated, and a signal sounded from Emilya's laptop. The location arrow lit up and a message appeared at the bottom of the screen.

"You see? We'll get the alert that you're in danger." She typed a command and the message and signal vanished. "Now if we detect something, we can also notify you." She typed a command and the tracker vibrated again.

"Got it."

Stan nodded. "I have faith in this plan. We'll get you and Jonathon out of there."

I wanted to trust them, but I was scared and used to working alone.

Emilya leaned forward and helped me bandage the entry wound from the tracker. When she finished, she cupped my chin in her hand and looked me in the eye. "We'll find you. I promise."

-37-

MINA

Michael and Emilya docked the Oyster and stowed the ropes. Though Michael had been able to fix the hydraulic lift on the aft swim platform, the teak steps and the sail still needed repairs.

Emilya put her arm around Michael. They stood near the gate on the port side. "I called ahead and ordered some parts we need to repair the Oyster," he said. "The rest will have to wait until we go back to Athens."

"I owe you so much. Please let me help with the costs." I pulled a thick stack of euros out of my bag.

Michael backed away. "I told you I was all in for this rescue mission. I don't need your money."

I pressed it into his hand. "Use it to fuel up and restock provisions."

"I can't accept this."

Emilya intercepted the transaction and took the money. Then she gave me a generous hug. "I am grateful. Thank you."

"When this is over, I'll compensate you all. Jonathon would want it."

"Like Michael said, we're not in it for the money," Greyson stated. He and Stan sat on the sofa in the cockpit. Greg had disappeared down below.

"You look beautiful today. Jonathon will see what he's been missing." Emilya touched my hip. Today I wore the green sundress Jonathon said matched my eyes. I wanted to remind him of what we were like together. What he meant to me.

"Thanks, Em. I hope so."

"We should be able to head back to the island by morning." Michael pulled Emilya close.

I lowered my sunglasses, even though the sun had gone behind the clouds. "I hope to be there by the day after tomorrow."

"We'll keep an eye on you via the GPS, Mina," Emilya said.

Greyson stood. "Godspeed, Mina."

"Stay safe. We'll catch up with you on the other side." Stan waved from the sofa.

"Why does this sound like goodbye?" Using his cane, Greg limped to my side. "Not like you'll never see them again." He stood beside me and slung my backpack over his shoulder.

"Where are you going?" I asked.

"I'm your bodyguard, remember? I'm escorting you to the airport." Greg wouldn't accept no for an answer.

The dusty roads on Thera wound a passage through the hills past scrubby grass browned with the coming of winter. The taxi stopped and started for light traffic, pedestrians, trailers pulling boats, and a herd of goats crossing the road.

"Are you nervous?" Greg asked.

"Not any more than usual." I tried to imagine traveling to jump from a cliff—Rory's cliff—but for some reason I couldn't get into my usual bold and fearless headspace.

"You're usually nervous?" Greg and I sat shoulder-to-shoulder in the cramped back seat of the tiny European car.

"Just high-strung. I'm worried about Jonathon."

"Don't be. I'm sure he has a strategy."

"You didn't talk to him, Greg. I think the strategy is history. I'm afraid she's gotten to him."

"But he never loved her."

"I'm not so sure anymore." *I'm with her. I'm with Rory now.*

Gray clouds covered the sky. We passed small square houses and a stone fence. Rusty cars sat in the tall grass. The road narrowed to about the width of a bicycle path. The central part of the island was barren and rocky.

We rode in silence, taking in the surroundings. Greg seemed to be gearing up to say something. I needed the quiet. To prepare. What would I say to Jonathon when I saw him? I imagined spotting him at the end of the tarmac and running toward him. Maybe he would stride toward me like Mr. Darcy at that iconic moment at the end of *Pride and Prejudice* when he and Elizabeth finally decided to be together. When Darcy meets Elizabeth under the ancient elm at dawn. I wanted to take Jonathon's hand and ask him to marry me. With his resources we could escape Rory. We could disappear into the crowd and slip into a taxi. We could go into hiding.

If, however, Jonathon was *with* Rory, what would I say then? I looked down at the green dress and wished I hadn't worn it. Conflicting emotions surfaced. It angered me to have come all this way. To rescue him! And have him decide to dump me and go along with her evil plan? I wanted to smack the smug look right off his face. I took a ragged breath and tried to calm down.

On the other side of the plateau, the astounding view overlooked the city of Santorini on the populated side of the island. We eventually drove through the cute town with white Mediterranean-style buildings. Roadside vendors and beautiful homes lined the streets.

"Don't doubt it, Mina." Greg gripped the handhold above his head with a white-knuckled clenched fist. "Jonathon loves you. If he didn't love you—"

He was about to say something neither of us could unhear.

"Don't . . ." Blood rushed from my face, and I looked out the window. I suspected how Greg felt. I just couldn't reciprocate the sentiment.

We remained awkwardly silent until arriving at the airport.

"Be safe, Mina. You've got the most dangerous role in this."

"I will, Greg. I'm going to get him back." The surprising strength in my voice bolstered me. I hoped that my determination showed.

I took my backpack from him and walked toward the terminal with a new burner phone in my hand. That morning, I'd called Leo Thibodeaux. He said he'd meet me with the jet on the other side of the security checkpoint.

The sundress swished around my knees as I walked through a crowd of sunburned tourist in tank tops and straw hats. Small children clutched the legs of family members. Elderly travelers sat in a limited number of rigid plastic chairs. I soon realized there was only one departure gate in the small airport. Most of the terminal was exposed to the elements with palm trees and open walls.

Once through security, I stepped outside into the cloud-filtered daylight and put my sunglasses on. Across the runway, the wind whipped the green Aegean Sea into a white-capped turbulent froth. A mountain peak on another island poked through a cloud in the distance.

Out on the runway, Leo stood beside a sleek Dornier Seastar amphibious airplane. I recognized the airplane from the social media posts Emilya found. It was the same style and type that Rory's pilot, Vedran Kolak, flew to Rethymno beach. I wondered briefly why we weren't taking the Gulfstream G650 and didn't think any more of it as I walked toward Leo.

He wore a white shirt and dark slacks and the gold and black stripes on his shoulder glistened. But the closer I got to him, the clearer his features became. He wasn't smiling. He seemed stiff, and I wished I could see his eyes behind the dark lenses of his shades.

When I reached out my hand to greet him, a crisp pinging sound pierced the air. Something hit me in the face and arms, and I flinched. Leo clutched his chest and a red bloom appeared on his white shirt. In slow motion, his mouth opened in utter shock as he sank to his knees.

I reached for him and gasped. "Leo!" I gripped his shoulders and kneeled, holding him upright. I pressed my hand against his as the red bloom grew too quickly, soaking his fingers and mine.

Adrenaline coursed through my veins. He was losing strength. His blood covered my hands and face. I glanced left and right—where had the shot come from? Movement in the cockpit of the Diamond Star caught my attention. I looked up.

Another man—with too-perfect facial hair—had the barrel of his gun pointed directly at me.

"Who—"

"Get in." It wasn't a request.

Easing Leo down onto the concrete, I stood and wiped the blood off my chin with the palm of my hand. I hesitated—wanted to run.

The man leapt out of the plane and took me by the arm. "Get. In."

~38~

JONATHON

"**H**e's got her. She's on her way." Rory hung up her jeweled cell phone and slid it into the deep pocket of her floor-length black skirt.

Knowing she'd killed Leo added to the rage growing inside me. "Good," I said it as if I meant it. I stood back from the balcony to keep the bear from waking. As long as I kept my gaze on the horizon where the sea connected with the sky, my phobia remained under control. It didn't help knowing what lay at the bottom of the cliff. Boulders, stones, and the sea lapping against them. Mina would like it. And she was out there somewhere. None of this was her choice.

I had no idea how that man had treated her. Was she hurt? Scared? I didn't doubt Mina could hold her own. She was more likely to be elevated—her senses heightened—by a little fear. She'd told me about diving, the last seconds in the air, the free fall. As much as I feared her retelling, she lived for those moments—the excitement, the thrill, the fervor, and triumph of tombstoning.

I would have met Mina in Dubrovnik. I would have held her and given reassurances that all would be okay. I would have kissed her deeply and told her how much I missed her. And I would do my best to protect her.

"Jon." Rory snaked her arms around my waist and rested her head on the back of my shoulder.

I placed my hand on top of hers. "I was just thinking how grateful I am to end that part of my life."

"Which part?" Her voice was dreamy, as if she were a young girl in love. I knew how quickly her emotions could change, and I was cautious.

"The part without you." I turned in her arms and gazed into her dark blue eyes. I let her believe I was hers again.

She put a hand on my chest. "I missed you. I missed us. Together."

A commotion in the hallway caught her attention. We both turned to face the walkway as several men strode into the room.

"Króshka. Darling. How are you?" A small, round man in black dress pants and a white dress shirt walked into the living room. Two men in dark gray suits followed closely. They looked like CIA. No, KGB.

"Papa." Rory glided toward him with her arms wide. They greeted in Russian and embraced for a long moment. I would have considered it a tender reunion if I hadn't known who he was.

He held her at arm's length. "You are beautiful as always, króshka."

"Oh, Papa. Come sit down. Have a drink with me." She snapped her fingers in the air and the staff scurried to set up a table and chairs. A woman in a white uniform wheeled a tray to the patio and set the table with linen and flowers. The KGB twins with curly wires dangling from their ears whispered into lapel coms and took positions around the room. Within moments, we took our chairs. I sat across from Artur Protsenko, the most powerful international crime boss in the world.

A waiter poured wine.

Artur asked for scotch and three of the waitstaff hustled to answer his request. He unbuttoned his cuffs and rolled up the sleeves on his shirt. "Introduce me to your friend."

"I can't believe you've never met before. This is Jonathon Heun, one of the wealthiest men in Chicago. He and I dated years ago, Papa. He's come back to me." Under the table, Rory put a hand high up on my thigh. She squeezed, and I blew her a kiss. All for show. I wanted Artur to think I cared about his króshka. His darling daughter.

"Jonathon, this is my father," she said. I struggled to see similarities in their features. Rory was slender. Angular in all the places that Artur was rounded.

I reached across the table for a handshake.

He made a sour face. "I never shake hands. I never know what viruses you've been exposed to. And at my age—"

I withdrew my hand. "I understand."

He turned to Rory. "I can't get you to come onto the boat, so I decided to visit."

"I know, Papa. I've been so busy."

A staff member came around the table with a tray. She set a crystal carafe, a bottle of fine scotch, and three glasses on the table then offered to pour for Artur. He pushed his glass toward her. "Doing what, Rory? You have the perfect life, do you not?"

"It's perfect, Papa," Rory said dismissively.

The girl, Sitaara, entered the room with a platter filled with appetizers. She shuffled to the table and offered Artur the plate.

"What's this?" He took the plate from her and handed it to the staff member. "Sitaara. How is my daughter treating you?"

Sitaara's nostrils flared. She stiffened, seeming to hold back.

I watched their interaction closely, wondering how Sitaara got here. Surely my friend Alawi el Attar didn't arrange for his daughter to stay here. Sitaara was leverage. She was Artur's assurance for some business deal.

"I'm not sure she speaks English," I said, knowing full well that she did. My friend Alawi was educated at Cambridge and spoke nine languages fluently. He would make certain that his daughter knew English as well as Chinese, Japanese, and the Romance languages.

"How would you know?" Artur asked.

"She looked after Jonathon when I first brought him here. He'd been injured." Rory conveniently left out the part I had been her prisoner and she had me tortured.

Artur reached for the girl, but she backed away. He said something in Arabic to her, and her eyes went wide. She spat at him and ran out of the room.

Shock and distress reached his eyes. He turned on Rory. "Aren't you caring for my pet, Rory?"

His pet? I vowed to myself to free her when I got out of here.

"Like any of my staff," Rory said, "I am caring for her. She has a place to sleep. Isn't that enough?"

Artur gripped the edge of the table and stared Rory down. "She is not a servant. She's the daughter of a powerful man. An oil mogul. She deserves to be treated like a princess. With kindness."

"Papa, you brought that girl here and left her with me. I'm not her mother. I have no desire to care for that child."

Artur stood so quickly his chair fell over. He leaned forward and gripped Rory by the throat and her eyes went wide. He said, "You will treat Sitaara as your own family. Or I will disown you." His fat fingers locked around her thin neck. "Understand, króshka?"

Rory clawed at his fingers. Her eyes teared up with fear.

So this was her loving father. I felt sick but remained quiet. Observant. While her lips paled and turned blue, he waited for her to respond.

Finally she nodded. He released her, and she sank into her seat, choking. "As you wish, Papa."

Artur downed his scotch and refilled the glass. The silence following the father-daughter confrontation made me uncomfortable. Clearly, he controlled Rory in ways I couldn't imagine. Rory poured scotch into her glass, then mine. She drank hers in one gulp.

Needing courage, I sipped the scotch.

"I'm getting something—someone—for you, Papa. For your pleasure." Rory seemed to be trying to smooth the rough edges. "She arrives in about an hour. She is my gift to you."

A chill went down my spine. I covered it with a cough and then forced a smile. "Mina?"

"Of course," Rory cooed. "I know we talked about selling her on the black market. But I want to give her to Papa. It's my way of thanking him."

Artur looked over his whiskey glass with great interest. "Tell me about her."

Rory tipped her chin and gave him a coy smile. "She's a powerful Chicago businesswoman. A successful criminal lawyer. She would be a wonderful ally, and if she's as smart as Jon says, she'll do anything you ask her to do. *Anything.* Because she's also a slave."

"Intriguing." Artur sipped black coffee. "A criminal lawyer and a sex slave?"

I tightened my fists under the table. I didn't like where this was going.

"It's my understanding that she likes it rough," Rory said. "Maybe you know someone who needs a submissive—"

"Chicago? I'd like to have a legal expert from Chicago on my staff. When will she arrive?"

"Any moment. I sent a plane for her an hour ago." Rory touched my arm. "Don't be upset with me. I wanted to make it easier on you."

Artur squinted, and his gaze shifted from me to Rory and back to me. "You know this Chicago lawyer?"

All eyes were on me. Rory waited for me to show what I was made of. To prove I was on her side. "I know her well. She was my lawyer for a brief time. She's brilliant in the courtroom. Never lost a case."

"Tell me her name again?"

"Wilhelmina Green. She's with Milton, Wallace, and Edwards."

His face widened into a sly smile. "Ah. I know this woman. She defended the traitor, Bohdanovyan Mykajlenko." He dabbed his mouth with a white linen napkin then crumpled it up and put it on the table.

I added, "He changed his name to Bohdi Michaels. From what I heard, he received a very light sentence for money laundering. She won the case over well-known U.S. prosecutor—"

"Harvey Slater. I also know him well." Artur nodded.

"Did Mykajlenko make investments for you?"

Artur leaned forward and put a weighted hand on my shoulder. "Jon. May I call you Jon? You should know that I have never needed to launder my money."

I understood I'd overstepped a boundary. I looked him in the eye. "Of course not."

He held on to my shoulder as if he thought he could control me too.

"Neither have I." I grinned back at him.

Artur released me and threw back his head. His loud laughter echoed off the plaster walls and ceiling. "I can't wait to meet her. To see what she can do for me."

Almost on cue, the sound of a single engine plane buzzed overhead.

Rory had done this to her. I'd do everything in my power to stop it.

-39-

MINA

I watched out the window of the mid-sized seaplane as we approached an island—the one we'd suspected was Sotoris. The steep cliff on the west face was instantly recognizable and unmistakable. Above it, the iconic Grecian-style buildings of Rory's villa looked like an elegant place to stay . . . if Jonathon wasn't being held prisoner there. If I wasn't handcuffed to the passenger seat behind the pilot of this seaplane.

But was Jonathon a prisoner? I was about to find out.

As we buzzed by the island, I got a close-up view of the square, limestone formations of the rock face. Where the sea was shallow, I could see the green, rocky bottom. Dark water below the cliff indicated deep water. The tall cliff face seemed like a long distance for a solo climb without any ropes. Greg's idea of sport was my idea of torture, and I tried to examine it in a constructive way. It looked feasible, yet terrifying. The chimney near the top, a fissure wide enough for a body, was bigger than it looked from the Oyster.

Where was that obsessive drive to dive? Where was my passion for tombstoning?

The pilot landed with a splash in the sea alongside the cliff. As we motored past the cliff, I closed my eyes and tried to envision my toes curled over the edge. If I had to, I'd jump. If I was forced into a situation . . . I imagined the dry grass and stones beneath my feet. I saw myself prepared to squat and drop my arms.

"Follow my orders when we pull alongside the *Ivan*. Understand?"

The moment was lost. I glared at him. Why couldn't I muster the compulsion, the urge to dive? It had been an addiction. It had been my lifeline when times were darkest.

"Did you hear me? Understand?" The pilot glanced at me over his shoulder.

"I heard you."

"We'll take a dingy to the island. No funny business, okay?"

It was almost an invitation.

The pilot tied the airplane to the dock. Nearby, guerillas aboard the massive yacht, the *Crazy Ivan*, looked over the gunwales at us. They held Uzis and wore army fatigues. Mounted on the top of the bridge, the array of satellite dishes and antennae put Emilya's setup to shame.

The pilot talked while we disembarked the plane and climbed onto the dock. "My name's Kolak. They call you Mina?"

I didn't answer.

"It's a pretty name," he said. "A Russian name. Are you Russian? I was born in Kyiv long before Ukraine declared independence. When I was young, my family moved to suburbs of Moscow, to one bedroom apartment. I shared room with four sisters and brothers."

"Why do I care?" The blood on my green dress—Leo's blood—had dried. I rattled the handcuffs.

"Artur Protsenko saved me. He pulled me out of the slums and gave me a purpose."

A pair of burly men waited where the dock met the island. Cut into the rock behind them a long stairway led up to the villa on the northeast side of the island. My gaze was drawn up there.

The pilot continued with his story, but I wasn't listening. Only looking for my lover.

Kolak tied a rope to the handcuffs and pulled me forward like a dog on a leash. We walked up the steep staircase, probably five or six flights, and then through the white stucco halls and arched doorways of the villa. Near each entryway, another armed guard silently eyed us. At the end of a long hallway, the late afternoon sun shone brightly through two sets of arches. Blinding me. Kolak had taken my shades and thrown them aside in the seaplane. I lifted my cuffed wrists to shield my eyes as we entered a room facing the sun.

A woman called his name. "Kolak." She approached from a patio, but with the sun behind her, she was a tall, dark blur. Two other figures followed her. One stocky and the other, notably taller. I couldn't see anyone's face with the low sun directly behind them.

"Lady Protsenko." Kolak stepped forward as if he expected her to hug him.

"Don't call me that. That's my mother's name, for God's sake."

"Apologies. I have done what you asked. I brought Mina Green to you." The pilot shoved me forward and I stumbled on the sharp edge of a tile. I landed hard on my elbows and knees on cool black marble. There would be bruises later.

"Don't treat our guest like she's a dog." The short man walked toward me. "This woman is an accomplished lawyer and businesswoman. Give me the key to the handcuffs."

I tried to push myself to my feet as Kolak apologized and gave the stocky man a set of keys. The man took the keys, then strode toward the nearest armed guard. Swiftly, he took the Uzi from him and pointed it toward me.

The blast dropped me to the floor again.

Have I been hit? I covered my head in fear.

Kolak landed on the floor beside me. The side of his face was gone.

My heart was in my throat and my ears rang. I shook as the man helped me to my feet and examined my skinned knee. He gently unlocked the handcuffs and handed me a handkerchief. "For your knee."

I thanked him with a strangled voice and looked down at my body. Two men had been shot and killed in front of me today. Leo's and now Kolak's blood covered my dress. Was I intact? A quick assessment, and I seemed okay except for the shaking. My hands. My ragged breath.

"I am Artur Protsenko. You must be Wilhelmina Green." Still in shock, I looked at his outstretched hand.

The woman and man in the sunlight approached us and once under the shadow of the arches, I could finally see their faces. The woman was dark-haired and striking. She reminded me of Gisele, the famous Brazilian model. Beside her, with his arm at her waist, stood Jonathon. He'd grown a beard and was thinner than I remembered. I hardly recognized him.

"Hello, Mina."

~40~

MINA

Unbelievable! Jonathon's smug look of superiority angered me. Heat and pressure built in my chest until I was ready to explode, but my voice came out in a low rasp. "What's going on?"

Artur dropped the handcuffs that had been on my wrists on the floor beside Kolak. A dark puddle of blood surrounded Kolak's head and his missing face. Artur swept his hands toward the staff—some kind of signal. Two guerillas moved in behind me and carried dead Kolak off, trailing blood across the black marble floor.

Artur stepped carefully around the puddle and pulled me away. "Come in, my dear. My daughter was just telling me about you."

My gaze remained on the trail of blood behind the pilot as Artur led me, wobbly, to a table. My knees gave out from under me. I sat.

Rory whispered into Jonathon's ear. He leaned in and smiled like she'd said the most precious words.

"What's going on?" I repeated a bit louder.

Someone poured scotch and Artur pushed the glass in front of me. He sat in one of the cushioned chairs and dragged it closer to me. I noticed the linen tablecloth. The empty bottle of Perrier—Jonathon's signature drink—and the laptop on the table.

"Welcome to the family, Mina. May I call you Mina? It's such a pretty name."

I would rather he didn't but knew I didn't have much choice. I nodded and picked up the scotch.

Artur said, "You are well known for representing some very vicious criminals, Mina. I see that you are also a talented lawyer and have gotten acquittals for most of those men. They all could not have been completely innocent, no?"

My brow lowered. I was cautious. "Lawyer-client privacy. It's a thing."

Artur laughed. "I knew I would like you. You're like me. You take your job seriously."

"What's your point?" I glanced toward Jonathon, and he met my eyes. I would have held eye contact, but he looked away. He looked at Rory who gazed up at him like a woman in love. They were *holding hands!*

"My point?" Artur asked. "I want to make you a member of my family. I'm going to make you an offer you can't refuse because I want you to work for me." Artur patted my leg, then rubbed it gently.

Through the fabric of my blood-spattered sundress, goosebumps rose on my leg. "What offer?"

"I want you to be my lawyer. I occasionally have some . . . how shall I say—" He looked at the ceiling, thoughtful. "Uncomfortable dealings with law enforcement. I want you to represent me. You can give me legal advice. Help the law to see that I am not a criminal."

A chill shot up my back and arms. "But I'm licensed in the U.S. I'm not entirely familiar with international law."

"That's okay. I have business dealings there too." I knew exactly the kind of man Artur Protsenko was. He reminded me of men who were killers. Of sociopaths and cold-blooded murderers. Of clients I'd represented for Milton, Wallace, & Edwards.

His reputation was well known. Artur was just like those people I'd helped to acquit. He was asking me to do the kind of work I wanted to get away from. My gut clenched and the smell of whiskey mixed with the metallic scent of blood turned my stomach. Artur Protsenko was not *asking* me to work for him. Still, I had to retain my sense of self. "I'm not sure—"

"Let me tell you a story." His kind smile belied the nature of this conversation.

I sipped the scotch with a shaking hand and glanced at Jonathon.

"A man I know," Artur said. "Clark Daugherty is his name, is gifted with banking and investment skills. Much like your friend Bohdanovyan Mykajlenko. You like Bohdi, no?"

I nodded.

"I like Clark Daugherty. I like the way he does business so much that I welcomed Clark into my family. Much like I invite you today. Clark said he already had family. Too much family. Too much commitment for him to add my family. But I told him I needed him. I asked him very nicely to help me out with an investment problem."

"You asked him to launder money." I wanted to get to the point and speak to Jonathon.

"Laundering is illegal. I would never ask anyone to do something illegal."

"Then what do you call it?"

"I call it creative financing." Artur's chair squeaked as he sat back. "My friend Clark disagreed. So I brought him and his wife and three children to Greece and showed him the life he could have if he worked for me. Clark understood. He returned to the States and made a few business deals. He made good investments and saved me money. But after a few years, he wanted to stop. His children were in school, and he was worried that my family wasn't good enough."

I had a feeling I knew where Artur was going with the story, and I glanced at Jonathon for confirmation. He stared at the floor, or his shoes. I couldn't read him.

"Clark and I had a disagreement. You see, my family is more precious to me than anything."

"What did you do?"

"Me? Nothing. I sat on my yacht and watched the sunset while Clark learned what it meant to be a part of my family."

I knew the extent of Artur's reach and what he was capable of. "What happened?" I whispered.

"Someone killed Clark's children and his wife. I don't know who. I don't know the details. But now Clark works for me. Now, he understands what it means to be a part of my family."

Relief flooded my neck and chest. I thanked God that I didn't have children. So what was the rub? What would Artur use against me?

"I want you to be a part of my family, Mina." He turned the laptop toward me and tapped the screen. There in full color was a video of my brother, James, and his wife, Sienna, sitting on a bleacher in an Illinois stadium. Next to them, his two boys, Mattie and little Mikey, wore Bears football jerseys and sipped juice from straws. James silently cheered and threw his fist in the air.

"How—"

"It doesn't matter how. But you will notice the video is in current time." He pointed to the corner of the screen.

I took a breath.

He clicked a new tab where my youngest brother, Eddie, sat in a cozy coffee shop in front of his laptop. Eddie lived in Cincinnati. James lived in Normal, Illinois, where we'd all grown up. The message was clear as purified water.

"I have a big family, Mina. And I want you and your family to be a part of it," he said.

"It's in your best interest to work for my father, Mina." Rory came to my side and held out her hand. Her fingers were long and thin like a pianist's, and she wore a ring with a huge red jewel on her index finger. "We haven't met but I know everything about you. My name's Rory."

I didn't know whether to shake her hand or spit in her face. I did neither. Coffee shop noises from the laptop drew my eye back to the computer screen. Eddy hunched over a table and typed on his computer.

Rory withdrew her hand and pulled up a chair. "At one time, I didn't want to meet you either. It seems we share something in common. We both love Jon."

He went to her side and placed his hands on her arms. "Rory's right, Mina. We all want you to become part of the family. It's in your best interest."

I stood so fast my chair tipped over. I slapped Jonathon hard, knocking him back a few steps. "Don't you ever. Ever. Speak to me again." He backed away. His cool blue eyes had fire in them now. And something else. Sadness? I couldn't tell.

Rory laughed and Artur joined in. "She's feisty, Jon," Artur said. "I like her."

I rubbed my stinging hand and clenched my teeth.

Rory stood and moved to Jonathon's side, but she addressed me. "I was in your shoes a few months ago. Now you know how it feels when someone is taken from you."

"Everyone sit." Artur topped off my glass of scotch. "We are family now. I can tell."

My breath came in short bursts.

Artur put a hand on my thigh. "Drink your scotch. Today we celebrate."

I picked up the glass and thought of Eddy, James, and Sierra. Little Mattie and Mikey were only four and seven years old. Their beautiful young family was irreplaceable. Fragile, now that I saw how vulnerable they were. And dearer to me than my own life.

I looked Artur in the eye and gave the tiniest nod.

"To family." Artur lifted his glass.

With a shaking hand, I picked up my glass. If I didn't, I had so much to lose.

–41–

MINA

I barely remembered the rest of the afternoon. By the time the sun set, I was drunk. The blood trail from dead Kolak's body had been cleaned—not a trace remained. As if Kolak never existed.

Artur held my arm as he took me down the steep stairs toward the shore. "We sail for Croatia tonight. At dinner, I'll introduce you to my wife." Artur kept talking about his plans for the next few days. About problems he had in the U.S. About the ways I could help him. I didn't listen. He escorted me onto the *Ivan*, past his armed guards and deep into the belly of his yacht.

We stopped at the door to an elegant berth without windows. "There are clean clothes in the closet." His gaze slid down my body and landed near my hips. "I think we got your size right. Small. Freshen up. Change into something nice. I will see you on deck two in one hour."

I wanted to puke.

"Dinner is served at nine o'clock sharp. You need to eat, Mina. It will help clear your head. I need you to be focused for our long discussion." Artur closed the door and left me in peace.

I staggered to the bathroom and crouched over the toilet. After my stomach emptied, I turned on the cold shower and walked in with my clothes on. Bloody, brownish water pooled at my feet. The smell of iron gagged me, but my stomach was empty. I sank to the floor and put my head in my hands.

Artur was a murderer with power and money. The most dangerous kind. And I had put James and Eddy in danger.

Then there was Jonathon . . . Tears mingled with the shower water. My hair matted and the dress clung to me wet and cold.

I finally wanted to jump from that cliff.

-42-

JONATHON

It killed me seeing Mina like that. When she came into the villa in handcuffs and with so much blood on her dress, I worried at first it was hers. My heart caught in my throat when I realized it was not and a bad feeling it was Leo's arose. Still, I dared not reveal how my heart ached for her. That I wanted to hold her. To hug and caress her and let her know everything would be okay. When Artur pulled up the video of James and his family, the pain and anguish on Mina's face made me look away.

I could have gotten Mina out of there before something—anything—happened. Now that Artur Protsenko had her, I struggled to see another way. I was alone. Rory had set me figuratively adrift with no paddle or sail. Without resources or connections to my people. And now Mina suffered a similar fate. I started drinking when Artur threatened Mina's brothers, James, and Eddie. I couldn't help thinking if anything happened to them, it was my own fault.

After Artur forcefully took Mina to the *Ivan*, Rory and I went to her bedroom for some privacy. "Why didn't you tell me?" I slammed the door.

She set her jeweled cell phone case on the dresser and backed up to the bed. "Tell you what?"

"What happened to the plan? I thought you wanted to sell Mina at an auction. To recover the millions from the loss of your fentanyl?"

"Careful, Jonathon, dear. You almost sound like a man in love."

Her warning sent an electric shock through my body. Because I was *in love*. Not with Rory, but with Mina.

"Not in love. I consider her my property." I gazed directly into her eyes. I needed to keep up this pretense until I could destroy her.

"Did you really think I was worried about the money? It's more important to please my Papa. You see that, don't you?"

I did. After watching her with her father today, I gained more insights into why Rory was so broken. Because Artur, her father, was a sadistic bastard. The fruit doesn't fall far from the tree, they say. She craved abuse because it was the only thing she'd ever known.

"Papa has many uses for her. Besides, this way he will always have someone watching her. This way, I'll know if you so much as call her."

Muscles all over my body tightened. I made a fist and clenched my jaw. It took a moment to release my teeth so I could say, "No. You're right, this is better."

"Mm. I love it when you get angry, Jon. Your blue eyes shine so brightly." She lay back on the bed and her high-heeled shoes hit the floor with a clunk.

We'd both had too much to drink and too little to eat. I kicked off my shoes and moved in on top of her. I needed her to believe I was on her side.

Rory wrapped her arms around my neck. She placed one hand over my cock and unzipped my pants with the other. My kisses were fierce and angry—like they'd always been with her. Hers were passively aggressive. Needy. She wove a hand through my hair and pulled me down.

I dragged her dress over her head and left her arms tangled in it. I twisted the fabric around her wrists and held her hands above her head. I yanked her panties down to her knees.

She laughed and sounded like a crazy woman. "Are you angry? Are you pissed at me? Fuck you, Jon."

"No, fuck you, Rory." I slapped her tiny little tits until they were bright red. Her nipples grew hard. Then I spit on her.

She laughed again. "Fuck me, Jon. I have wanted you for years. Fuck me like you'll never let me go."

I didn't want Rory, but my cock decided it needed her. It eagerly rose to the challenge. "Fuck you, Rory." I spat on her again.

"Yes. Yes." She arched into me. Her pussy tightened on my cock. "Fuck me like I'm the only woman you'll ever love."

She thrust against me again and again, and I lost control. I closed my eyes and pictured Mina the last time we'd made love. Her long light-brown hair framed her high cheekbones. Mina's narrow hips and muscular legs wrapped around my waist. I moved my pelvis faster. I braced myself.

Rory gripped my arms and slammed her hips into me. "Oh, Jonathon." I imagined Mina's voice because I was drunk. The feeling of Rory's wet sex overtook other sensations. She lay back, calling my name, and I rode her. I closed my eyes and thought of the one woman I loved. Thought of Mina's smooth skin scented with sunflowers and ylang-ylang. The thought of her clever conversation and the way she called my name made me rise up. I peaked.

"Oh! Mina!"

The sting of Rory's hand on the side of my face sobered me up. I pulled out and rolled over as I spasmed into my hand.

Rory ducked out from under me and gathered her clothes. As she rushed to the bathroom, she cried, "Get out!" She said, "Get out of my room." The door slammed.

I used my shirt to wipe my hands and cock, then left it on the floor of her room. At least I had the presence of mind not to come inside her. God only knew if Rory was on the pill.

Behind the closed door, water ran in the bathroom. I pulled up my pants and looked around the room. Her clothes lay in a heap on the floor and there . . . on the dresser. I palmed her cell phone and stuck it in my pocket. Then I left and closed the door.

The cloudy effects of the scotch were wearing off. I badly wanted another drink but needed to remain lucid. I needed a plan.

Armed guards stood in every corner of the house and at every exit. I dared not make a call here. I went toward the balcony and stopped ten feet from the rail. From here, I could clearly see the superyacht. It didn't surprise me that Artur Protsenko named it after one of the cruelest Russian rulers of all time, Ivan the Terrible. The white-and-black ship was all lit up and as the sun set, it glowed against the darkening water.

The two-hundred-foot *Crazy Ivan* was built for speed and for negotiating the large oceanic swells. The sleek yacht sat low in the water. I bet it had the horsepower of a racing boat. Along its sides, blackened banks of windows like the eye slits in a warrior's helmet stared ahead with a menacing glare. If it were mine, I would have installed bullet-proof glass. Artur probably had.

From the balcony, I had a nauseating bird's eye view of the three decks. But I ordered the bear—my phobia of heights—to stay in hibernation. I needed to get to know my enemy.

On *Ivan's* top deck, a small helicopter was parked on a helipad. Lined up in rows behind it were what appeared to be dozens of drones. Weaponized, I guessed. Artur had thought of everything.

On the middle deck, an armed guerilla paced back and forth along the rail. He tossed a cigarette into the sea, and I watched the orange coal snuff out in the water. Staff bustled around a table set for dining on the well-lit top deck. I wondered if Mina would sit with Artur and his guests. I longed to be there with her.

A blue swimming pool glowed on the lowest deck. Framing it, two deadly missile launchers aimed into the dark. *Ivan's* motor rumbled to life and my senses came alert. Artur had not told Rory his plans to set sail tonight.

I watched in horror as the anchor chain reeled into the stern compartment. The engine pitched up and the yacht started forward. The *Ivan* pulled away from Sotoris, leaving a foamy white trail in its wake.

In my pants pocket, my thumb drew across one gemstone on Rory's silly cell phone case. I dug the phone out of my pocket and furtively pried the case off with my fingernails. Thirty feet to my right, a guard smoked a cigarette and looked out at the yacht. Twenty-five feet to my left, another sat in a chair tipped back against the stone railing. When neither were looking at me, I stepped to the deck railing made of solid white marble, and I flicked the sparkling case out into the water below.

Moments later, the guard to my right heard the splash and looked down over the ledge. Then he looked at me. I backed away from the edge because nausea threatened to overwhelm me.

Ivan turned southward and moved out of my view. "I'll come for you," I whispered to Mina.

I strode back to my tower bedroom and took the steps two at a time. I closed my door and left the lights off. In the dark, I pulled Rory's cell out and tried to guess her password. My name didn't work and neither did my birth date. I tried the acronym for her favorite sex game, BDSM, and I was in. I opened the settings. GPS tracking was turned off. She had state-of-the-art anti-tracking software installed and privacy shields everywhere. I wasn't sure what to expect, but this—all her safeguards and anti-piracy protection—was perfect.

I dialed Mayhem's number.

~43~

MINA

Every last tear wrung from my body and washed down the drain with the last of the bloodstains. I rested my head in my hands. The sobs stopped. My hair dripped over my shoulders. At some point, I realized my teeth were chattering. As I made my way to my feet, I noticed the familiar sway of the yacht and heard the thrum of the engine. We were at sea.

I needed to get my shit together.

I turned the shower faucet to hot and peeled the soggy, ruined sundress from my body. I shampooed and scrubbed my skin until it was red and raw. Like my emotions. The washcloth brushed against the bandage where Emilya had inserted the GPS tracker.

A lifeline stretched out for me. I peeled the Band-Aid away and dropped it. The wound was tender and slightly swollen. I drew my finger along it, gently pressing the outer edges of my hip muscle and the border of my tattoo and the jeweled ring flashed in the light. The panic button was there if I needed it. I depressed it now. Emilya and Michael knew where I was. They would come for me. How much time had passed since I left the Oyster? How soon could they get to me? Greyson had connections at Interpol. Would he notify them?

They could not get here quickly enough.

I prepared to join Artur for dinner. In the bathroom drawers I found a hairbrush, hair dryer, and lotions. There were small samples of Clé de Peau Beauté, and Guerlain makeup—foundation in a half-dozen colors, eye powders, mascara, and dozens of shades of lipstick—tucked into a drawer. Mine for the taking. I dabbed a little foundation under my eyes to hide the circles. A dark shade of red lipstick reminded me of the pool of blood under Kolak's head. It drew attention away from my puffy eyes.

Breath filled my lungs, and I let it out slowly.

The closet was stuffed with dresses for every occasion. Who did they belong to? Did Artur keep them in case of unexpected company? Or were they the last remnants of women he had killed? I found suitable undergarments and a black sheath dress in my size and put them on. My blood-splattered Sorels completed the outfit—there was no other choice. As I checked myself in the mirror, someone knocked on the door.

"Dinner is served. Mr. Protsenko requests your presence." I opened the door to a stick-thin woman whose head almost touched the ceiling. She wore a black uniform and held an electronic wand in her hands. "Raise your hands over your head."

She must have seen the quizzical expression on my face.

"Weapons check."

I did as she asked and she waved the wand from my shoulders to my waist, then down my legs. "Turn around."

The snug dress left little to the imagination. I spun with my hands in the air. She waved the wand, and it passed over my hip without a sound.

Still she tucked the wand under her arm and patted me down with flattened hands. "Hmph," she said. "Follow me."

I closed the door to my room and followed the tall woman—her hair pulled into a severe bun at the base of her skull—as she moved quickly down the narrow chrome and plexiglass hallway. I couldn't see past her but somehow I got my bearings and realized my cabin was in the middle of the ship. We took two flights of steep marine-maple stairs to the upper deck. She stopped and allowed me to pass. "Mr. Protsenko waits."

The night air cooled my cheeks. Out on the open deck, a generous table was set for ten with an enormous bouquet in the center. I wondered if Jonathon and Rory would join us. Had they boarded the *Crazy Ivan?*

I examined my surroundings for an escape route. Armed guards stood in various corners of the deck. Beyond the trailing wake of the

Ivan, Sotoris was but a speck on the horizon. We seemed to be heading southeast.

Artur stood with his back to me near the railing. Smoke blew away from him as he turned with a cigar clenched between his teeth. He removed the cigar and with a grand sweeping gesture said, "Mina. Welcome." His gaze settled on my hiking shoes as he stubbed the cigar on a gold-rimmed plate at the corner of the table and approached with his arms out.

I backed away.

"We are family. Nothing to be afraid of." He touched my arms and kissed both cheeks.

I shivered.

"You are more beautiful than I realized." He took my arm, and I followed him. Behind the table, a fully stocked bar ran the width of the boat. Chrome and plexiglass reflected the running lights. Artur took two tumblers from the bartender and handed one to me.

"Tonight we'll discuss all the things you can do for me. I hear you have talents beyond the courtroom."

"Mr. Protsenko . . ." I thought of James and his sons. Of Eddie. But I no longer had it in me to argue.

Women's voices arose from the staircase. Two striking women joined us. The elder said something to Artur in Russian. He laughed. "This is Wilhelmina from Chicago," Artur said. "She's an acquaintance of Rory's. A brilliant criminal defense lawyer. Mina, my wife, Olena, and her friend, Tonya."

Olena wore a turquoise damask kimono-style dress. She touched my shoulders and kissed each cheek. "Artur says you are family now. I expect nothing less." Gray curls framed her strong jaw and angular, Eastern European features. I instantly saw the resemblance to her daughter.

"So nice to meet you." I returned her kisses, pretending I didn't hate being here.

Tonya nodded and kept her distance. She pulled a cigarette out of a silver box and placed it between bright pink lips. "Nice to meet you," she said with a French accent.

Artur lit her cigarette. "Wilhelmina agrees to be my American counselor."

"Maybe she could be mine." Tonya waved smoke away from her face.

I wondered what crimes she had committed.

A staff member in a black uniform appeared at my side with a tray of filled champagne glasses. I gripped the tumbler of scotch and tried not to think about how many would get hurt when Interpol attacked the *Ivan*.

Olena took a glass and sipped. "How do you know my daughter, Rory?"

Through my lover? Through her terrorist acts against me and my friends? I hoped I didn't have to discuss details with Rory's mother. "She's a friend of a friend."

"You look familiar. Tell me about your most recent case," Olena said. "Who have you defended? Anyone I know?"

"Most recently I represented Bohdi Michaels. He was charged with money laundering, among other things."

"She means Bohdanovyan Mykajlenko. You never met him, Olena." Artur walked past us, and I turned to keep my eye on him.

Tonya blew cigarette smoke into the dark. "I know of him. Bohdi was exiled from France, but he narrowly escaped execution. The organization wanted his head."

"That's not it. I feel like I know your name." Olena studied me with her head tilted to one side.

We took our drinks to the table and sat. Artur at one end and Olena at the other. With eight chairs in between to choose from, Tonya and I took opposite sides somewhere in the middle. Three staff members quickly cleared the extra place settings and moved the enormous bouquet to the bar.

After we were all settled, Artur turned to me. "I want to ask your advice, Mina. I have a thriving business in Chicago. I own several night-clubs and a theater downtown. I want to make one into a casino."

"Gambling is legal in Chicago. It's regulated by the gaming commission. You'd have to comply with zoning regulations as well."

"I see. How can I bypass the regulators?"

I thought for a moment. "Riverboat casinos are allowed. I suppose you could buy a riverboat and offer trips out on Lake Michigan. But if you're using it to launder money, a casino is the worst way to go about that. The FBI takes extra precautions with casinos. There are more legal hoops to jump through than any other type of business."

"Let's get past that. I want you to help me to turn my nightclub into a casino."

"You're better off opening casinos in New York or anywhere on the East Coast—where you're allowed to own and operate up to seven casinos." *And far away from me*, I was thinking. "Because unless you fall under Native American tribal law, you can't do it in the state of Illinois."

"I know where I heard your name." Olena set down her glass. "My daughter has spoken of you."

I raised my eyebrows.

"You stole her lover's heart."

I looked Olena in the eye. "I don't know what you heard, but every word is a lie."

Olena leaned forward and pointed a bony finger at me. The veins on the back of her hand bulged as she whispered, "If you hurt my daughter, I will have the skin flayed from your face, but I will keep you alive. You will become a monster. You will be so hideous that no man will ever want to be with you."

My skin crawled as I sank into my chair.

Artur laughed. "Welcome to the family, Mina."

~44~

JONATHON

The call to Stan went to voicemail. I wasn't sure if Mayhem didn't answer because he didn't recognize the number, or if he was away from his phone. I pocketed Rory's phone and paced the well-worn path in my room.

I needed to reach him quickly. Mina was in danger.

Perhaps an hour later, the phone rang in my pocket. Mayhem's number appeared on screen, and I answered quickly to silence the loud opening notes of Mikhail Glinka's *Valse-Fantasy*.

"Mayhem?" I kept my voice as low as possible. "What took you so long?"

"Jon? Is that you, old boy?"

"Who else?"

I heard him tell someone and in the background there were cheers and shouts. "In a minute!" Stan said. "Jon, I'm putting you on speaker-phone. Everyone's here."

"Yo, Jon!"

"Greg? What are you doing there?"

"Long story."

"I'll introduce the rest later," Stan said. "Where are you?"

"I'm on Sotoris, but I'm well-guarded. I have to keep my voice down, or I'm afraid Rory will find out I have her phone."

"Got it. We're on our way, but we're about three hours out."

"On your way? To Sotoris? How—"

"There isn't time. Have you seen Mina?"

"She was here on the island, but she's with Artur Protsenko now. The *Ivan* set sail an hour ago. I need to get her off that yacht. There's no telling where he'll take her."

"She's wearing a GPS tracker. We saw her travel away from the island. What's the situation?"

"Bad. Artur threatened to kill her family to get her to work for him." Disheartened, I updated Mayhem and Greg. "I'm in no position to help. I was lucky to swipe Rory's phone, but it won't be long before she realizes it's gone. We need to get Mina out of there."

"Jon, it's Greg. If we're going to save her, we need to stop the *Crazy Ivan*. Otherwise, we could be following them all the way to Cairo, for all we know."

"No. Mina's aboard that ship. I don't want her to get caught in a terrorist war."

"The *Ivan* is a San Lorenzo 64 Steel. It weighs 1600 tons and has a max speed of 17 knots. My ship will never catch her."

I recognized the voice. "Who is speaking?"

"Michael Bettencourt. How are you, Jon?"

"God, Mike, I heard you bought a yacht, but I didn't think I'd ever see you again. Now I can't wait to hear how you all got together." I sat on the bed. "I'm running out of time. How can we stop the *Ivan* without risking Mina's life?"

"We can't catch her unless we hit a steady high wind," Mike said. "The *Ivan*'s moving south at about ten knots. But we wouldn't be able to maintain that speed for more than a day. I don't have the manpower. We won't be able to catch up to her once it gets out into the Mediterranean, but my friend Greyson has connections with Interpol. He notified them of the kidnapping." I thought I heard voices outside my door.

"Interpol will send the Hellenic Coast Guard to intercept the *Ivan*," Greg said.

"Artur will find a way out of it. I want him to pay for what he's done. I may know a way, but it's dangerous," I said.

Mina was so brave. I thought about her tombstoning expeditions. She was a good swimmer, and I knew she'd fight for her life. "I know someone who would love to get his hands on Artur Protsenko."

"What do you need us to do?"

Voices were at my door. After giving Stan a name, I threw Rory's phone as far as I could out the window. It soared out over the edge of the cliff, but I didn't watch it. My stomach couldn't take it.

Rory barged in. "My phone is missing." She squinted suspiciously at me, and her gaze darted around the room and stopped at the open window.

I shrugged. "I haven't seen it. Where did you leave it?"

"Where did *I* leave it? Maybe you took it to call your *lover!*"

"Rory." I touched her shoulder.

"I hate you, Jonathon." She turned to go, but I pulled her close.

She pounded on my chest. "I hate you!" She was crying.

I held her, and she buried her face in my chest. "Let me help you find it," I said.

~45~

MINA

Like preparing for a trial, I tried to compartmentalize my thoughts but couldn't escape the one major difference between my clients and this fucked-up situation.

I was the victim.

Despite the flowing champagne and the drinks, I didn't sleep. The previous day kept circling and circling in my thoughts. Olena's knobby finger and the evil tone of her voice. Artur shooting Kolak in cold blood. Leo Thibodeau dying in my arms.

Jonathon holding Rory's hand.

I couldn't close my eyes. Lying with a sheet over me, not even the yacht's steady rocking relaxed me. Deep inside the belly of the ship, I listened to the humming of machinery and tried to quiet my thoughts. The ventilation system blew cold air. I turned to feel it on my skin. The ticking sounds and creaking wood marked seconds, minutes, hours. It counted the distance in knots as we moved away from Jonathon and away from the life I knew.

Footsteps pounded down the hall past my cabin. Did I hear warning shouts or was it my imagination? I sat up in bed searching the black darkness for a clock and pulled the sheet to my neck.

An explosion shook the boat and rolled me out of bed. In the aftermath I heard doors opening, slamming shut, and men shouting in Russian.

I staggered to my feet as the yacht lurched and red emergency lights came on. Quickly, I put on the dress from last night and my shoes and stepped out into the hallway.

Crew members in boxers and nightshirts opened their doors as gunfire sounded from above. The yacht was under attack. The *Ivan* shook with another explosion. Flames shot down the hall from the stern, where the engine must be. The yacht was taking on water.

I darted to the stairs and climbed them two at a time. I didn't understand the shouts in Russian and other dialects. But I understood the tone of fear. I kept moving.

At the top of the stairs, I leapt back. A fleet of drones on the deck looked like giant bugs. Two took off into the night sky. Several hundred feet away, an explosion lit up another yacht. I thanked God it wasn't the Oyster, but we were under attack. Guerillas fired Uzis into the darkness as the *Ivan*'s stern took on more water.

I slid to the floor and back toward the stairs. More guards climbed up from the lower levels. I scrambled to my feet and grabbed the rail. A warm wind blew back my hair. To my left, the Aegean—were we still on the Aegean?—was a black abyss in the moonless night. To my left, faint lights dotted the shore of whatever land mass we were passing. The Greek island Karpathos? Sotoris Island seemed far away.

Artur, in a T-shirt and shorts, tripped past me. His wife in her nightgown and Tonya still in her cocktail dress ran like scalded cats as they climbed to the top deck. One heavily armed guerilla trailed them. I tried to follow.

"No!" The guard raised his weapon at me. I let them go. From the top of the steps, I watched Artur and the rest climb into a small chopper. Other crew members tried to clamber on board the small aircraft. The guard shot them as the propeller came to life.

The chopper lifted into the air just as the *Ivan* took another missile hit.

How far were we from land? Could I swim there before morning? No one paid any attention to me as I searched storage lockers for a floatation device. When I found what I was looking for, I strapped it on.

The yacht kept tipping, sinking deeper, and I lost my footing. Another explosion knocked me to the deck.

$-46-$

JONATHON

Rory's phone lay at the bottom of the cliff. I'd chucked it out the window of my room and watched it sail over the rocky edge. I knew she'd never find it, but I had to display my show of support. We were turning over pillows in the living room when a guard ran into the room.

"Your mother tried calling you. The *Ivan* is under attack," he said.

Rory's eyes met mine and a look of horror came over her face.

My only thought—*Mina!* We ran to the balcony so fast, my stomach didn't have time to do flips. All I could think of was Mina.

"Papa set sail tonight. Why didn't he tell me?"

Caught up in the search for her missing phone, I hadn't told Rory the *Ivan* had pulled up anchor and sailed. My heart sank. By instructing Mayhem to call Artur's enemies, I'd started a terrorist war. Stan said they'd reported the kidnapping to Interpol and the Hellenic Coast Guard. I scanned the dark horizon for any sign of another ship. For rescue aircraft. For a response team.

The guard waited for her orders.

"Call the coast guard," I said.

"Are you kidding? They'd be happy to get their hands on Papa."

"Your family might die."

"I'm not getting the police involved! Shit. I need a fucking phone!"

I needed to have faith that Mina would escape. I couldn't bear to think of the alternative.

Rory snatched the guard's cell phone out of his hand. She dialed as she walked swiftly to the door. "Get the helicopter ready!"

"No, Rory, it's too dangerous." I ran after her through a maze of tunnel-like hallways. She didn't stop. "You can't go after them! If the attacking vessel has missile launchers, your chopper will end up at the bottom of the sea."

We emerged from the hall and swiftly crossed to the well-lit helipad on the east side of the island. A man in a helmet ran toward us. "We heard their radio call for help. The ship attacking them is Arab," the pilot said.

Behind him, a handful of technicians prepared a Russian Hind helicopter for flight. Maybe I'd been wrong about her chopper ending up at the bottom of the sea. The Hind was a helicopter gunship equipped with bombs and heavy weaponry. Alone, it could take on the Arab attack ship and win.

"Send reinforcements." Rory said. "My father's in there. And my mother. We need to save them!"

"Mr. and Mrs. Protsenko deboarded the Ivan on the helicopter. They escaped and are safe." The pilot signaled and the guerrillas climbed aboard the chopper. "There's more," the pilot said. "Mr. Protsenko believes Alawi el Attar is behind this. Your father wants you to kill his daughter."

"What? Now?" Rory looked like she'd been slapped.

I wouldn't allow Rory to kill Sitaara.

Did she hesitate? I wanted to give her points for discretion.

"Yes. He says, kill the girl."

"She's a child, Rory. She's innocent!" *Never underestimate Rory Protsenko,* my inner voice said.

"This is your fault, Jonathon." Rory stormed past me. "Vaolym!"

The huge guard stood nearby. "Take Jon back to his room and lock the door."

Vaolym and another guerilla took me by the arms.

"Rory, don't do this!" The guards dragged me back to the house.

Over her shoulder, Rory said, "Go and cry for your dead lover."

I dug my heels in as the guards pulled me back to the prison bedroom. But what of dear little Sitaara? I pounded on the door and shouted, "You can't kill the girl!"

When they locked the door, I prepared for war.

~47~

MINA

The sea looked like black oil. Like it would swallow me up and kill me. The flotation vest I'd grabbed was a few sizes too big. Though I tightened it around my chest as far as it would go, it chaffed my chin and armpits as I swam.

On my right, faint lights of motorboats and search helicopters dotted the horizon. I kept swimming north. On my left, a tanker cut through the water. Too far away to pull me under or drag me along in its wake. I needed to trust the GPS tracker. I pressed the emergency signal ring again. Faith that Emilya and Michael would find me faded with each passing minute. I grew tired and struggled to keep my eyes open. The horizon turned pink.

The rumbling motorboat engine woke me. I was shivering and could barely keep my head out of the water. The bright sun crested the horizon, and there, a shadow moved in front of it. Beyond exhaustion, I didn't care who or what. I lifted my heavy arms out of the water and waved.

The boat turned toward me, and a spotlight hit my eyes. Temporarily blinded, I shielded my eyes and heard someone calling my name.

At last.

Michael and Greg helped me up onto the swim platform, and I lay there like a beached seal, catching my breath and resting. Goosebumps covered my arms and legs. I'd lost my hiking shoes and the black dress stuck to my hips. No one spoke for the longest time.

When I finally caught my breath, I said through chattering teeth, "Someone attacked *The Ivan*. At first I thought it was you. It was sinking fast. I had to get off before it went under."

Michael looked at Emilya and smiled. The rest huddled around me on the swim platform. She said, "We think it was an Arab vessel. Greyson notified the Hellenic Coast Guard and Interpol."

Stan said, "You'll be happy to know, Jonathon called. I don't know how, but he got Rory's phone."

Jonathon? The image of him holding Rory's hand was burned into my mind. But a flicker of hope lit behind the veil.

Emilya brought me a clean towel and a blanket. "Let's get you out of that."

My cold fingers fumbled with the clasp on the life vest. Emilya helped me take it off.

"Jonathon told me Rory is holding a girl named Sitaara al Attar captive," Stan said. "He asked me to call a friend of his, and I told him about the girl."

"I swear Jonathon knows everyone." Greyson peered over the stern.

Stan continued, "I told him where to find Protsenko, and where to find the girl. They went after Protsenko, I guess."

Emilya handed my dripping life vest to Michael. "The radio noise from the coast guards is all about the search and rescue mission for two sunken yachts near Karpathos. They say pirates attacked a Russian superyacht. Is Artur Protsenko dead? They are all wondering if the TOC leader was killed in the attack."

I pulled the towel over my shoulders and shivered. "Artur escaped. He and his wife fled in a helicopter shortly after the first missile attack. The *Ivan* exploded. I jumped off because it was taking on too much water."

Emilya helped warm me by rubbing and patting my arms and back. "I'm so happy you're alive! I followed your GPS tracker signal. We got to you as quickly as we could. I thought you were on a lifeboat or dinghy. We had no idea you were swimming."

"The Port Corps-Hellenic Coast Guard would have taken you in for questioning," Michael said. "Since you're American, they might have turned you over to Interpol. You would have been held for questioning. The bureaucracy might have taken weeks."

"We don't have weeks. I need to go back to Sotoris."

Greg helped me to my feet. "You need to rest."

"If what you said is true, then Rory is still holding Jonathon captive. I have to go back."

-48-

JONATHON

*W*as Mina dead?

I had to believe Mina survived the blast. I had to picture her swimming to safety. *Stan will rescue her* I kept repeating to myself.

Every few minutes, I stopped to listen through my door. Sitaara's room was right down the hall, but I heard nothing to indicate Rory had taken her. Once I was free, I'd do everything in my power to return Sitaara to her father. I had to rely on Mayhem and my friends. I had to maintain hope.

What seemed like hours later the helicopter returned. Sometime after that, I heard them in the hall outside my room. A key jiggled in the lock. They threw the door open, and it crashed into the wall behind it.

Rory stood in the doorway with her hands on Sitaara's shoulders. Sitaara's mahogany brown eyes glistened with fear.

Vaolym and two armed guerillas crowded into my small room. They scooped me up from the bed as I fumbled to my feet. "I'm not fighting you!" I said.

"Search every corner," one said.

"It must be in here!" Rory was still looking for her phone, but she'd never find it.

Vaolym locked my arms behind me and shoved me forward. Another guard tossed my bedding on the floor then hefted the mattress off the frame. They tossed the chair, turned over the desk, and manhandled my clothes.

"Where is the phone, Jon?" Rory's voice cracked.

I debated the wisdom of playing ignorant, then decided holding back would likely draw Rory's attention from Sitaara to me. "I don't know what you're talking about."

I was right. She pushed Sitaara aside and flew at me. "You do know! You orchestrated the attack on my father's ship last night. You revealed Papa's location to the Arabs. You set him up!"

"Even if I could have notified Abu Alawi el Attar, I wouldn't have. Mina was on board that yacht. She's an innocent victim."

Rory slapped my face. "You lied to me."

I wouldn't admit to anything.

"Attar is indebted to my father for protecting his assets during an attack on his homeland. My father made a business deal with him, and Sitaara is his assurance that Attar won't back out."

The same kind of business deal he'd made with Mina.

Fire shot from Rory's eyes. "There's only one reason those Arabs didn't attack the island."

Sitaara.

Rory stepped closer to me. Close enough to kiss me. "I knew you were too good to be true, Jon. I kick myself for trusting you and your . . . lies!" She spit on me.

"Lock them up together!" She pushed Sitaara into my arms.

The guards climbed awkwardly over the mattress and furniture tossed on the floor. They exited the room.

Sitaara tightened her arms around me.

"I'll keep you safe," I said. "I promise."

Please let that be true.

-49-

MINA

So Jonathon stole Rory's cell phone and contacted Stan.
The story gave me hope as I recalled the evening when I arrived at Sotoris.

At Rory's side, Jonathon had avoided eye contact with me. *He drank scotch!* And he agreed with everything she and her father said. Jonathon never drank. Without blinking, he agreed that I was the perfect legal tool for Artur. Rory seemed to hang on his every word, to put his suggestions first. In the subtleties, I noticed the power struggle between them. He gave in to her. He let her take the helm during the entire discussion. She allowed him few opportunities to speak to Artur. When she did, she twisted Jonathon's words.

Jonathon was powerless. I wondered what else she took from him.

There was one moment that Jonathon suggested they send me back to Chicago. Rory replied with an absolute no and approached me with something like compassion. She dragged her hand across my cheek and jaw. She flirted with me. But by then I was drunk. Speechless. And Jonathon gave Rory a look that was filled with such venom.

Rory and Artur missed it. And while they conferred by the balcony, Jonathon asked if I was okay.

Far from it. But what could I say? I was still in shock. Before I had a chance to answer, Artur took me by the arm and walked me to the *Ivan*. When I looked back at Jonathon, I thought he mouthed the words, "I love you."

Did I dare hope that there was still a chance? My heart swelled.

During the darkest moments of a trial, when it seemed the prosecuting attorney held all the cards, I would rise from the ashes like a phoenix bird. I'd bring in the golden ticket, a witness who could vouch for my client's whereabouts or their good character. Someone who could prove to the jury that no matter what evil act my client had done, it was done with the best intentions. It was passion. It was love. Or it was nothing at all.

Had Jonathon acted out of love? I needed to believe it. Because if Jonathon didn't love me, I would tell Michael to turn the yacht around and take it back to Milos or Athens or Rethymno. Or I would jump from the cliff on Sotoris and take my punishment, however it came.

I slept like a baby for four hours, then tossed and turned for two more. When I woke, I felt strongly that I'd made the right decision.

I needed to rescue him from Rory's clutches.

Michael anchored the Oyster on a tiny rock of an island about thirty knots from Sotoris. Red sunset rays hit the rock face in the distance and made it glow like a fortress. We stayed below deck in the saloon and discussed our next move, while Emilya served feta and olive salad with pita crisps, tahini, and baba ghanoush.

"Without the *Ivan*, Sotoris is more vulnerable. They lost missile launchers and a dozen or more guerillas. There was a fleet of drones on that yacht. They all sank with the ship." I plunged a crisp pita into the creamy eggplant dip Michael made.

Emilya nudged Michael over and sat beside him on the couch. "The RF blockers are keeping us safe for the time being, but we're highly visible on the Oyster. We can't approach the island in this yacht."

"We need the cloak of invisibility," Greyson said.

"If only it weren't fiction." Stan shoveled olives and dip onto a small plate.

"It might not be." Greg grabbed a pad of paper and began sketching out something. "We have much better chances if we approach from an unexpected access point."

"I was thinking the same thing," I said with my mouth full.

"We'll have to approach the island from the southwest." Michael shoved an olive into his mouth and washed it down with sparkling water. Tonight, none of us drank alcohol.

"He's right," I said. "On the north side, we'd be exposed. There's a short pier and a long stairway leading to the top. But armed guards are stationed up and down the steps keeping lookout and keeping anyone from approaching. If we try to get to the villa from there, we'd be shot on sight."

Grayson speared an olive with his fork. "Even at night, we'd be shot before we made it to the shore."

"There is another way." Everyone's gazes landed on me.

"She's right." Greg sketched shapes on the paper, turning it at angles while rubbing his knee. I caught a glimpse of what appeared to be a map forming on the page.

"The west wall," I said. "The rock face."

Greg sketched fast. "If we take the dinghy and approach quietly from the southwest—"

"The guards patrol that side of the villa on foot," I said.

"Two of us could make it to the top."

"Count me out," Greyson said. "I'm not climbing that cliff. I have terrible vertigo."

"I've performed infiltration tactics like this when I was in the military," Stan said. "It's been a long time though and I don't know if this old body—"

"I'll do it," I said.

Emilya held a chip topped with baba ghanoush in front of her open mouth. Greg raised an eyebrow. Michael said, "No, Mina. It's too dangerous."

"A few months ago, Greg taught me how to climb. Besides, I've done enough free climbs to know what I'm capable of."

"When?" Emilya asked.

"That's not important." I wasn't about to tell them about my tombstoning adventures. "The problem isn't getting up the wall, it's getting past all the guards on the inside. I suspect Jonathon is still her prisoner. I just don't know. He was there last night when Rory and Artur captured me. But I don't know what kind of freedom he has. And I don't know the layout of the entire building."

Greg finished his sketch and turned the paper toward us. It was an arial view of the villa with the steps on the north side, and the cliff on the west. The rocky approach on the south, and the helipad on the east. "I have a pretty good eye for architectural structures. This isn't the highest wall I've ever climbed. If we go up here, we can probably find an access point on the south side. We'll find Jonathon. I think he'll be waiting for us."

I could only hope.

-50-

JONATHON

Sitaara stood at the window while I put the room back together. "Did you really call him? Did you call my father?" she asked. In the weeks Sitaara had cared for me, she never spoke to me in English. As I suspected, she understood every word.

"I didn't call him," I said. "I called a friend. He's the one who called your father." I smoothed the blanket on the bed.

"Do you think my father is still alive?"

"Of course he is. Your father is a powerful man. I'm sure he sent the ship. His faithful men and women attacked Artur Protsenko, the man who's holding you prisoner."

"Did they all die?"

I didn't know. But I wanted to give Sitaara hope. "No. I don't think so. The coast guard will rescue some of them. Others will have escaped."

"What's she going to do now?" She meant Rory.

"I don't know, Sitaara. But I'll do everything in my power to get us out of here." I sat on the side of the bed and Sitaara hopped up beside me.

"Me too. I want to see my father and mother again." In the dark, her eyes shown with determination.

-51-

MINA

After a light meal, I put on black yoga pants and a long-sleeved black T-shirt. Tucking my light brown hair under a black baseball cap, I felt like a ninja, getting ready to wage war on Rory. It was a good feeling.

Once the sky was pitch dark, around ten o'clock, Greg and I loaded the inflatable dinghy with ropes and carabiners. We filled our backpacks with pistols, an Uzi, and the appropriate ammunition. Stan wore his bullet-proof vest and brought a dazzle gun—don't ask me where he got it—and a missile launcher. The three of us motored to Sotoris under the cover of stars. It was slow going with the small three-horse engine. On the way, I used high-powered, night-vision binoculars to view the top of the cliff. No one patrolled the perimeter of the villa. I wondered where Jonathon was or if he expected us to be there tonight.

The water near the island looked dark during the day, which meant it was deep. Unlike the sandy and smooth-bottomed Caribbean, the Aegean Sea is made up of so many islands, the underwater topography is like a sunken mountain range.

We beached the dinghy on the rocky shore. Mossy boulders of all sizes made terrible footing. Greg clambered ahead with a small flashlight in his mouth and his hands on the ground. He almost made it to the rock face when he twisted to the ground.

"Shit," he whispered. He tried to sit down, but his leg was stuck.

I scrambled to his side. His foot was stuck between two tire-sized boulders. "Can you get it out?"

He pulled and grabbed his still-healing knee. "Dammit," he whispered. He tugged one more time and his bare foot popped out of his shoe.

"Are you okay?" He rubbed his knee.

"I twisted the knee. But I'll be all right."

I reached into the crack to retrieve his shoe. "Are you sure?" I whispered.

He massaged his leg. "It's just so dark. We'll need to be extra careful."

I handed him his shoe. "Take your time then. Try to watch your step."

"I will. But it's getting late." He turned his head and peered up the cliff face. "It will take us an hour, maybe more."

"Then let's get going," I said. I was anxious to get to Jonathon.

He began setting ropes for our climb. Stan mounted the launcher on a flat rock near the shore while I adjusted the heavy backpack.

Out across the sea, a green light, like a beacon swept the sky.

"Don't look at it," Stan said. From the Oyster's stern, Greyson was manipulating the laser beam, a blinding green light that would disorient the guerillas. The idea being, if their attention was on the horizon, they wouldn't be watching for our small craft to come ashore.

"I won't." I kept my gaze down.

Since my swanky hiking shoes had been lost when I leapt off the *Ivan*, Emilya gave me a pair of her gently used Converse. They were one size too small, but we hoped the rubber toe and flat soles would be ideal for rock climbing. I made sure the laces were tucked in.

Greg began to climb and set ropes for the descent along the way. Once he got about ten feet up the wall, he pulled pins, anchors, and locking carabiners out of his pockets and hammered them into the cracks. My eyes had long since adjusted to the moonless night. I began to climb after him and stayed about ten feet behind.

At first, I needed his guiding reassurance. "That first rock is a big one. Place your foot on the grip at the right, then grab the top of the stone and pull yourself up. It's wet from the sea spray, but there's a handhold on the back side. You'll find it."

I found footing and pulled myself over the top. The movement lit up muscles sore from the long swim yesterday. My triceps and pectorals burned, but I pushed through it.

Greg guided me through the initial steps, and as we climbed, I gained confidence and found ledges and jugs, easy handholds that worked for me. As we ascended, the crag became drier. The cooling rocks became less slippery. I pressed my body into the face and clung to the squared off rocks like a bug.

When we reached a midpoint with a nice ledge, Greg stopped to rest. I plopped down beside him.

He panted, "I'm done," and rubbed his knee.

"What do you mean, you're done?"

His face glistened, even in the dark, like he'd worked up a sweat. "When my shoe stuck down there, I twisted my knee. I think I tore the meniscus."

"You're kidding, right? How did you make it this far?"

"I don't know. Adrenaline? That wore off about fifteen minutes ago. I can tell, if I go any farther, I'll just be a sitting target once we get to the top."

I thought about the options. Turning back was not one of them. "Can you make it back down?"

"That's why I set ropes. But, Mina..." He looked up the wall above us. We had a good twenty five feet to go.

"But . . . ?"

"Once you get to the top, I'll throw you the rope. Find a secure place to tie it off. You remember the knots?" he asked.

I did.

"I'll secure the ropes for your descent on this end. Jonathon is good at many things, but climbing isn't one of them."

"He'll do fine." I dismissed Greg's warning right away. Jonathon was capable and strong. He'd do fine.

"What I mean is, he has acrophobia. He's afraid of heights."

I squinted to see Greg's face in the dark. "Are you joking?"

"Nope. He has a very healthy fear of falling. He told me about his phobia years ago. When we flew to Japan together, he took the aisle seat and insisted on keeping the shade drawn. I didn't think anything of it until we were on a train heading to Hideo Ryushi's dojo. The roads to the Bujinkan master's dojo followed the slope of the mountain. I was looking down the steep mountainside when I caught Jon out of the corner of my eye. He had paled to a sickly shade of green. Later he told me why, but I'll let him tell you the story."

Acrophobia? This plan was doomed to fail. "What if I can't get him to go down this way?"

"Radio me when you're ready. Stan and I will pick you up near the stairs on the north side."

My gaze was drawn to the sea lapping the stones below us. I thought how much easier it would be to dive into the deep water below. "Not a problem. I'll do whatever it takes." I just hoped Jonathon would be on board.

~52~

JONATHON

Sitaara slept while I sat in the chair. Hours had passed since we heard about the attack on the *Ivan*. Hours without knowing whether Mina lived or . . . I couldn't think about that now. I tried to focus on getting out of here. I tried to focus on my anger at Rory. My hatred of Artur. I tried to focus on what they'd done. At my rage about what they planned to do to Mina *and* Sitaara.

By the time Rory returned with three armed thugs, I was seething.

"I wanted to believe you were on my side, Jon. God, I wanted to."

"Pardon the pun, but that ship has sailed." I couldn't help it. I hadn't had a clear thought since the *Ivan* exploded.

She touched my cheek tenderly and looked in my eyes. "Right. There was a reason I left you the first time. Now, I like knowing where you are. I like keeping you caged like this and knowing you can't hurt me anymore."

Sitaara sat up in bed and rubbed the sleep from her eyes.

Rory pushed past me and grabbed Sitaara's arm.

"Leave her alone!"

Vaolym put me in a chokehold. Though I clawed at his arm, his grip lifted my feet off the floor.

Rory yanked Sitaara out of bed and took her to the door. "No more chances, Jonathon. This is your life now. Like Sitaara, here. Nowhere to go. No life to live except the one I make for you. Comply, Jon. And you will be a king here. But cross me—" Her eyes turned to stone-cold marbles. "And I will make your life miserable." She turned sharply away.

I lunged forward, but Vaolym firmly held me back. "Where are you going with Sitaara?" I asked. "Where are you taking her?"

"Papa asked me to do something."

Anger heated my face. *Was she going to kill Sitaara?* "Rory. Don't you dare. She's innocent. Leave her out of this."

Rory seemed to be listening. I continued, "I'm here because I want to be. Do you think for a moment that I couldn't escape if I wanted to? Do you think I don't have the skills and the connections to overcome you if I wanted to? You underestimate me."

"I don't underestimate you." She placed her hands on Sitaara's shoulders. "First, I know you have the *skills and connections* to pull off an escape. But I'll never let that happen. Do you know why? Because I'm the dominant one now. And you are *my* submissive." She pushed Sitaara forward and then turned and took my chin in her clawlike hand. "You stopped caring for me a long, long time ago, but I've been stupid to hold out hope for you. I know what you're capable of. Why do you think I'm well-guarded twenty-four seven? Why do you think I keep my distance from you? The truth is this. You. Underestimate. Me."

When she released my face, her thumbnail cut me. I touched the scratch under my scruffy beard as she walked away. This was the Rory I remembered. The Rory from our final days as a couple. Volatile. Crazy.

"You'll pay for it, Rory. Believe me you'll pay."

She stopped at the stairs with Sitaara's arm in her grip. The pleading look Sitaara gave me fueled my anger.

"Give him something to think about," Rory said. "Beat the shit out of him." Then she disappeared with the frightened child in tow.

She claimed to be the dominant one in our *relationship*. But she'd forgotten one crucial detail. *The submissive has all the power.*

Two guards grabbed my arms from behind. Vaolym came for me with his soccer ball- sized fists out front. I did what any man trained in martial arts would do. As he came at me, I launched a flat-footed front kick aimed for his gonads.

Because of his forward momentum, he still struck me in the chin, but he doubled over after delivering a weak punch. The guard on my left, Number Two, loosened his grip and I yanked my arm away from him and backhanded him in the nose. My second strike, an elbow to his jaw, dropped him to the floor. I took the guard on my right, Number Three, by gripping his face and throwing him on top of Vaolym.

Three and Vaolym fell to the floor as I spun to receive another attack from Number Two. I upended the mattress to block him and pinned him in the corner. The huge guards occupied half the small room.

Three crouched like an ape and reached for the Uzi hanging by a strap over his shoulder. Apparently, he didn't want to fight fair. We'd see about that.

I egged him on. "Bring it." I didn't know if he spoke English but the *come here* flick of my fingers should have been clear enough.

Vaolym nursed his wounded pride and Two climbed out from behind the mattress. I ducked behind it and pushed it on top of them. Number Two fired at the mattress. Twitchy trigger finger, I guessed. I crept out from behind and squatted underneath the Uzi. Clutching Two's legs, I threw him off balance. The physical movement exhilarated me. He wasn't expecting it when I hopped to my feet and popped him in the jaw with the butt of the Uzi. Three went down. I wanted a fair fight, so I threw the gun down the hall.

Number Two untangled himself from the mattress and made it to his feet. I swung my leg at the side of his knee and heard a sickening snap. He collapsed.

Three clawed his way to his feet. I was ready as he took a pistol out of its holster and aimed it for me. We stood eye to eye in the doorway of the tiny room.

"That's not fair. You're so much bigger than me. I bet you can take me," I said.

He cursed in Russian and pulled back his arm to strike me with the butt of the gun.

I raised my left hand in the air and wiggled my fingers. *Mitzubish.* It's a little-known martial arts move used to distract your opponent. It worked. Three's gaze flicked to his right.

I knocked the gun away and pushed my fingers into his eye sockets. Three backed away with his hands clutching mine. I didn't let go until I drew blood. I released him with a shove, and he landed on Vaolym and the mattress.

I dove to retrieve the gun and came up facing Rory and Sitaara. Vaolym's whimpers filled the silence.

"Well, well. You do have skills." Rory held Sitaara tightly against her body with a pistol to her temple.

Sitaara's big brown eyes filled with tears.

"Let her go, Rory," I said. "She doesn't need to be part of this."

Rory dug her painted talons into Sitaara's dress and cocked her weapon.

Vaolym picked up the Uzi. If I fought back, Rory might shoot Sitaara. "What are you going to do, Jon?"

It came as no surprise when Vaolym jammed the barrel of his weapon into the back of my head. I raised my hands in the air.

Sitaara put her head in her hands.

"She's a child, Rory. Let Sitaara go," I said.

~53~

MINA

So Jonathon was afraid of heights. *Huh.* The perfect man, the man who had it all, was afraid of the one thing that gave me a thrill. Was it one of those *opposites attract* things? I smiled. The phobia endeared him to me. It made me want to hug him.

And wanting to hug him fueled my climb.

Scaling the top half of the crag was easy due to the block-shaped rocks. As I neared the top, the chimney I'd seen from Michael's yacht loomed over me. In climbing terminology, a chimney is a narrow, three-sided gouge in the rock face. Hence the appropriate name. Above me, two massive boulders nested with a twenty-inch wide gap between them. Wide enough for me to squeeze through. But did it give me enough room to maneuver my way to the top?

Only one way to find out.

I found a toehold and pressed myself into the opening. Once fully inside the chimney, I felt for grips and jugs to wrap my fingers around. My left arm met the back of the chimney, so I reached overhead with my right and found a grip. Bracing my left knee against the stones, I inched my way up until I could pull my body higher using my arms.

I gained about a foot and reached up again. This time I touched something cold and slippery. Whatever-it-was moved beneath my touch. I screamed.

A snake! As it slid out from under my fingers, I screamed again and withdrew my hand so quickly, I bumped my elbow on the inside of the chimney. "Ouch!"

"What's going on? What happened up there?" Greg called from below.

"It's a—" A clear hissing sound quieted me. I looked up. The snake rose up like a cobra and flared its throat. I tried to back away but couldn't find the foothold.

"What's happening?" Greg asked.

I lost my footing and a spray of gravel fell down the rock face. The snake loomed above me like it would strike any second. I scrambled down and slipped, catching my back on the sharp edge of a rock. "Shit!"

"What's going on up there?"

"It's . . . It's a cobra!" I pressed my shin against the chimney wall and my ankle sheath and tactical knife bit into my leg.

"Mina."

The scrape burned, and I knew the rock had drawn blood on my back. "Are cobras attracted to the smell of blood?"

"Mina! It's not a cobra!"

I locked my gaze on the threat. The snake flared its winged hood and hissed at me. "It is! It is a cobra!"

Greg laughed. "There are no cobras in Greece. It's a common grass snake, I assure you."

"No way." I didn't take my eyes off the slimy little thing. "How do you know?"

"Because I have ophidiophobia. I'm terrified of snakes. I learned everything about them in case I cross paths with something venomous. The Grecian grass snakes have a hood like a cobra, but they're harmless."

"You're sure?"

"Positive."

The slippery little guy backed away and slithered off, but I was still shaking. My back hurt. I twisted my arm behind me and felt moisture on my shirt. *Shit.*

A little blood wouldn't stop me from reaching Jonathon. I took a deep breath and tried to calm my racing heart.

Slightly winded and sore, I reached the top of the crag and looked around. The stone wall surrounding the villa was about twenty yards away. The main residence was several dozen yards beyond the wall. I imagined gardens and pathways inside the wall because I couldn't see a way in. There were no gates or openings on this side. And luckily, no guards.

I flopped onto my butt. "I made it," I called softly, hoping Greg heard. He was about twenty-five feet down the cliff where I left him.

A length of rope landed by my side, and I grabbed the loops before it fell back down. There were few boulders, let alone trees to secure the rope to. I located a shrub growing from a rock. At least it had thick branches. I hammered a metal pin between two stones and knotted a loop of rope over it. When I was done, I signaled Greg the line was secure and looked out over the horizon.

"Call if you need anything, Mina!" Greg worried.

As cool breeze blew my ponytail over my shoulder, my confidence grew.

Up close, the villa seemed like a fortress. With my Browning in my hands, I made my way along white walls surrounding the structure, hoping to find an entryway. Stan had fitted my Dad's old service weapon with a silencer. Though it wouldn't decrease the sound of a gunshot by much, I needed all the help I could get. Also, Greg had given me his Walther PPK and that was jammed into the back of my pants. I crept along the south side until I came to the well-lit helipad.

I crouched against the wall, scanned the area for guerillas and counted two. One sat against the doorway smoking a cigarette and the other paced along the far side of the helipad. He passed behind the chopper, so he didn't see me as I swung around the wall and squeezed off two shots.

The guard in the doorway flopped over.

My heart raced. I'd never killed anyone in my life. I thought of Leo Thibodeau and Vedran Kolak bleeding out in front of me and erased the images from my mind. *Focus*, I told myself. I imagined holding Jonathon. His steely blue eyes gazing down at me. His wavy black hair tousled.

As the other guard walked away from the chopper, I darted to the door. I gave a quick glance and saw no one inside the long white hallway.

Inside, I pressed my back against the wall and kept my gun pointed at the floor like Stan and Greg had coached me. As I held my breath and slowly rounded the curve, another guard stood facing the interior. He looked at his cell phone and swiped. He didn't seem to hear me, so I raised the pistol and aimed.

He looked my way as I fired off the shot and missed. The bullet ricocheted off the walls. He was out of his chair and coming for me. I didn't give him time to put down his cell phone and reach for his Uzi. I fired again. He ran three more steps. I fired again, and he slowed.

He put a hand to his chest and looked me in the eye. He seemed bewildered as he coughed blood. He sank to his knees and pointed the Uzi at me. I squeezed off one more shot, but he tightened his grip on the Uzi trigger.

A loud report echoed through the chamber, and I dropped to the floor. I flattened out and put my hands over my head as the spray from his gun drew circles on the ceiling. The Uzi stopped firing, but the noise had drawn attention. I leapt to my feet and ran to the nearest doorway.

Down that arched pathway, two more guerillas ran toward me. I ran the other way.

-54-

JONATHON

"**D**on't be stupid, Jon." Rory's cold gaze didn't frighten me. It only drew rage.

"You have no idea who I am anymore," I said. "I'll kill everyone who works for you."

Vaolym pressed the barrel of his Uzi into my back. It seemed like I was at a disadvantage, but I'd mortally wounded two men. Vaolym didn't know what was coming.

Rory laughed. "You can't possibly kill them all. I have an army of terrorists who will fight to the death for me. There's no way for you to win."

Brave Sitaara stood tall beneath Rory's touch. The sight of Rory clutching that child to her chest—using her against me—fueled my anger. "That's the thing, Rory," I said. "It was never about winning or losing."

"And that's why you're weak, Jonathon."

The sound of gunfire echoed through the house. I wanted to believe Stan and his army had come to help me fight. Rory looked over her shoulder at the stairs. I used the distraction and turned on the guard. Taking him by the arms, I looked him in the eyes as if I would kiss him. I never said martial arts was about fighting fair. My knee connected sharply with his crotch.

Vaolym doubled over. One kick in the balls—excruciating. But two? I couldn't imagine. He loosened his grip on the Uzi. I took the weapon from him and clocked him in the face. He let out a groan and fell to the floor.

I turned the gun on Rory. Peering through the scope at her face, I said, "Sitaara, come here!"

The gunfire below stopped, but from somewhere in the compound, a man shouted, "We're under attack! Stop them!"

Sitaara pried Rory's hands off her shoulders and came to my side. I took her under my arm and closed in on Rory. "Go down the stairs. Move!"

Red-faced with anger, Rory walked ahead of me down to the main level. Open to the Aegean breeze, the unlit passageway at the bottom of the steps was oddly quiet. No guards were present at the far end where an arched door led to the spacious living area.

"Where did they go?" Rory dragged her feet. The high heels of her silly flowered sandals scraped the floor. For the first time, she appeared frightened.

-55-

MINA

I'd used up the Browning's ammo, so I tossed my father's gun aside and I ran. Three more guards chased me out onto the helipad, but they were slow. I darted beneath the fuselage, tugged Greg's gun out of my waistband, and fired shots at everyone who approached. The Walther was surprisingly light and accurate. Considering this was my first day of killing another human being, the body count was rising. I tried not to think of them as people, but as moving targets. My escape and Jonathon's depended on eliminating them.

I lay on the ground beneath the chopper waiting for the next wave of militia. When they didn't come, I cautiously made my way to my feet and loaded the second clip into Greg's Walther. Scanning the area for movement and not seeing any, I sped to the door.

Strip lights along the walls gave off an ambient glow as I moved through the hall. If I had the time, I'd stop to enjoy the beautiful house and feel the cool Aegean breeze on my face. But my heart pounded as if trying to break out of my chest. I had to find Jonathon.

-56-

JONATHON

"Keep moving." I prodded Rory with the Uzi.

"They're coming to rescue me, Jon," she said with a sneer. "I called Papa's militia. They're bringing a chopper."

Ivan's Militia. Artur's terrorists. "Well, they aren't here now, are they? Keep moving."

I shoved her forward. In the dojo we trained in bare feet. Now, the feel of the sidewalk, of each piece of sand and pebble beneath my bare feet gave me confidence and a heightened awareness of my surroundings.

Sitaara clung to me. Her small body pressed against mine and thin arms hugged my waist. I squeezed her shoulder reassuringly with my free left hand. I would put her behind me if necessary.

We entered the dark living room and heard gunshots again. Footsteps and shouting made us all turn toward the outer hall leading to the helipad. I pushed Sitaara behind a marble urn. "Stay there until I come for you." I wished I could reassure her everything would be okay.

Sitaara was a smart kid. She did exactly what I asked.

Rory bolted for the far doorway. "Help!" But her ridiculous high heels slowed her down.

I caught her in three strides. "Shut up." I snatched her by the throat and dug the barrel of the Uzi into her shoulder blade. I held her in a lock with the gun jabbing her. Someone ran toward us from the hall that led to the helipad. A black-clad ninja emerged from the shadows with a pistol pointed in our direction.

They stopped and stared at us.

I couldn't believe my eyes. Mina stood before me, gun raised, face set and stern, a vision of strength and courage. I wanted to let Rory go and run to her. But I dared not release the devil.

"Come out of the shadows," Mina said.

I pushed Rory forward. She said, "You've got to help me! He's gone mad!"

"Mina?" I stepped into the soft ambient light coming from the patio.

~57~

MINA

*W*as that *Jonathon's voice?*
I peered through the darkness and ahead of me a shadow moved. Someone shuffled toward me.

"Don't shoot!" said a woman's voice. Her hands were in the air.

Gripping the Walther with two hands, I raised my arms straight out in front of me, just like at the shooting range. "Who's there?"

I peered down the length of my arm through the sight. Rory emerged from the shadows. She wore an elegant white dress and a pair of high-heeled Dolce and Gabbana floral sandals. At first, I was jealous that she had a pair of the rare designer shoes. But then I realized she wasn't alone. A bearded man held her from behind in a chokehold. As she stumbled forward, I saw his gun.

"Stop where you are!" I said.

The man pushed her toward me, his Uzi jammed into her rib cage. *Not* pointed at me. They stepped into the moonlight. And I gasped.

Jonathon! He was barefoot and wore a plain white T-shirt and striped pajama pants. "Mina, you're alive."

Joy and happiness sped through my veins. I suppressed a smile at the sight of him. I needed to be sure he was on my side. "Why wouldn't I be?"

"The *Ivan* . . ."

"Sank. Did you—" Using every ounce of willpower, I halted a few feet from them.

"I had Mayhem call an old friend. I was worried—"

"Can we stop with the touching reunion?" Rory struggled to get free.

He kept her locked in a chokehold. "What are you doing here? Are you alone? Where's Mayhem?"

"He doesn't climb. And Greg hurt his knee again halfway up the cliff. They're waiting at the bottom."

"Oh." I thought Jonathon paled. "How many guards—"

"Seven. But there are more—"

"I know. I incapacitated three. That means—"

Almost on cue, we heard them coming. I turned my weapon toward the hallway.

"Miss Protsenko," someone called. Five guerillas entered the living room.

"You'll never win, Jon." Rory clawed at Jonathon's arm.

I took a wide stance and aimed my gun at them. They raised their Uzis.

"Stop right there or I'll kill her!" Jonathon tightened his grip.

The huge man stepped forward, sopping up blood from his nose with a small towel. "Let her go." He aimed an Uzi at Jonathon.

-58-

JONATHON

Vaolym staunched the blood from his nose with one hand and held Mina at gunpoint with the other. And he looked angry.

Mina lowered her gun.

"Throw it across the floor." Vaolym sounded pissed.

Mina tossed her pistol across the floor, and it landed beside the marble urn. I hoped no one else saw Sitaara's shoe behind it. And I prayed that Sitaara would stay put.

The other guards closed in and took the Uzi from me. I released Rory. She stepped in front of Mina and slapped her in the face. "You bitch. You think you can come into my home and hurt me? Who do you think you are?"

Someone fired a round and Vaolym went down. Two guards fell to the floor and the rest scattered.

"Jon? You okay?" Stan Mayhem stood in the hallway, an Uzi in one hand and a Sig in the other. He was a sight for sore eyes.

"I missed you, Mayhem."

Mina lunged at Rory. She grabbed her hair and yanked her to the floor.

The other guards fired on Stan, and he ran to cover me. I picked up Vaolym's Uzi and covered Mina. "Get out of here."

"Not without you," she said.

The remaining guards had taken cover behind pillars or the couch. When they began shooting, Rory scrambled to her feet and ran.

Mina followed her to the patio.

I moved backward, with Mayhem at my side. We both shot at guards hidden in the dark. "I'm right behind you, Mina. Don't let her get away!"

-59-

MINA

I chased Rory out to the patio. She stopped briefly to pull off her shoes, then darted left and flew down a flight of stairs. She ran along the outer perimeter wall. I didn't think she had any way to escape, and I was almost upon her, but I hadn't seen the gate at the far northeast corner.

The sound of my sharp breaths and the crunching dry grasses beneath our feet punctuated the night. Rory disappeared through the opening in the wall, and I followed.

Bam! My shin slammed into something, and I dropped to my hands and knees. The bitch tripped me as I rounded the corner! By the time I looked up again, she had put significant distance between us, but she was limping. I hopped to my feet and ran after her. I gained on her as she rounded the curve of the cliff.

In the distance, the moonlight streamed across the surface of the Aegean. She stopped, and doubled over neared the cliff's edge.

I slowed and approached cautiously. "You have nowhere to run, Rory."

She rested, panting hard, with her hands on her thighs. "Do you think I'll let you have him? Do you think I'll let you win?"

The humor in the situation bubbled to my throat. I couldn't help laughing. "It's not just about Jonathon."

"Oh?" She straightened.

"Are you mad? You and your thugs have been fucking with me for months. You kidnapped my best friend and wounded her. You shot and killed Jonathon's dear friend and personal assistant. Because of you, hundreds—if not thousands—of people will die from fentanyl overdoses and poisoning. Sure, some if this is about him. But it's also about stopping you from killing more innocent people."

"Wow. Who knew you were such a Goody-Two-shoes. What perfect world do you live in anyway?" Her back was to the cliff, and she put her hands on her hips.

"I live in a world where justice reigns." And as the words left my mouth, the years of guilt and remorse for helping free murderous villains rose to choke me.

"Right. Says the woman who helped acquit Phil Peterson and the South Side Slasher. You're no better than me. We are cutouts from the same book of Disney evildoers. The only difference is, you have *his* heart."

She got to the point. I'd give her that. "It's not my fault. You lost him a long time ago."

"I want him back!" She ran at me, and I braced myself. She gripped my arms and tried to throw me down. I had better footing, but she clamped on to me like a linebacker. Her fingernails gouged the bleeding scrape on my back. We spun near the edge of the cliff.

"Rory! Stop it!" Jonathon appeared in the straggly grass with Mayhem behind him.

Jonathon's presence seemed to increase her determination. As her claws dug into me again, I grabbed a handful of her hair and threw her to the ground a few feet from the cliff edge. I pinned her with my knee on her throat and drew the knife out of my ankle sheath.

She clawed at my leg. When I pressed the blade of my knife into her neck, she stopped moving. "Fine." She panted and slowly relaxed her arms.

"It's over, Rory," I said.

"You're right." She seemed to give in. I didn't trust her not to lunge at me again.

Jonathon approached with an Uzi pointed at her. "Let Rory get up." He stopped about twenty-five feet from the ledge.

I backed off and let him have her. She was, after all, his nemesis.

"Get up, Rory." He stayed back from the edge of the cliff but aimed the weapon at her. The look in his eye was nothing like I'd ever seen before. His gaze was stone-cold and full of rage.

She slowly made her way to her feet. "Go easy on me, Jon. You know I always loved you. Even now. Especially now."

"Move," he said, urging her to come away from the cliff. I had nothing but pity for her.

$-60-$

JONATHON

They were too close to the cliff. My feet froze in place as the old bear, my phobia, finally woke from its slumber. I kept my gaze aimed through the narrow sight to keep from peering over the cliff. "Move this way, Rory! You have nowhere to run."

Mina stepped to the side away from Rory, then got behind her.

Rory reluctantly put her hands up, raising them to about waist level. "Okay, I'm coming."

I backed up. The farther away we got from that ledge, the better. I wanted to get Mina back to the house. Back to the safety of the walls blocking my view of the cliff. My plan was to lock Rory in the same room she'd held me captive in until I could reach Interpol.

Mayhem stood at my side with another gun trained on her. "You heard him, lady. Move."

We flanked Rory, Stan circled around behind her. I dared not take my eyes off her as I walked backward toward solid ground at the center of the island. As long as we kept moving in that direction—away from the cliff—my nausea abated.

A whimpering noise behind me stopped me in my tracks.

"Jonathon?" The whites of Mina's eyes glowed in the darkness.

I didn't want to take my eyes off Rory but flicked my gaze over my shoulder. *Sitaara*. The child held a pistol out in front of her like a pro.

"It's all right, Sitaara," I said.

The girl came forward. It was hard to tell whom she was aiming at. "Sitaara, we've got Rory. Put the gun down. Rory will never hurt you again."

Still whimpering, she froze somewhere behind me.

"Put that thing down, dear. You don't know how to use it." Rory lowered her hands.

"It's okay, little girl." Stan lowered his weapon.

Sitaara walked toward us, the gun waving wildly from Rory to Mina. As if she didn't know who to trust.

"Sitaara, come to my side," I said. "I'll take care of you, I promise. I'll send you back to your father in Dubai. I'll send you home."

Tears streamed down the girl's face, soaking the hijab at her neck. Rory took a few steps toward her. Artur had nearly strangled his own daughter for not properly taking care of the girl. The fact remained, she was a child and deserved to be treated kindly.

"Come here, Sitaara." Rory held out her hand to her.

Sitaara aimed the gun at her. "I hate you."

"Put your hands in the air, Rory," I commanded.

Rory looked from Sitaara to Stan and then to Mina, who stood six to eight feet behind her and about ten feet from the cliff edge. Too close for me. Rory spun. She sprinted toward Mina, and Mina dropped to a linebacker squat.

Stan launched into a run too. Perhaps he thought he could stop the inevitable.

Rory hit Mina with the force of an angry rhino, pushing her backward toward the cliff.

"Stop!" I yelled.

A gun went off.

Rory and Mina fell to the ground inches from the precipice. Inches from death.

Sitaara burst into tears and dropped the smoking gun.

-61-

MINA

Rory lay on top of me. Unmoving.

Huffing and out of breath, Stan skidded to his knees beside us. "Are you hurt?"

"I'm okay," I said. Just before we fell, something warm and wet hit my face. I cautiously pushed Rory to the side. The shot had hit her in the back and went right through her heart. She was dead.

I rolled painfully to my side, aware that the fall opened up the wound on my back. About a foot from my head lay the cliff's edge. Rory had almost run us both into the water.

"Close call." Stan looked down the cliff where waves splashed jagged rocks below.

My gaze tracked his to the water. The cliff was about twenty five meters high. Approximately seventy feet. I'd jumped from a similar-sized cliff in Acapulco, Mexico. From this height the impact would take the wind out of you. The water's surface felt like concrete if you hit wrong. It could break your limbs or—worst-case scenario—break your neck.

Stan helped me get out from under Rory. "You're a mess." He handed me a handkerchief to wipe my face.

I pushed to my feet and Stan pulled me away from the ledge.

Hugging the girl, Jonathon kneeled in the grass about thirty feet away. He seemed to be consoling her. And I wanted to hug her, too, for saving my life.

The horizon in the east had turned orange. "Give us a few minutes, will you please?" Jonathon said to Stan. He had asked Stan to take Sitaara back to the house. Sitaara hugged Jonathon once more before going with Stan.

I took his hand. "Jonathon."

"Mina. I've missed you so much." He lifted me off the ground and swung me around in a circle.

"I was so worried about you—"

"You came for me!" He set my feet down on the ground.

"You put me through hell! What were you doing holding Rory's hand? I thought—"

"I couldn't compromise my position. Rory had me under lock and key." Jonathon held me at arm's length and painted me with his gaze. Then it was just as I suspected. He was a prisoner. He said, "It was so hard not to go to you."

I stared into his blue eyes. Jonathon was tanned and his hair had grown. Slicked back on top, his black curls hung past his ears to his neck, giving him a sexy lion's mane. The beard made him look wise and sophisticated. His strong arms embraced me as I fell into them. "I missed you."

"It's so good to finally see you again. God, you look stunning."

I was covered in Rory's blood. I'd wiped as much off my face as I could.

"I was so worried . . ." I never finished the sentence. With one hand holding the back of my head, he kissed me firmly on the mouth. His touch felt so familiar. Like going home. My heart raced again, this time with love for Jonathon. My pulse pounded in my ears.

His lips came away from mine. "Do you hear that?"

I took a breath and opened my eyes. The pulsing noise grew louder.

"There." Jonathon pointed upward and I saw the chopper headed toward the island.

"Has help finally arrived?" I asked.

His voice sounded suddenly hoarse. "That's not Interpol. That's a Russian Hind helicopter. That's the enemy."

It hovered over the villa. Guerillas hung out the open side door carrying Uzis. One held a pair of binoculars to his face and as he swept them toward us, he pointed. The chopper turned toward us, and gunfire sprayed the ground at our feet.

"Run!" Jonathon took my hand and ran toward the wall.

The chopper came down between us and the house. The unmistak-able rat-a-tat of automatic weapons stopped us. We were trapped.

There was only one way to escape. "Do you trust me?" I looked into Jonathon's stormy sea-blue eyes. He paled as if he'd had the same thought, but I didn't wait for an answer. I gripped his hand and ran for the cliff.

Ahead of me, I recognized the spot where I'd climbed up here. On the other side of the chimney, the water was deep and dark. It was our only option. I prayed there were no submerged rocks.

Jonathon squeezed my hand and dug his heels in. He stopped, so I did too. "I—" He hesitated.

"Come on!" I said urgently. I couldn't give him time to think about his fear of heights. "Trust me!"

Gunfire sprayed gravel beside us, and I gripped his hand and ran. Jonathon tightened his handhold and kept up with me. We quickened our pace—the faster the better—to get some distance between us and the wall. "When we get in the air, stay upright and draw your feet to-gether," I shouted.

I don't know if he heard me.

As I reached the edge, I launched off the rocks into the air. I didn't let go of Jonathon's hand until we were in free fall.

$-62-$

JONATHON

I thought I was going to die.

When Mina looked at me that way, I knew what she planned to do. The bear, my phobia, rose from its slumber and gnawed at my guts.

As gunfire pelted the earth behind me. I weighed the choices. Death by machine gunfire, or death in Mina's arms.

I choked down bile. I needed to trust her instincts. She'd done this before, right? She lived to talk about it. *Right?* The conversation with my inner demons didn't get far.

A bullet grazed my shoulder. We ran. I didn't look back. "Go! Go! Go!"

Then I screamed like a little girl.

When I hit the water, it knocked all the wind out of my lungs. I sank into the deep, dark sea. The bear shook its head and walked away.

I woke floating in Mina's arms. Her legs moved in the water. She was swimming to shore. "Breathe, Jonathon. I've got you. You're all right."

I sucked in the breath of life like it was my first. I coughed, and she held me.

"I've got you." She pulled me onto a stony beach at the base of the cliff. And I lay there with my heart pounding.

The helicopter hadn't chased us. The pulsing rotor of the chopper echoed off the island and faded away.

Mina sat on a boulder beside me. "We made it." She took my hand and kissed it. As the sun rose and our clothes dried, we held each other tightly.

I'd never leave her again. And I promised myself, I'd never let her go.

-63-

MINA

The night we escaped Sotoris, an Interpol aircraft chased the Hind chopper away from the island and intercepted it. Stan safely took Sitaara to the dinghy at the bottom of the staircase on the north side. Emilya radioed Greg and told him my location. They picked us up on their way back to the Oyster.

Greyson had contacted his associates, and they arrested nine men belonging to the terrorist organization known as Ivan's Militia. Artur Protsenko and his wife were never located.

In the days following Jonathon's rescue, no news reports emerged regarding Rory's death, but her fentanyl factory in Izmir was officially shut down. Decontamination units bagged the entire facility. It would be months before all the drugs were destroyed in a hazardous waste incinerator.

The Oyster's patched black sails filled with wind. Michael had sewn a piece of royal blue tarp over the damaged area before we cruised westward, away from Sotoris.

Jonathon set a pillow on the deck, and I lay back on it. A large bandage covered the outside of his shoulder where a bullet grazed his skin. He wore Greg's pink flamingo shorts. "Emilya, can we reinsert the GPS tracker in Jonathon's thigh? That way, I'll never lose him again."

Emilya laughed as she prepared a needle full of Novocain.

"I promise to never leave the woman who threw me off a cliff." Jonathon smiled that dark, knowing grin I missed and loved so much.

"You'd better not." Unable to keep the anger out of my voice, I said, "If you ever put me in a situation like this again, you're on your own, Mr. Heun. You put us all in danger!" Because of him, I'd become a killer. Not like the criminals I represented. But I couldn't deny that part of me was dead because of it.

Jonathon looked down at the deck. I'd struck a nerve.

"I'm sorry I put you—and everyone here—in danger, Mina. I'm eternally grateful for the help. If you hadn't come, I'd still be on Sotoris." His gaze seemed more introspective than hardened. Rory had put him through trials no man should ever have to suffer.

I sensed a change in him, and not only because of the scars on his chest and on the back of his hands. He seemed to be scarred inside as well. Did I have regrets? Was I angry? Perhaps. But I was strong. I still loved Jonathon, despite all he'd put me through.

"And I love you," I said. I took his jaw in both hands and kissed him. Jonathon kissed me back.

Everyone on deck hushed for a moment while the wind fluttered the sails.

Greg said, "Get a room, you guys."

Emilya wiped my hip with rubbing alcohol. "He loves you very much."

I looked him in the eye. "I know."

Jonathon held my hand as she stuck me with the needle. The numbing effects would soon allow her to gently excise the GPS tracker. I had no more need for the device.

She readied her scalpel and kneeled over my side. "Can you feel this?" Emilya poked the tattooed skin on my hip.

"Not anymore. Go for it."

As if she had nursing experience, Emilya carefully cut a slit near the implanted device.

"You continue to amaze me, Emilya," I said. "You're a computer whiz, navigational engineer, security expert. You're good at everything,"

"It's nothing. You dove off that cliff! You're a goddess," Emilya said with a grin.

Despite my discomfort with the attention, they couldn't stop talking about it. "My secrets have been revealed."

"Very few people do what you do." Greyson sat in the captain's chair with the wind in his face.

"They call it tombstoning. There must be a reason for that moniker." Michael manually tightened the halyard.

"She's crazy," Greg said bluntly but followed with a wink. He wore neon green shorts and a blinding, shiny yellow shirt. I could hardly look at him without shielding my eyes.

"Not crazy," Jonathon said. "Brave and fierce." He squeezed my hand as Emilya pulled the tracking device from my hip with a long pair of tweezers.

She held up the half-inch device for everyone to see. "It worked so well, I want to inject one into Michael's skin." She smiled brighter than the sun. "I'll do it while he's sleeping."

"I heard that!" Michael kneeled down beside her. "Besides, I figured you already had. You always find me."

Emilya closed the hole with a few drops of super glue. The adhesive was originally designed for human skin, after all. Then she handed me a bandage. Jonathon helped me put it over the tattoo, then ran his fingers over my ink. "I love this new tattoo."

I took off my T-shirt and shorts, uncovered my bathing suit, and dabbed sunscreen on my shoulders. Jonathon wore a pair of Greg's wild pink shorts. The flamingos with sunglasses suited the Mediterranean vacation vibe today. He rubbed lotion on my back and Emilya gave me a wide-brimmed sun hat. At last, I felt like a tourist on a much-needed Mediterranean cruise.

The Oyster moved forward like a butter knife through frosting. Smooth and easy. Now we were just a group of friends out for a Sunday cruise. At least that's what it looked like. No drones or terrorists chasing us. No missing billionaires or kidnappings. No shipments of fentanyl to intercept.

"I've finally thought of a worthy name for the Oyster," Michael said.

"What did you decide?" Greyson asked.

"*Cliff Diver*. After our good friend—someone I greatly admire."

"It's perfect," Emilya said.

I squeezed her hand. "I'm humbled."

When Stan came up from the saloon, Sitaara followed. "Please play another game!"

"No." Stan frowned. "You're too lucky."

Sitaara's sunflower hijab brightened her eyes. Stan plopped down on the couch in the cockpit, and she sank down next to him with a deck of cards in her hands. "Oh, come on. Just one more? Please?"

"You're a shark. I thought you didn't know how to play."

"Beginner's luck." She smiled and shuffled the deck like a Vegas dealer.

Stan caught my eye and grumbled, "I taught her how to play Go Fish, and she's kicking my butt."

"I'll play," Jonathon said. His steely eyes lit up. I could tell he had a real affection for Sitaara. They seemed to share a deep bond. But there was something else. That twinkle in his eye when he gazed at me was new.

Emilya watched me watching him. "You should marry him," she said.

"I'm going to," I said. And I meant it.

~64~

MINA

*D*ays later, we dropped anchor and swam at Lover's Beach on the north side of Mykonos. The sails were down, and the anchor firmly rooted in the bottom of the sea near the island. Stan, Jonathon, Sitaara, and I took the dinghy to a pier and tied it off. Sitaara's finely woven, damask butterfly dress shone in the sunlight as she ran up a long walkway to the entrance of a modern Grecian mansion.

Abu Alawi el Attar met us at the end of the walkway. He embraced Sitaara and a half-dozen elegantly dressed women and young ladies wearing colorful kaftans and hijabs surrounded the father and daughter, each vying for their turn to hold the beloved girl.

I felt underdressed in a calf-length, pale-orange cocktail dress, but it was the only thing I'd brought with me. It warmed my heart to see Sitaara reunited with her family. After the tearful reunion, everyone wiped their eyes.

Jonathon held out his hand and greeted his acquaintance. "Abu al Attar."

"Mr. Heun." The oil mogul wore a white European-style suit and shirt with the traditional red and white head covering. He took Jonathon's hand in both of his. "May I call you Jonathon?"

"I'd be honored."

"No. It is I who am honored to hold the hand of the man who saved my daughter. And please. Call me Alawi." He held his arms wide, inviting an embrace.

"Alawi, apologies for the shoes. I'm stuck with borrowed clothes for the time being." Jonathon wore Greg's flip-flops because no one else shared his shoe size. Today's outfit was a pair of Greg's pink flamingo shorts and Michael's tight, short-sleeved white shirt. At least it had a collar. Though Jonathon preferred to wear a tie, no one on board the Oyster had one.

"You are welcome in my home no matter what."

Jonathon embraced him. Once introductions were made all around, we followed the family into their lavish home. We drank mint tea and ate delicate pastries on a shaded patio overgrown with heavy bougainvillea and orchids. The well-kept flowers bloomed all around us, despite the late season.

Surrounded by her five older sisters, Sitaara told stories of Jonathon's heroics and Stan's rescue.

I was surprised to learn she'd been hiding behind a massive marble urn when I entered the living room where I first discovered Jonathon and Rory. She'd seen everything.

No one mentioned Sitaara had fired the gun, killing the TOC leader's daughter. When the Hind chopper arrived and began shooting at us, Stan and Sitaara hid deep inside the villa until it was clear to run to the boat.

"We are so happy you are home safe, little Sitaara." Her mother wore a royal-blue beaded gown with a matching shayla scarf draped over her head. Tears pooled in her eyes as she pulled Sitaara close.

"If it weren't for Mina's determination, we'd still be captives on Sotoris." Jonathon put his hand over mine. He told the story of our rescue mission, and the harrowing escape from the Hind. Since I'd never developed a phobia, I had no idea jumping from the cliff was so terrifying for him. The feared he admitted facing at the cliff edge infused me with heightened respect for him. It also gave me faith that he trusted me.

"The terrorists would have killed us. Jumping into the sea was the only way to escape the gunfire." I realized not everyone would draw that conclusion.

"She saved our lives," Jonathon said.

My gaze dropped humbly to my lap while Jonathon's proud gaze remained on me.

"I don't know how to thank you," Alawi said. "I must reward you all."

Stan humbly accepted a monetary gift. I gratefully received a gorgeous dark green silk kaftan and matching shayla scarf. Jonathon refused a gift but accepted an open invitation to stay at the mansion on Mykonos. As we walked back to the dinghy, Alawi told Jonathon they would fly back to Saudi Arabia with Sitaara later that evening. And I saw the idea bloom as Jonathon stopped him on the pier.

"Do you mind if Mina and I take you up on the offer to use your home? Could we stay here at your house tonight?"

"I'd be honored! Stay for the week. Stay for the month. The house will be empty until January." Alawi seemed overjoyed he could give something to Jonathon to show his appreciation. Something that Jonathon could use.

~65~

JONATHON

Mina packed her bag while I said my goodbyes. Greg parted with a pair of flip-flops, his baby-blue T-shirt, and the hideous pink shorts. I had nothing else to wear and couldn't wait to get back to my own clothes. I had no suitcase and no toiletries, yet somehow that made it harder to leave. To say goodbye.

"Not goodbye, old friend," Stan said. "Farewell. Well met. Cheerio." I welcomed Stan's strong and friendly handshake, then pulled him in for a hug.

"I don't know how to thank you for not giving up on me." Emotions choked the words. "I owe you my life."

He patted my back. "You'd do the same for me."

"Count on it."

Greyson held out his hand and I cupped it in mine. "Any friend of Michael's is a friend of mine."

"Thanks to you, Interpol has shut down a major fentanyl operation," Greyson said. "You helped stop an international terrorist organization. I am honored to have met you."

I embraced him then turned to Greg.

"You had the most important job, and you didn't let me down."

"What was that?" He leaned on a cane. While climbing the cliff with Mina, he'd ripped apart some of the scar tissue in his knee. We figured it would set him back about a month of physical therapy.

"You had her back. You made sure she didn't do something foolish."

Greg nodded. "She's headstrong, that's for sure."

"Outspoken," I agreed.

"Opinionated."

"Tenacious."

"So courageous," he said. "I respect that about her."

"It's hard not to respect her . . ."

"Don't let her get away." The intense look in Greg's eye told me he cared deeply for Mina.

I patted Greg on the shoulder. "You'll be the best man?" I said.

Greg pulled me in for a hug. I thought he wiped away a tear.

"Who are you whispering about?" Mina came up on deck with her luggage. Emilya followed.

"You guys make it look like they're taking a rocket ship to outer space," Emilya said. "It's not like we'll never see them again."

"She's right," I said.

Michael offered his hand. I slapped it and he slapped back. We waved our thumbs and lifted our hands in the air with a roar. Then he swiftly put me into a headlock and let me go. It was something we learned at the dojo in Japan. I smiled at the memory. "You endured a lot, my friend. What do I owe you for damages to your yacht?"

"I don't want anything," Michael said.

"Has Mina compensated you?" I asked.

Mina came to my side. "Emilya and I have taken care of things down below."

Michael gave Emilya a stern look of disapproval.

She put her hands on her hips. "Michael Bettencourt, you wouldn't have anything left if it weren't for me."

"When did you become my wife?"

Mina and I stepped out from between them.

"When have I not been?" She waved a finger at his face and launched into an angry Greek speech.

Michael shouted over her tirade. "I love it when you talk like that. It makes me want to . . ." He took Emilya in his arms.

She softened at his touch. "It makes you want to what? Tell me."

"It makes me want to marry you." Michael lifted her off her feet and swung her around. Emilya shrieked with joy.

"Are you asking me now?"

He set her on her feet. "Yes, I'm asking you to marry me!"

Her teeth shone brightly with her wide smile as she gazed up at him. "The answer is yes!"

While they kissed, I said to everyone, "We'll be back in Chicago in a week. Please stay in touch."

"The world is a smaller place with video calls. Call me any time." Mina sounded choked up, but she turned away from us and walked to the stern.

Stan, Greyson, Greg, and I silently followed her gaze out to the sea. "I won't forget this," she sniffed. "I won't forget any of you." Tears ran down her cheeks.

-66-

MINA

B oth dressed in silky pajamas, we ate a lavish seafood dinner on Abu Alawi el Attar's veranda.

Several boxes had been delivered containing slacks, shirts, and undergarments for Jonathon. He seemed delighted that Alawi not only knew his size, but also guessed his color scheme—blacks and jewel tones. He'd thought of everything, even a pair of hand-crafted Italian leather shoes.

Tivoli lights twinkled around the shrubs and framed the arches. The meal started with tomato and seafood bisque and oysters on the half shell. I sipped dry champagne while Jonathon had his traditional Perrier water with a lime wedge. Alawi's staff served lobster thermidor to Jonathon and sole almondine to me. We felt pampered and thoroughly spoiled by eclairs afterward.

Before we'd finished, the doorbell rang, and our butler, Stephano answered.

"Who could that be?" I asked.

Jonathon shrugged and we both turned as Stephano returned with another man. Jonathon leapt to his feet. "Javier!"

I never tired of seeing Jonathon embrace his friends. Javier wore a blue-and-white arm sling over his tailored suit. "So good to see you again," Javier said.

"You have no idea." Jonathon introduced us. "Are you here to stay?"

"Yes. I'm back to work. And I have a special delivery for you."

"From Abu Alawi?"

"You guessed it." He handed Jonathon a small white bag with ropey black handles.

Jonathon took the bag and walked Javier to the foyer while I waited. When Jonathon returned, without the bag, dinner was cleared.

"Javier is a good man. I'm happy to have him back. I had the butler arrange a room for him. We'll catch up in the morning. Tonight is for you, Mina."

I cherished my alone time with Jonathon, so I was grateful he'd sent Javier away. We moved to the patio outside and sank into a sofa to watch the sliver of a waxing moon travel westward in the sky. Soon we would head west to Chicago. After all the melodrama of the past weeks, I had trouble imagining what our lives would look like.

Tonight we stood on the edge of an abyss. I was ready to take a leap of faith with the man I loved. However, I could never return to my life as a criminal defense attorney. More than ever, I wanted to protect people from criminals. Since I had the means, and Jonathon would willingly help me, I vowed to give myself time to figure it all out. And time to draft a plan. For now, I looked at the stars. Listened to the sea lapping the shore. And felt my lover's warm arm wrapped around me.

"The night is almost perfect," he said.

"I finally feel like I can relax." I rested my head on his shoulder.

"I'm so sorry, Mina, for all the trouble."

Now that he mentioned it, I had something to say. I sat up. "You know, I'm still angry with you, Jonathon."

"I would expect you to be." He folded his hands into his lap.

"I traveled halfway around the world to find you. I was chased by drones, guerrillas shot at me, a psycho bitch almost threw me off a cliff, and a Hind helicopter gunned us down." I looked him in the eye. "I killed for you, Jonathon."

"I told you not to come." He lowered his voice. "You didn't listen!"

"Oh, you're angry?" I asked. "You're the one who went off on some vendetta. You're the one who got captured. I should have left you to her!"

He smiled softly. "But you didn't. You came for me, and you kicked ass."

I looked away. I'd almost lost Jonathon. Angry tears rolled down my cheeks. I wiped them away with the palms of my hands. When I looked back, Jonathon held a black velvet box.

He slid out from under me, off the sofa, and onto one knee. "This is for all that you've done. For all that we will do. For all that is to come." His eyes sparkled with a million stars as he pushed the box into my hand.

My eyes filled with more tears and suddenly I couldn't see.

"Marry me, Mina. I won't take no for an answer."

My hands shook as I fumbled to open the box. I could only make out brilliant rainbows of glittering sparkles at first. I squeezed tears from my eyes and saw the diamond ring.

I smiled and my throat closed on the rush of emotions. I swallowed. "Yes. Yes."

"I can't go on without you, Mina." He took the sparkling gem from the box. I gave him my hand and he slipped the ring onto my finger. "I always want you by my side."

Words wouldn't come. I flung my arms around his neck and we both stood.

Jonathon held me tightly. "You are everything to me, Mina. I love you so much."

"I love you, Jonathon. I'm incomplete without you."

"Now the night is perfect," he said.

And it was.

EPILOGUE

We heard that Karolos Samaroulis and Luna had recovered from their injuries after the bombing. For his troubles, I gave him a gift from Jonathon's expense accounts, the value of the Dragonfly. I also paid the balance of his hospital bills after insurance. With this gift, Karl and Luna partnered together and bought a seventy-five foot catamaran. And with a little help from Michael and Emilya, they installed anti-piracy equipment on the boat for added protection. Months later, Karl and Luna were offering Grecian cruises and getaways, and just like before, they were back in business.

My aunt and Traci helped arrange a small wedding at an old church in Lake Geneva, Wisconsin. My friends, Steph and Jenn, came. Jonathon's partners, Jack and Darren, were there. Darren's wife, Maddie, held their new bundle of joy, Marshal Phillip Ward, in her arms. Emilya and Michael, with shiny new wedding rings on their fingers, flew all the way from Greece for the event. Even Greyson made an appearance before catching a flight back to Germany. His ongoing work for Interpol kept him hopping.

Standing in the small Wisconsin church, I said, "I do," surrounded by bouquets of white roses with paperwhites, sprigs of rosemary flowers, and lush trails of English ivy. Jonathon stood before me in a royal purple shirt and black tuxedo decorated with a boutonniere—a single white rose with a rosemary flower sprig. When he kissed me, he dipped me over his arm.

His breath smelled of cinnamon and his trim beard tickled my face. The sweeping motion and swoon-worthy kiss made me more light-headed than jumping from the Sotoris cliffs—which I learned towered almost thirty meters, eighty-five feet—the highest jump I'd ever made.

After the ceremony and before the festivities, Greg, Javier, and Stan managed to distract the paparazzi as we slipped out the back door. We sank into Jonathon's Astin Martin and raced back to his Lake Forest mansion before anyone knew we were gone.

That night, I sat back on the red bedspread on the four-poster in the center of his dungeon room. My white satin gown and Jonathon's tux jacket and shirt lay in heaps near the doorway. Wearing only his tux pants, Jonathon knelt before me. He peeled one sheer stocking off, then the other. When he reached for the garter belt, I stopped him and helped him to his feet.

"It's my turn," I said.

He looked at me with that wicked glint in his eye. "Do I need punishment?"

"Yes." I pushed him back on the bed and leapt on top of him. I straddled his waist. "I'm going to bind your wrists to the bed . . . here." I took his hand and fastened his wrist to the headboard. "And here." I fastened his other hand to the headboard.

"Are you going to spank me?"

"Yes." I hopped off the bed and walked to the wall where most of his paddles and whips hung on display. "How about this one?" I dragged my fingers along the leather flogger.

"No."

"This?" I lifted the studded paddle away from the wall.

"Not that one. I think you'll need to use the Japanese reed with the red ribbon." He held on to the bedposts. His chest rose and fell.

I went to a narrow dresser and opened a drawer. "This one?" I held up the thin bamboo reed with red ribbons trailing from it. "You must have been very bad."

He nodded. "I made you chase me all the way to Greece. I put you in danger."

I was long over that. But I wanted to christen our marriage with the thing that started it all. Bondage and discipline.

Jonathon's steely blue eyes locked on mine. "Take off your bra."

I swished the reed in the air, and it whistled. "I'll give the orders," I said.

I took my time unfastening his belt and pulling off his pants. I kneeled on the mattress over him and traced the reed along the soft flesh of his inner arms, and his chest. I spread his legs wide. Goosebumps rose from his skin and his cock swelled.

I struck his thigh with the reed.

"Again." Jonathon tugged on the bindings.

I smacked his thigh again. And again. Until his thighs were red and I thought I heard him gasp. I held the reed in the air and watched his face for signs of pain.

"What are you waiting for?" he asked.

I shook my head and set the reed down. "We can't continue this way."

I went to the dresser and found a blindfold. I slipped it over his eyes and fastened it behind his head. I said, "Each time you feel the strike of the reed, you'll say, thank you."

He nodded. "Yes, councilor. Thank you."

Councilor? I'd been his lawyer once, but we tore up that contract almost a year ago. "Call me *Mrs. Heun.*"

His lips curled into a smile. "Yes, Mrs. Heun."

I knew the blindfold heightened all other senses. Without sight, every sound became a tell. Every touch a symphony. I watched Jonathon cock his head and listen to me pacing like a hungry cheetah around the bed. I traced the reed along his cheeks and chest then slapped his nipples until they stood erect like his cock.

"Thank you," he said.

I circled the bed and touched his shoulders with the reed. I pulled on the ropes holding his wrists tight and made him wait for the sting. When the impact came, he said, "Thank you, Mrs. Heun."

I set the reed down and climbed up on the bed and straddled him. I traced his scars with my finger and took a nipple in my mouth. He tensed at my touch, and I thought of how Rory tortured him with her games. The scars on his chest from cigarette burns had healed to pink circles. I kissed each one. I kissed the places he'd been injured—where the bullet grazed his shoulder, where the blast from the car bomb burned his hand. I kissed his shoulders and kneaded his thighs. I took his length into my mouth and made him harder. And though I loved being in charge, I wanted us to be equal.

I untied his wrists and Jonathon removed the blindfold. Then I slowly removed my bra, my garter belt, and my thong. He laid me gently down on the bed. He spread my legs wide and dove between them.

My folds were wet, anticipating his warm breath and tender kisses. I peaked quickly. My back arched, and I cried out again. This time with pure ecstasy.

When I finally straddled him, I moved my hips slowly. I ran my fingers through his hair as he thrust his hips in a rhythm. I met him with equal force. He stiffened and cried out, and I rode the wave and brought myself to another sensuous orgasm. When it ended, I collapsed beside him. "I love you, Mr. Heun."

Jonathon took me in his arms. "I love you, Mrs. Heun."

How I loved him. I loved his dominant nature, but also loved how our relationship had evolved. I loved the give and take. I loved submitting to him, but also loved it when he gave me the authority. The chance to choose. In that way we were balanced. Neither of us held power over the other. And I looked forward to sharing a life with my equal, my partner, Jonathon.

THE END

ACKNOWLEDGEMENTS

My writing community is my support, my nourishment. Many thanks to the Dark and Stormies for your first reads and for helping me tell Mina and Jonathon's story in the best way possible. Blackbird Writers will always have my heart. I'm grateful for your support and your shared knowledge of this industry. You all inspire me. Once again, Stacey Donovan had a hand in developing the story. Karen Hrdlicka helped with this and *that*. Most of all, my unwavering husband held my hand through the most tortuous times. I couldn't have done it without you. I would sail seven seas to rescue you too.

A Message from the Author

If you loved The Client, Please write a review on Amazon, Goodreads or Bookbub. For more conversation with the author, find me online at Karissaknight.com. I'm also on Instagram as @karissaknightauthor and Facebook as @Karissaknightauthor. I'd love to chat with you!

Karissa Knight is a pseudonym for published author Tracey S. Phillips. If you love Mina, if you love fearless women who embrace their shadow side, you may love books written by Tracey S. Phillips. BEST KEPT SECRETS won a Hugh Holton award in 2018.

Link to Tracey's books here: https://traceysphillips.com

Link to *Best Kept Secrets*

PRAISE FOR BEST KEPT SECRETS!

"Beautifully put together. Look out...there's a new female detective (and talented author) in town. Tracey S. Phillips's *Best Kept Secrets* is a twisty, tantalizing read."

—<u>Karen Harper</u>, *New York Times* bestselling
author of *Dark Storm*

"*Best Kept Secrets* will have readers breathlessly turning pages until the final twists and turns."

—<u>Rosalind Noonan</u>, New York Times
bestselling author of *The Sisters*.

"A thrilling ride!"

—<u>Sarah Meuleman</u>, author of *Find Me Gone*

"*Best Kept Secrets* is a gritty and absorbing story from a promising author."

—<u>Libby Fischer Hellmann</u>, author of the
Georgia Davis PI novels

An excerpt from *Best Kept Secrets –*
A psychological thriller by Tracey S.
Phillips

– 1 –

MORGAN

Detective Morgan Jewell outpaced her partner by several car lengths. "Hold up, Mo. I didn't get enough sleep, thanks to you. You could at least wait for me!" A seasoned detective, Donnie James had been Morgan's partner for ten years. Now he was fifty and would rather ease into retirement than take any risks.

Morgan snapped over her shoulder, "I can't wait. This is the one, Donnie. I know it." Pulling the front of her jacket closed against the cooler than normal temperatures, she took in every detail of the rural street. On one side of the road, oaks towered over Victorian-style houses. Across from them, fields of tall, end-of-season corn browned in the sun.

Fresh country air filled her lungs with the bright smell of autumn. "Is that what you think?" Donnie strolled along at a slower pace.

He and Morgan had been partners for almost ten years but his time as a detective was drawing to a close. He had been offered the position of their lieutenant, who was retiring at the end of the year. Donnie hadn't accepted yet but was seriously considering it. Morgan had called him before five this morning. She had had to dial his number three times before he answered, groggy and resistant to taking a case outside of their jurisdiction. Furthermore, it was Saturday. He would rather have stayed at home with his wife and two teenaged daughters. Behind him, farm tractors kicked up dust clouds that dissipated in the breeze.

Half a dozen police cars in the road indicated that most of the law enforcement in this little farming burg had come out for the show. In the driveway, EMTs were trying to console a hysterical woman sitting on the bumper of an ambulance with the back doors open. Morgan heard her cries and winced.

The night before in Hendricks County, dispatch had reported a 911 call. Upon returning from an out-of-state work trip, Rebecca Harrington, the weeping woman, discovered her partner's broken, blood-covered body in their bedroom. Because of this crime's similarities to an ongoing Indianapolis investigation, Detective Morgan Jewell of the Indianapolis Metro Police Department, Homicide Division, had been granted special access to this crime scene in Danville.

Fueled by coffee and self-confidence, she bounded past a group of officers gathered around the steps of the light-blue, Victorian house. This little town had never seen a murder so gruesome, and Morgan didn't like the attention it was getting. She snarled at them, "What is this, some kind of party? Have some respect for the dead, will you?" A pair of them took the hint and peeled away.

Inside the house, the officer on duty greeted her. "Morning, Detective Jewell." Behind him, several Hendricks County cops milled around the living room. Too many crime-scene investigators were dusting, tagging, and labeling every surface.

Donnie ambled in a few minutes later, his voice booming, "Who's in charge?"

The officer nearest the door updated them. "Nothing in the lower level was disturbed according to Ms. Harrington," he said. "We've sealed off the crime scene. Forensics is on its way."

Morgan wandered past the officer, who had seated himself in a chair near the front door. Behind him, an oriental rug covered the living-room floor beneath an IKEA-style smooth-as-swede couch and matching chair. The ottoman was topped with a flat blue tray holding a candle and a stack of coasters. A vase of flowers sat in the corner. Little china cups and saucers filled the gaps in an ornate bookshelf. On a side table, a photograph of two women posing cheek-to-cheek and smiling widely took prominence. Morgan looked closer without touching. They looked so happy. She remembered feeling that way once.

"What's upstairs?" she asked.

"Upstairs . . . Lieutenant Werner is upstairs. That's where . . ." Color left the young officer's face.

Donnie had come in and was standing in the doorway texting someone on his phone. Morgan asked, "Your daughter?"

Donnie nodded and followed Morgan up a narrow staircase. At the top of the stairs, the lieutenant greeted them. "We've been here since midnight. What took you so long?"

"Got caught in that construction traffic on I-465." Donnie was bending the truth. In fact he had dragged his feet and taken his time, his way of showing Morgan that he didn't want to be there.

"They're always working on something, aren't they? Even on Saturday." The lieutenant looked past Morgan at Donnie.

"Especially on Saturday," Donnie concurred.

Morgan felt like a ghost as the lieutenant chatted casually with his same-sex peer.

"I've heard a lot about you, Detective James, but no one mentioned your stature. Did you ever play ball?"

"Too clumsy. Call me Donnie."

"Lieutenant Werner." He reached past Morgan to shake Donnie's hand—indeed as if she wasn't there. "Call me Tim."

"I'm the detective in charge." Morgan intercepted the handshake. "And I'd like to see the body."

Limp and cool, the lieutenant's hand slid from hers as he looked her up and down. She was wearing a black fitted suit with a red blouse. Her long brown hair was pulled into a tight ponytail. Thick black lashes framed dark-brown eyes emphasized by her porcelain complexion.

"Hope you haven't had breakfast yet, Detective," he said to her. "Burger and fries on the way here, lots of ketchup." She privately hoped to see the lieutenant pale at the thought. When he didn't, she continued. "What have we got?"

Werner led the way down a tight hallway wallpapered with pink flowers. The trim, painted periwinkle-blue, bordered hardwood floors that groaned under Donnie's weight. Werner stopped before entering and held up a hand.

"Her name's Hallie Marks. She's the owner of Hit the Mark Design. I heard she was one of the best interior decorators in the state."

"Yes." Impatient, Morgan wanted to go into the room. "It was her partner who found her like this, isn't that right?"

"Rebecca Harrington," Werner said, "is the owner of the house. She said she's been out of town for a few weeks."

"How long ago was Hallie Marks killed?" "Probably in the past day or so."

Donnie lifted the back of his hand to his nose. In the airless hallway, he looked a little pale.

The lieutenant gave a final disclaimer. "This is ugly. Just warning you."

Morgan pushed past him. "I'm ready for it."

Light colors and country lace decorated the small master bedroom. It looked like no one had slept in the antique four-poster bed the night before. Eyelet curtains framed the bay window where dark, dried spots of blood splattered the light-blue cushion on the window seat. Outside, the sun shone on ripe cornfields across the street.

Beside the window, the body of Hallie Marks sat strapped to a Queen Anne chair. Her bloody face hung down forward between her shoulders. A drying red stream ran from her destroyed face down her chest and between her breasts. Hallie's broken bloody hands were tied to the arms of the chair. Her bare feet rested in a sticky pool of blood.

Morgan's hand grazed a soft spiral notebook in the pocket of her pants. Donnie stood beside her looking down at the body. As he shook his head, she knew he was thinking about retirement. In the car he had let her know how upset he was to be riding along with her. It wasn't even their jurisdiction, he'd said. But Morgan wanted Donnie's opinion. She had enormous respect for him and his ability to solve crimes. And crazy as it sounded, Morgan hoped this case could be the connection to her past.

"What do you think?" She asked him.

"The killer is an animal," Werner said.

Riveted to her spot, Morgan answered, "Not an animal, Lieutenant. A sick-minded, fucked-up human being. Animals don't behave this way." She squatted down for a closer look. She had seen these kinds of injuries before. The memory made the hair on the back of her neck stand at attention.

At least the victim was wearing underwear, a lacy red pair of panties and fancy bra. Her clothes, a pair of jeans and a plain white shirt, were laid on the bed as if she had been getting ready to go out. Or perhaps she'd just taken them off?

Gazing at the female victim's smashed, bloody face, Morgan shivered. Blood covered most of the injuries, but it was clear that anger had driven the killer to destroy this woman's face. Years ago, Morgan's best friend, Fay Ramsey, had been murdered similarly. Every day since her death, Morgan had scanned the news for possible reports of the killer's capture. And she still looked for the killer herself, needing closure. But for now she pushed the horrid memory aside to focus on the task at hand.

The victim was wearing a braided silver ring with a malachite stone on the pinky finger of her left hand. But her crushed metacarpals had caused the long, slender fingers to lie askew. Swollen, black-and-blue flesh indicated that those injuries had been inflicted hours before her death. That, Morgan thought, seemed to be the killer's mark.

On her face, numerous impact sites were about two inches in diameter. One blow had crushed Hallie's nose. Another took several teeth.

Fay's killer had done the same things to her.

Under her breath, Morgan muttered, "So much hate and passion."

"Passion isn't the word I'd use." In the doorway, the lieutenant watched her work.

"Me neither." Donnie went out into the hallway.

Morgan took a pair of gloves from her pocket and slid them onto her hands. She lifted Hallie's cold, stiff fingers to examine her fingernails. They were long but not painted. All were trim, filed, and clean, except for the index and middle finger, which had something dark underneath them.

Had Hallie clawed at her attacker? Is that his blood? A chill went down Morgan's spine.

"Have forensics swab her nails and send me the results." "Sure thing, Detective."

"Do you study serial crime, Lieutenant Werner?" she asked, standing. Werner picked at his own fingernails. "Nope. Not my thing."

"The killer has done this before. There is precision in each knot, each loop of rope, and in every blow." Morgan removed her gloves.

"Can we get the body out of here?" Donnie called from the hallway. "We were waiting for you detectives. Hey, Richardson!" Werner hollered out to the officer stationed at the bottom of the stairs. "Go tell Lemay that we're ready for the coroner."

Donnie started for the stairs and Morgan followed. "I want to talk to Rebecca," she said.

"Wait." Lieutenant Werner touched the back of Morgan's arm. "We found a possible murder weapon."

Morgan turned on her toes. She wondered what hard object had been used. Something sturdy and heavy would do it. The butt or barrel of a gun. A mallet. A hammer.

"There's a meat tenderizer in the dish rack by the kitchen sink. It's been washed. We're spraying the sink for traces of the woman's blood."

Best Kept Secrets by Tracey S. Phillips

9 781736 852453